Golden Bloodline 2

Golden Bloodline, Volume 2

Richard Moorman

Published by Richard Moorman, 2024.

GOLDEN BLOODLINE 2

First edition. March 25, 2024.

ISBN: 979-8224153107

Written by Richard Moorman.

Table of Contents

Prelude 1

Chapter One 3

Chapter Two 8

Chapter Three 14

Chapter Four 18

Chapter Five 22

Chapter Six 26

Chapter Seven 29

Chapter Eight 34

Chapter Nine 37

Chapter Ten 42

Chapter Eleven 49

Chapter Twelve 53

Chapter Thirteen 58

Chapter Fourteen 63

Chapter Fifteen 69

Chapter Sixteen 75

Chapter Seventeen 80

Chapter Eighteen 86

Chapter Nineteen 90

Chapter Twenty 94

Chapter Twenty-One 99

Chapter twenty-Two 105

Chapter Twenty-Three 110

Chapter Twenty-four 116

Chapter Twenty-Five 120

Chapter Twenty-Six 125

Chapter Twenty-Seven 131

Chapter-Twenty-Eight 135

Chapter Twenty-Nine 140

Chapter Thirty 146

Chapter Thirty-One | Sixteen Years Later in Ballarat City: 152

Chapter Thirty-Two 157

Chapter Thirty-Three 162

Chapter Thirty-Four 166

Chapter Thirty-Five 170

Chapter Thirty-Five 175

Chapter Thirty-Seven 180

Chapter Thirty-Eight | Three years Hence. 185

Chapter Thirty-Nine 191

Chapter Thirty-Nine 197

Chapter Forty 203

Chapter Forty-One 210

Chapter Forty-Two 217

Chapter Forty-Three 223

To Those who read Historical Fiction

Prelude

In this city, where the echoes of the gold rush still whisper through the streets, an extraordinary discovery is poised to bring its storied past roaring back into the limelight.

The headlines in the Ballarat Local News Bulletin ripple with excitement throughout the community. A treasure has been unearthed, a beacon from the past shining bright in modern times. A prospector, his identity shrouded in secrecy, has chanced upon a relic that could rewrite history.

Local News Bulletin: *"Gold Found Near Ballarat"*
Published December 17, 2021 – 11:14 am By Dick Bonnard.

In the depths of Nerrina Forest, an unassuming ginger beer bottle contained a discovery worth a small fortune. Six troy ounces of gold flakes and several nuggets glinted within it, a legacy of Ballarat's once-abundant riches. This find defied all expectations.

Burt Rigg, the entrusted gold buyer, marvels at this extraordinary event. Only five kilometres from Ballarat's heart, buried a mere twenty centimetres beneath the earth, the treasure was discovered with a Minelab Equinox 800 – a modest metal detector that led to an astonishing find.

The bottle, embossed with the name "Rowland," harkens back to the golden era of 1853-1856. Its contents, valued at A$15,000, might fetch even more due to its rarity. Rigg emphasises the find's historical value: "Melting down this gold would be a crime. These nuggets are a piece of history, their worth transcending mere monetary value."

The prospector, a veteran of over two decades scouring the Ballarat region, had never found anything larger than a 5-gram nugget before this. The discovery, hidden in a land once called the district of Little Bendigo, overgrown with gorse and wild blackberries, emerged following a controlled burn by an FFM-VIC Crew. His metal detector, which had accompanied him on countless fruitless searches, finally sang the song of triumph.

"This find brings hope," the prospector shares with Rigg. "It's the culmination of a lifelong dream, a testament to perseverance. I never imagined finding such a treasure."

A history enthusiast, Rigg sees this discovery as starting a new adventure. He plans to explore Ballarat's Mechanic Institute library archives and Project Gutenberg Australia. His mission is to uncover the story of the person who hid or lost a treasured Rowland bottle over a century ago.

Ballarat stands on the cusp of a new era, where the past's whispers become a chorus, echoing through the present.

*From the 1860s to 1892, readers are again invited to journey through Riley's Legacy. Burt Rigg's archival research uncovered the owner of the ginger beer bottle through the writings of Levi Brody, Jack Riley's grandson. Their family saga, spanning generations, was initially chronicled by the author in an earlier edition titled "The Gravel Pits". The author has now revised that story with added chapters of discovery titled "Golden Bloodline - Unravelling the Riley Legacy," - the first of a new series, intertwining past and present in a dance of discovery and legacy. This book you are about to read is the second book in the series – Enjoy!

Chapter One

My story continues in the heart of the 1860s, penned with the ink of my heritage and Jack Riley's bloodline. I, Levi Brody, Jack Riley's grandson, chronicle the continuing legacy that intertwines with the tales of my father, Dan Farley. My mother, Alice Brody (nee Riley), also penned a manuscript for perpetuity. Their lives were synonymous within the raw cradle of the Ballarat goldfields, unravelling Jack Riley's enigmatic legacy and tracing it back to the Port Phillip Settlement of 1837.

As I etch these words onto my journal aboard a ship, I stand a fugitive of the Law amidst the grandeur of the SS Great Britain, a behemoth of the seas, poised to embark on a voyage laden with distance and intrigue. With its iron hull driven by wondrous steam power, this six-masted auxiliary steamer is my chosen escape vessel. It is not merely a ship but a floating microcosm of society, capable of accommodating hundreds of passengers and a dedicated crew, ever attentive to our myriad needs.

Beyond the human occupants, it harbours a menagerie, a vital source of sustenance for the impending long journey. Chickens, ducks, sheep, turkeys, geese, pigs, and even a milking cow with her calf reside in pens on the deck above the steerage passengers—those travellers are destined for conditions less than abundant.

My destination is the Swan River Colony, a mere pause in the ship's majestic voyage back to England. She had just completed a monumental task, depositing English migrants at Melbourne—a historic feat connecting Australia's first railway line from Flinders Street to the pier. These migrants, dubbed 'Four Pound Poms', disembarked in Melbourne, a town thirsting for labour, the goldfields having drained its workforce.

Yet, my journey is veiled in secrecy and peril. Falsely accused of murdering my grandfather, the notorious Jack Riley, I now wear the mask of John (Johnny) Cartwright, purchasing my anonymity with a hefty price – a pound of gold for a first-class cabin, a sanctuary from the gallows. The Purser, my sole confidant aboard, knows my true destination – Fremantle Port of Western Australia.

Before I settled into the cabin that shall be my sanctuary throughout the voyage, I diligently perused the guide program provided by the liner. Passengers are expected to be self-sufficient during this protracted sea journey. We are advised to pack essential items in a canvas bag, with the rest of our belongings relegated to a trunk stored in the ship's hold and only accessible once a week.

Life at sea, I soon discern, bears little resemblance to the comforts of home, especially for those who, unlike me, have opted for economical steerage accommodation. Storms in the stormy Southern Ocean are capricious, posing perpetual threats. Even in fair weather, hygiene conditions are deplorable, deteriorating to intolerable levels during storms. Using candles or oil lanterns is then restricted and, at times, forbidden altogether, a necessary precaution given the ship's combustible construction, comprising internal timbers, straw mattresses, and hemp rope. A solitary spark could engulf the vessel with horrifying rapidity.

In the event of a maritime disaster or a shipwreck on the coast, prospects of rescue are grim. Few passengers or sailors possess swimming skills, and the supply of lifeboats seldom matches the number of souls aboard.

The guide program enumerates each passenger's essentials—a survival blueprint. For a man, it advises six shirts, three Guernsey or flannel shirts, six pairs of stockings, one pair of sturdy boots and another of stout shoes, a suit of warm outer clothing, one of lighter attire: an extra pair of trousers, a soft hat, and a warm Southwester cap.

For an adult woman, the list comprises six chemises, six pairs of stockings, two flannel petticoats, two lighter petticoats, two pairs of suitable boots or shoes, a warm cloak with a hood, and a hat or lightweight bonnet for warm weather.

On the day of departure, I am conveyed to the docks in a handsome cab, the driver wisely positioned behind me, which avoids drawing attention to my identity. I meticulously orchestrated every detail of my escape by Fred Bailey, whom I entrusted after paying him a pound bar of gold (*introduced in the first *series, "Golden Bloodline 1"*).

Old Alby, Fred Bailey's right hand, ensured my seamless transition aboard, down to the provisioning of my meals and the modest garb of a gentleman of unassuming means.

As I stepped onto the vessel, the Purser, the gatekeeper of our floating citadel, surveyed each passenger with a discerning eye. Old Alby's discreet exchange with him cements my cover, sealing a silent pact with a nod.

A young steward guides me to my cabin, and I cross the threshold of the hatch marked 'First Class Passengers Only'. The ship, a marvel of its era, boasts six towering iron masts and a grand black funnel. Her hull, a striking contrast of black and white, is crowned with ornate golden scrollwork.

Though modest, my cabin is a haven of tranquillity. Bathed in natural light, it offers a respite from the noisy world outside. A two-seater sofa graces the outer wall, and a neatly arranged bunk bed completes the furnishings. A fold-down water basin is affixed to the entry wall, accompanied by pegs for hats and coats. Despite its compact size, there is ample space to change my clothing and store my two carpet bags.

As I settle onto the sofa in my cabin, my thoughts whirl like a stormy sea. Bailey's wise counsel echoes in my mind, urging me to remain within these four walls throughout the journey. This precautionary measure will help me avoid undue attention, preserve My privacy and security, shield myself from prying eyes, and prevent accidental slips of my identity in moments of drunkenness.

But with the grip of my addictions to alcohol and opium – I must now suffer the agonising grip of withdrawal symptoms upon my body, a relentless craving that claws at my sanity. The thought of liquor, its soothing caress, tempts me as my body's addiction longs for the solace of alcohol, with the withdrawal symptoms manifesting as agonising chest and stomach pains. My bones and head throb with the relentless craving.

I try hard to resist the temptation to leave my cabin, but the longer I sustain, the more my mind tortures me with the taste of liquor on my parched lips and the want of that first nobbler of rum with its soothing effect sliding down my throat, to flush my pains away.

I tear at my hair, beat my fists on my knees and against my head, and pace around my room with a feverish intensity. The absence of Laudanum to quell the torment leaves me restless and agitated. A desperate thought creeps into my mind—a fleeting notion that a plunge into the icy ocean might offer solace, a permanent escape from my relentless turmoil. Yet, reason battles against impulse, reminding me of my proficiency as a swimmer, a skill that renders such a drastic act futile.

Amidst the fevered chaos, fragments of my past assail me in my delirium. Visions of my beloved Ma, Alice Brody, her warm embrace and gentle voice calling me home to Ballarat, intertwined with memories of sweet Pol, my closest friend and confidant. Their spectral presence tugs at my heart, urging me to return to the solace of familiar faces and comforting arms.

But amidst these tender recollections, darker shadows loom. The image of Mr Lynn, my lawyer and erstwhile Trustee, flashes before me, his face contorted with fury as he chastises me for the murder he believes I committed. I see again the madness that consumed Jack Riley, his eyes ablaze with a deranged fervour before his final, fateful act of suicide. The echo of that gunshot reverberates in my mind, a chilling testament to the depths of his madness.

And yet, in his madness, Jack Riley orchestrated a final act of revenge—a twisted scheme to blame me for his demise. It was his retribution, a last-ditch effort to avenge the perceived sins of my mother, Alice, whom Riley disowned as his daughter.

She gave birth to me outside of wedlock - her transgression supposably disgracing Riley's family name. The weight of his vindictiveness hangs heavy upon me, a burden I cannot shake as I wrestle with the ghosts of my past and the spectre of false accusations.

Jolted awake by these phantoms, I stagger over to the wash basin and fill it from a pitcher to douse my face in cold water, seeking respite from my tormented thoughts. In my solitary chamber, as the ship prepares to cut through the harbour's expanse, I find myself wrestling with the ghosts of my past and the uncertain path ahead.

Chapter Two

As the SS Great Britain's mighty propeller churns into action, a jolt surges through me, the ship slicing through Port Phillip Bay's swells. Inside my cabin, I rummage through a carpetbag—not the one hiding the remaining three bars of gold grasped from Jack Riley, a lifeline from the noose, but another containing Old Alby's provisions. This bag reveals two coarse suits and undergarments, high brown leather boots, a wooden briar pipe, and a tobacco pouch.

Inhaling the unfamiliar tobacco, a poor substitute for my habitual opium smoking, I force myself to acclimatise, seeking any semblance of comfort. The smoke weaves through me, a temporary balm for my frayed nerves. Finally deciding to venture beyond my cabin's sanctuary, I tread the quiet corridor, tiptoeing past closed doors.

At the end of the long passage, I pass through a dual doorway that leads into a spacious dining floor. It contains polished bench tables with bench seats cushioned in purple satin and laid out in rows. Several splendid marble columns centre the dining room and support the upper deck.

The dining seats have hinged padded backrests that can be reversed to assist first-class passengers in sitting and looking towards the open space in the middle of the room when ball dancing or other entertainment is conducted within the same room.

On the tables, preparations have been made towards the evening meal. Each place setting contains crystal tumblers, a white cotton serviette held together by a gold ring, and a multitude of silver cutlery on either side of a large white dinner plate with a matching side plate.

A printed 'Bill of Fare' sits next to each setting, declaring the contents of a five-star dinner menu with a multitude of choices: beef, mutton, turkey, duck, mutton cutlets, tripe, ham, and pork. For desserts, a selection of pancakes, pastries, rice pudding, apple tart, fruit, omelettes, stewed prunes, and French pastry.

All food is included in the ticket price, but the drinks are provided at an exorbitant price. To accompany such fine fare is a choice of champagne, wine, brandy, rum, whisky, cognac, or ale. Pocketing a menu as a reminder of my cabin's entitlements, I beat a hasty retreat, my brief foray enough to satisfy curiosity and maintain my guise as Johnny Cartwright.

With my carefully maintained facade still intact, I make for my cabin, cautious not to draw any unnecessary attention. As I approach my cabin door, the door opposite mine opens abruptly, revealing a stout middle-aged gentleman. His head boasts thick, black, curly hair, and his complexion carries a rosy hue. A jovial smile lights up his face, and his attire, high-waisted black pants paired with a snug-fitting black vest adorned with a colourful cravat, suggests a pleasant character.

In a booming voice, he exclaims, "Good Day To Ya, Sir! Senan Doyle... be me name. I'm heading to the saloon for the ship's fine beverages. Would ya be inclined to accompany me... if ya don't mind the intrusion?" He extends his hand in a gesture of camaraderie.

This unexpected offer takes me aback, and my mind races with the potential consequences. My carefully preserved anonymity hangs in the balance. I weigh my options carefully, realising that refusing could draw even more attention to myself now that I am seen and possibly brand me as a hermit or someone struck down by illness if I don't reappear in the future. Accepting Doyle's company, on the other hand, might help legitimise myself as a familiar person among the other passengers.

"Johnny Cartwright," I introduce myself with a feigned ease. "I'm pleased to meet you, sir. I'll fetch my purse and be right with you." With a handshake and a nod, I quickly retreat into my cabin.

Once inside, I closed the door behind me, biting into my fist in frustration. I had been careless in leaving my cabin, endangering the anonymity crucial to my escape mission. I quickly regained my composure and exited the berth, finding Doyle waiting.

Doyle gives me a courteous bow and motions for me to follow. As we make for the saloon, we navigate the ship's labyrinthine passageways together. The other passengers, still acclimating to the voyage, cast curious glances in our direction. Yet, I do my utmost to blend in - a mere face in the crowd.

I maintained this charade the following days, often joining Doyle in the lively saloon. He's a character brimming with life, a true Irishman always pursuing merriment. His antics served as a welcome distraction for those around us, diverting their attention away from me and allowing me to become but a distant figure in their midst.

While the other passengers grow increasingly familiar to one another, forming bonds through drink and dance, I keep a respectful distance. I harbour no intention of making further acquaintances or forging other friendships. My mission demands anonymity, a pledge I'm unwaveringly committed to.

As the days pass, the saloon becomes a hotbed of activity, with drunken brawls frequently erupting. Offenders find themselves bound in irons, back-to-back, and serving a full-day sentence in the ship's hull as punishment.

Yet, as time progresses, Doyle's behaviour takes a noticeable turn for the worse. He indulges excessively in whisky and attempts to dance with every lady in sight, often without their consent. Surprisingly, he manages to elude the same fate as the other troublemakers. I distance myself from his increasingly erratic conduct, conveying my disapproval through heavy sighs and subtle hunches of my shoulders when eyes turn my way, offering a disapproving "tut-tut."

Doyle, it turns out, is no stranger to Australia. He regales me with tales of his life, originally hailing from England as a 'Four Pound Pom' who emigrated to this land in the late 1850s. He made his fortune in the Victorian goldfields by investing in several gold mining ventures. However, the tragic loss of his wife compels him to return to Ireland, his newfound wealth in tow, in search of a new beginning and perhaps another wife.

Before he ventured to the saloon this morning, I visited Doyle in his cabin. I engaged him in conversation, eager to learn more about the life of emigrants aboard ships bound for Australia, especially in contrast to those in steerage on our vessel who return home to England at their own expense.

Doyle doesn't hold back in his descriptions. "There isn't much difference," he begins, "between those who must dwell in decks below the waterline. It's a cramped, smelly, and perilous existence with nary a porthole to admit fresh air."

He explains that the cost of private steerage for those returning home is equivalent to half a farm labourer's yearly wage. The passengers in steerage sleep in narrow bunk beds lining both sides of a gallery, each bed separated by a flimsy curtain that offers scant privacy. Space is so restricted that changing clothes or stowing belongings is an exercise in acrobatics. Meals are served at communal tables placed at the end of each gallery.

Doyle grimaces, describing the rations under the emigrants 'Steerage 1855 Passenger Act: "Three ship's biscuits a day," he scoffs, "revolting things made mostly of flour and water, passed off as a substitute for fresh bread. Breakfast consists of one biscuit with a weak mug of tea or coffee, their weekly supply of tea leaves or ground coffee beans barely filling two dessert spoons.

"Lunch isn't much better: tea or coffee, another biscuit, some salted beef, rice, and a bit of potato. Then, for dinner, more weak tea or coffee, biscuit, and perhaps a simple pudding, like 'Plum Duck'—cheap and soggy, made of flour, water, and raisins. They're then allocated lime juice to ward off scurvy, and their weekly sugar ration is a paltry 6 ounces or 8 ounces of treacle."

Doyle continues to explain that government regulations: "Regulations dictate every facet of daily life on British emigrant ships departing English ports. Passengers must rise by 7 a.m., ensuring all children are washed and dressed before breakfast at 8 a.m., followed by the school for the young ones. At 9 a.m., the decks are meticulously cleaned, with passengers assigned to scrub areas not belonging to their mess.

"Dinner is served promptly at 1 pm," he continues, "followed by tea at 6 pm, and lights out at 8 pm. Steerage passengers are responsible for cleaning their berths, which starts their day. Regulations even dictate the timing of religious services, weekly musters for inspection by the Surgeon Superintendent on wash days, and the daily cleaning of the wash-coppers.

Doyle notes, "Afternoons are typically complimentary for emigrants to while away as they please, depending on the weather. Leisure activities include sewing, reading, writing letters and diaries, eating, drinking, and sleeping. It's a life characterised by routine, punctuated by the same everyday activities.

"Movement is restricted," Doyle continues. "Single men are typically berthed in the bow, married couples in the middle, and single women in the stern. First-class passengers like us have exclusive access to the poop deck, and we can entertain in our cabins or saloons. Lower-class ticket holders can only enter first class by invitation. The single women below are closely supervised by a matron responsible for their physical and moral well-being. They're physically segregated, often fenced off from the rest of the passengers and occasionally confined at night."

As he leans back, satisfied with his narration, I am left pondering the chasm that divides us, the stark disparity between the worlds within this single vessel.

Returning to my cabin, my mind races with the stories of those confined below, their lives a stark reminder of the inequalities that permeate even this floating microcosm. It's a revelation that stirs something deep within me, a newfound awareness of the broader world beyond my immediate concerns.

Chapter Three

On the fourth morning aboard the SS Great Britain, tragedy strikes. A passenger succumbs to a fierce bout of lung inflammation, and the solemnity of death envelopes the ship. His body, shrouded in canvas and weighted with iron, is draped in the Union Jack. Six sailors, dressed in their finest, carry him to the Lee Gangway. As Captain Gray solemnly recites the burial service, the board tilts, and the body descends into the sea's embrace.

A wave of unease sweeps the ship as thieves grow bolder. Just last night, a brazen rogue twice attempted to rob the inebriated Mr Doyle of his pocket watch and purse. Fortune favours Doyle as he stirs at each intrusion, though too dazed to give chase.

The fifth day dawns with unexpected liveliness, thanks to Captain Thomas, a retired military officer. His illustrious service during Tasmania's 'Black War' and the 'Eureka Stockade Rebellion' in Ballarat lends him a certain aura. Yet aboard the ship, he's embarking on a whimsical endeavour – forming 'The Great Western Rifle Corp,' a mock military unit.

I had a personal run-in with the captain when I left my friend Raffaello Carboni's tent the morning of the 'Eureka Stockade Battle' to assist any wounded miners. Sub-inspector Carter had advanced toward me with his pointed pistol and ordered me to fall in with a batch of prisoners behind him. I obeyed on seeing the look of his demeanour. As we were herded along, I protested to Captain Thomas within the gully, who said, 'Where you made a prisoner within the stockade, lad?'

'No, Sir!' I said, and he noted my paleness and astonished look as I lowered my head. After more explanation, he gave me a gentle stroke with his sword and said, 'If you are an honest digger, I don't want you. You are free to return to your tent.'

I keep my identity a mystery on this vessel, observing Captain Thomas from afar. I'm curious about his training methods, which I compare to those I witnessed with the Diggers before the Eureka Rebellion.

Thomas arranges his make-believe army into two ranks: the mock Dragoons, comprising first-class passengers, and his Regimental Troopers from the second class. I watch from a distance, stifling laughter as these untrained men clumsily collide and stumble, their mock weapons - mops and brooms - bobbing comically overhead. Their training at dusk, a time chosen for its cooler air but also when most men are tipsy from afternoon libations, turns into a farcical display.

The crescendo of this spectacle comes when Thomas orchestrates a mock battle against the ship's 'Sailors Corp.' The battle, a chaotic blend of manoeuvring and mock charges, devolves into chaos when the sailors open fire with 'Lucifer matchhead' loaded into their muskets. The flares from the muskets singe several Dragoon's beards, and the resulting melee is a whirlwind of flailing fists, brooms, and mops as most onlookers run for dear life.

On the fifth evening, the Southern Ocean's fury is unleashed. A tremendous crash shudders the ship, sending water cascading over the decks and into our cabins. I give myself up for lost, and I hear people rushing out of their cabins, so I charge out of my berth to see those all about with looks of absolute terror.

Doyle's cabin door is wide open, and I see him sitting there relatively calm until his lips start to move without sound, and I notice he looks as pale as death. The hatches have been battened down to keep out the water. Some young first-class ladies start screaming and try to climb up the hatchway, calling on the officers on deck to let them out. We don't know what the outcome is. Some think the tall spar mast has smashed, and the ship's structure groans and creaks as rumours abound about the ship's damage.

Braving the storm, a retired sea captain returns with news that soothes frayed nerves—"it's just part of the damaged bulwarks and hatching. The saloon is flooded, and all hands, even the servers, are drafted for bailing duties."

Late this night, the swell from the storm abates. Poor old Doyle is still green around the gills - badly in need of the 'hair of the dog', but with the saloon out of action, he is attended to by Mr Black, the ship's doctor, without relief.

I then decide to look in on Doyle; he looks up at me from his sofa with a sour face and says, "Johnny, it is enough to pitch me insides out. It's now all up to our own survival. I can't stir, but the good doctor can give me no relief, but I'm not surprised. He's very young, has never been to sea, and is just as ill as all the rest of us."

I don't feel the effects of seasickness for whatever reason. I find solace on the poop deck, the mainland visible on the starboard side, and I ask an officer seated nearby where we are on our journey.

'We're one day from reaching King George Sound, lad, named by Commander George Vancouver in 1781 onboard 'Discovery' when he sailed into the sound and named it for King George the Third. Then, in 1832, the Governor of the Swan River Colony himself, Sir James Stirling, visited the convict settlement there. There was even the possibility of moving the Western Australian Capital of Perth to King George Sound, which never happened, and he renamed the town Albany after the Duke of York and Albany.'

As the officer moves away, I thank him, "Thank you, sir! I am much obliged!"

Late this particular night, with the saloon still closed on drinks and entertainment, I venture outside the hatchway onto the poop deck, reflecting on my good fortune in escaping Melbourne Town and my presumed appointment with the hangman as Jack Riley's assumed killer. A full moon casts shimmering light beams around the frothy churning wake trailing the ship. The shoreline is visible as an inky painted silhouette off at a distance, and the sea around the boat is now spent from its earlier turbulence from the storm.

I begin filling my pipe for the pleasure it will afford me when my attention is overtaken by the sudden cast of two shadows before me upon the deck. I quickly turn to see the form of two burly sailors moving stealthily towards me. One raises his arm, and before I have time to contemplate my next move, I feel the blow of a wooden baton and hear my skull crack, which resonates through my whole body. Stunned, I collapse to my knees and try unsuccessfully to get up.

One of the offenders holds onto me from behind as I am on my knees, and the other fronting me begins to slap me about the face, saying, "Stay alert, lad and listen well. The Purser has cold feet towards yuh. Yuh, a liability he no longer wishes to carry. It's known that the Coast Guard at Albany might come onboard for a Customs visit with a head count from our passenger register checking for unregistered persons onboard – for Ta' likes of an accused murderer such as yerself.

'Now, with yuh skylarking about the ship as bold as brass, we can no longer stow yuh away as invisible. Do ya understand where I'm coming from, lad? Had ya stayed in your cabin, out of sight, as expected... that is? Now yuh gonna be missed by the other passengers during any headcount."

I hear the words as if spoken through a bullhorn, and my head throbs; I reply mournfully, "Yes, I Hear You!"

The rouge sailor continues, "Now the Purser, being an honourable man, and yuh have paid good money for yuh escape... so he's gonna compromise with yuh! Yer is about to go over the side, but given this 'ere lifebuoy, See! Yer can then make for shore in yuh own good time. If yuh makes it, and help comes yuh way... well, we'll be long gone.'

Chapter Four

Cast Into the Wilderness
A canvas life-saving ring, buoyed by cork, descends over my head before I plunge into disoriented darkness. Still dazed from the blow, I lack the strength to resist as the ring tightens around my body. I begin flailing my arms wildly, but they are quickly pinned down as the lifebuoy is forced down to my waist.

My arms are yanked free and dangle limply over the ring's sides. Strong hands seize me, hauling me toward the ship's stern railing. Panic surges through me, and I jerk my body about to break free from my captors, but their grip remains unyielding.

"Stop... Wait!" I shout desperately as they hold me aloft. "If you can keep me hidden from the Purser until we reach Fremantle Port, I promise you a reward of gold. Enough to buy your freedom from your voyage contract. Let the Purser think I went overboard! You don't have to do This!"

A harsh, mocking laughter fills the air. "Too much risk, lad, for both the Purser and us," he replies with a sly grin. "And what gold are you talking about, eh? The gold yuh had stashed away in yuh cabin. It's already been found, Lad, and confiscated in your absence to be divvied among all of us involved in this dirty deed... Ha, har! All I 'ave left to say is farewell, me Hearty, and may yuh 'ave a fortunate landin'!"

I am immediately tossed overboard, plunging into the ship's tumultuous wake. The impact with the water is jarring, my feet making contact first. There is a distinct thud followed by a Plop as the lifebuoy's cork-filled interior breaks apart within its canvas cover. The ring surrounding me, once rigid, now becomes a limp sponge, tossed about by the ship's turbulent wake.

My head is submerged below water, and I am propelled within the churning turmoil with alarming speed. The sheer volume of seawater

I swallow threatens to overwhelm me, and for a harrowing moment, I fear I might succumb to drowning.

As the ship's wake gradually loses grip, the sea reverts to a gentler, rhythmic roll. I muster every ounce of strength and begin dogpaddling to keep myself afloat. It becomes painfully clear that if I am to escape this watery abyss, I will have to swim to the shore unassisted. Now torn and filled with seawater, the lifebuoy proves more hindrance than a help, so I remove it and watch it disappear, being washed away.

The memory of learning to swim in Lake Wendouree, Ballarat, now serves as my lifeline. Those days spent mimicking the overarm crawl of Aboriginal children in the shallow waters have prepared me for this desperate moment. The chill of the Southern Ocean strikes a stark contrast against the day's scorching heat. I hastily shed my brown boots, knowing my clothes are my only shield against the wilderness that awaits me onshore.

With each overarm stroke, I push through the water, setting a rhythm that must carry me further than I've ever dared. The ocean's relentless swells toss me, intensifying my disorientation and nausea. Then, a chilling thought grips me – the memory of sharks trailing the ship, their dark fins slicing through the water.

I pat the pocket of my pants, reassured by the presence of my folded pocketknife, its blade ready to unfold into a formidable weapon. The thought of facing those primeval predators hastens my strokes, fuelling my desperate escape from the ship's ominous wake.

As I swim, a distant glimmer of light on the shoreline becomes my beacon of hope. It signifies human presence, perhaps settlers or sealers, and my potential salvation. I navigate the currents, aiming for the light, alternating between vigorous overarm strokes, dog paddling, and fleeting moments to rest on my back.

Suddenly, a presence collides with me from the depths – a solid, slick entity nudging against my side. Panic surges through me. I fumble for my knife, twisting in the water, blade poised in defence. After a moment of heart-stopping fear, the sea calms, leaving me alone in my desperate swim.

Time blurs as I battle the ocean. My body trembles from the cold, exhaustion clouding my senses. I focus my mind, willing each stroke to bring me closer to safety. Occasionally, I pause to realign myself with the distant light, ensuring I'm still on course.

My strength wanes as the shore draws nearer, but my resolve does not falter. Each stroke becomes a testament to my determination, a silent vow to reach the safety of land. The night's cloak envelops me, the moon's light my only guide as I swim towards the unknown - towards a chance at survival.

A roar shatters the night's silence, jolting me from my exhaustive rhythm. I pause, straining my eyes in the darkness, seeking the source of the furore. The numbing cold of the ocean is a relentless adversary, threatening to sap the last vestiges of my strength. The sea's icy grip will claim me forever if I don't reach the shore soon.

Then, as though heeding my silent plea, the full moon breaks free from the cloud cover, bathing the tumultuous waters in a ghostly luminescence. The chaotic scene before me comes into sharp relief – the churning whitecaps crashing over a surfaced reef. Beyond this barrier, perhaps a hundred yards away, lies my salvation: a sandy beach kissed by moonlight and the enigmatic flicker of artificial light.

With this beacon beckoning me, a burst of adrenaline ignites within. I marshal every ounce of my waning energy, pushing towards that distant shore with renewed urgency. Nearing the reef, an immense wave rises like a monster, its fury enveloping me. It flings me into a whirlpool of foam and water, my body a mere plaything in its powerful grasp.

Beneath the churning surface, I battle desperately, my limbs flailing against the water's ferocious pull. When I finally break free, gasping for air, I'm swept along by the thunderous tide. Pain sears through my thigh as it's torn open by the jagged reef, and my arm, thrust down to slow my relentless forward motion, is grazed raw.

My mind, however, remains fixated on the mysterious light that has beckoned me through the night. As I drag myself onto the reef, scanning the shoreline, the elusive light remains just that – elusive. Perhaps it was nothing more than a lantern, now abandoned, its temporary guardians swallowed by the darkness of the bush.

With every fibre of my being crying out in protest, I clamber to my feet, each movement a battle against the exhaustion that clings to me like a second skin. Despite the pain and fatigue, my resolve stands firm. I need to uncover the truth behind that solitary light—to find out who or what awaits me on this unknown shore.

Chapter Five

Exhausted and battered, I stagger towards the elusive sanctuary of the shore, which now lies tantalisingly within my grasp beyond this reef. Each step is a battle against the relentless current and jagged coral beneath. In sheer misfortune, a cruel piece of coral pierces through my right stockinged foot. Pain surges through me, but almost mercifully, a powerful wave sweeps me over the reef, casting me into deeper, calmer, inshore waters.

Gasping for air, I crawl towards the shore, the water gently washing over my torn, blood-stained right stockinged foot. My entire body is a symphony of pain and weariness. Overcome by exhaustion, I surrender to unconsciousness, the comforting lull of the sea coaxing me into a deep, dreamless slumber.

Dawn greets me with a soft light, but the sight of bloodied water and sand around me mars the tranquillity. My foot and arm wounds, though not life-threatening, bleed profusely. With trembling hands, I fashion makeshift bandages from my trouser legs by cutting them with my pocketknife just below the knees, staunching the flow of blood as best as I can.

Gritting my teeth against the pain, I embark on a laborious journey along the cove's embracing shoreline. The beach, flanked by imposing rocky outcrops and towering cliffs, offers a rugged beauty that's lost on my pained senses. Despite my agony, I press on, driven by the urgent need to find shelter and aid.

I veer right, instinctively aware that the currents must have carried me far from where I first plunged into the ocean. Each footfall on the coarse sand sends jolts of pain up my leg, relentlessly reminding me of my dire situation.

Amidst this arduous trek, I stumble upon a recent sign of life - the remnants of a fire. Charred wood, encircled by stones and mussel shells, tells of recent human activity. The sight of human footprints crisscrossing the sand confirms it. I recognise the signs of the land's indigenous inhabitants.

Approaching the abandoned mia-mias shelters in the bush, I am filled with trepidation and curiosity. These simple structures, expertly crafted from nature, offer a glimpse into a different life. Yet, uncertainty gnaws at me. I am a stranger here, an outsider who washed ashore and is now unfamiliar with these remote people's customs and disposition. The mia-mias, now empty, stand as silent witnesses to my intrusion. I wonder whether my presence will be met with hostility or understanding, a question that hangs heavily in the air.

As I cautiously navigate this unfamiliar territory, I reflect on my experiences with these indigenous inhabitants. I encountered similar dwellings in Ballarat's Little Bendigo District and learned to Appreciate their builders' skill and resourcefulness. But here, on this unknown shore, I face a new challenge: to bridge the gap between two worlds and find common ground with those who call this land home.

The closing redness of the sun casts long shadows, accentuating the stark beauty of the landscape and the isolation of my predicament. In this moment of solitude, I am acutely aware of my vulnerability, a lone figure standing at the crossroads of an uncertain future.

Huddled within the crude shelter of the mia-mia, the weight of my harrowing ordeal presses down on me. Thirst rages in my throat, and hunger claws at my belly, but these primal needs pale beside the overwhelming sense of solitude that swallows me whole. As nightfall shrouds the landscape, the shadows lengthen, morphing into ominous spectres that dance at the edge of my vision.

Every rustle in the underbrush, every whisper of wind, raises my awareness. The gulf between me and civilisation feels insurmountable, engulfing my senses and leaving me adrift in a sea of isolation. Restlessness grips me, a relentless force that drives me from the fragile safety of the mia-mia into the treacherous night, where it feels like unseen dangers lurk in every shadow.

Sleep eludes me, and instead, I'm haunted by memories. The tapestry of my past – Levi Brody's life – unfolds in my mind's eye. Scenes from my childhood in Geelong, the oppressive shadow of my stepfather Bill Brody, and the trials with my mother, Alice, are interwoven with my days as a tent-maker under Mr Crockett. Visions of the Eureka Stockade Battle, where I stood alongside one of the stockade leaders, Raffaello Carboni, flicker before me, followed by recollections of my school days under Master Crawley at 'The Melbourne Learning Academy', which was re-birthed as Scotch College in Melbourne.

In this whirlwind of memories, the figure of sweet Pol emerges, her aboriginal heritage casting an enigmatic allure, her presence marking my first brush with love. These fragments of my life, chronicled in "Unravelling the Riley Legacy," drift through my consciousness like ghosts.

The first rays of dawn pull me from this reverie, casting a golden glow on my plight. My lips are cracked and parched, and I am consumed by a desperate thirst. Hunger gnaws relentlessly. My wounded limbs, though painful, are the least of my worries.

Driven by a survival instinct, I follow the indigenous footprints etched in the sand. They lead me up a rocky slope to a cliffside cave, a haven above the restless tide. The cliff's natural incline facilitates the ascent, though arduous. I find myself staring at the vast ocean from the cave's mouth.

Pools of fresh water left by the previous storm around the cliff face quench my thirst. Over the days, I tend to my wounds with care, using my makeshift bandages and the healing properties of bruised Wattle Tree leaves, a remedy learned from Raffaello Carboni. The seawater, too, plays its part in staving off infection.

As I explore the clifftop, I discover a vine laden with ripe melons, their sweet flesh a welcome reprieve. Nearby bushes yield black and white currants, whose dried fruits will be crucial sustenance for my impending journey towards civilisation.

Each day, I grow stronger, my resolve hardening. Once a daunting adversary, the wild, untamed land around me now offers the promise of survival. With each passing moment, the memories of my past life in Ballarat and Melbourne become distant echoes, replaced by an immediate need to forge a new path to find my way back to a world I once knew.

Chapter Six

Perched upon a seaside boulder, I contemplate my next course of action, meditating upon the challenges ahead. In my reflective solitude, I remain oblivious to the world around me, save for the gentle lapping of the wavelets against the rocky shore and the dapple play of sunlight upon the beach. It is then that the chorus of human voices shatters my contemplative cocoon.

Startled to attention, I turn, only to behold three blackfellas standing atop the cliff above me. My instincts prompt me to seek concealment, for I am ignorant of these indigenous inhabitants' nature. Fearful of premature exposure, I scramble back towards the cave, uncertain if my presence has been detected.

However, the trio gracefully pursues me from rock to rock, eventually converging at the cave's entrance. They beckon and shout with unwavering determination, compelling me to emerge from my sanctuary. I comply, arising from the shelter to face their bewildering gazes. Their inquisitive fingers trace over my person, my tattered clothing, and my fair skin.

Resisting any inclination to fight, I allow their examination to go unhindered. Eager words flow from their lips in ceaseless chatters while their probing hands prod and poke my body. After several minutes, their scrutiny concludes, and the natives enact a series of gestures and actions that mystify me.

In a peculiar ritual, they thumped their chests and, in turn, mine. The symmetry of their movements puzzles me until they conclude their nonverbal exchange and step back. None possess imposing physiques; their lithe frames surpass those of the average white man, and innate agility characterises their appearance. Adorning their modest shoulders are cloaks fashioned from possum fur, its softness next to their skin. Their attire, reaching just above their knees, protected them against the elements.

Each trio bares spears of considerable length, weapons that arouse my apprehension. Had they intended to mark me as their target, my physical strength would have offered me little recourse. Yet, rather than malice, their curiosity seems to govern their actions.

As the initial astonishment subsides, the natives explore the comforts I have assembled within the cave. Without apologising or hesitation, one appropriates some of my dry grass bedding to kindle a roaring fire. Another venture into the sea, returning triumphantly with a sizable lobster, which is promptly dispatched into the flames.

The lobster is divided into portions upon roasting, and the largest share is generously offered to me. I accept the gesture with gratitude, my unease giving way to a glimmer of trust. Concluding our communal repast, the natives intend me to accompany them. Initially hesitant, I seek to express my reservations through gestures, stamping my foot, shaking my head, and gesturing toward my objective of the western coastline.

However, my protests meet their resistance, and I soon find myself concurring with their wishes. Our party begins a journey, guided by their watchful presence, which leads us into the bush as daylight wanes. The sun descends beneath the horizon as we reach two rudimentary mia-mias fashioned with bark and turf. Our group disperses, and all seek reprieve within these primitive shelters.

My assigned sleeping quarter is nestled inside the bark construct, affording me little personal space. My bedfellow, a singularly putrid individual, shares my confines. His dirt- and grease-clad form exudes an unpleasant odour that permeates the cramped space. Throughout the night, he awakes intermittently, muttering in fear of some unseen adversary. His restless vigil baffles my secret plans to escape within the night's cover.

As dawn breaks, painting the sky with streaks of gold, the natives signal their intent to continue our journey. Their impatience is palpable, yet I stand resolute, my foot firmly stamped on the ground, my head shaking emphatically, my gestures pointedly indicating my refusal to proceed. A silent battle of wills unfolds between us.

A tempest of frustration erupts among them, their animated gesticulations painting the air with their irritation. Despite their vehement protests, I remain unwavering; my resolve is an unbroken bastion against their persuasions. Ultimately, my steadfastness prevails, though not without their lingering desire to claim my ragged stockings as a memento of our strange encounter. But I stand firm, clinging to my long socks, symboling my defiance.

The irony of my situation does not escape me. Had I been in the clutches of the American Red Indians Vern the German spoke of in Ballarat, I might have faced a fate more dire than a mere tussle over stockings and perhaps lost my scalp. Yet, here, among these indigenous Australians, my obstinance pays off. After a fervent exchange, they depart, albeit reluctantly.

Unexpectedly, one returns, extending an olive branch in the form of a rush basket filled with berries. The offer, a gesture of goodwill, tempts me, yet I hold fast to my resolve. This blackfella, faced with my unyielding stance, leaves the basket and his fire stick, a smouldering torch I can use for my fires.

The craftsmanship of the basket is a marvel, intricately woven from split rushes, embodying both beauty and utility. The dew-kissed and inviting berries offer a welcome reprieve from my growing hunger.

Ensuring solitude, I make my way towards the coast. The landscape transforms, the sea crashing against the rocky and shingly terrain. A group of seals plays nearby, some lounging in the sun, others dancing in the waves. As dusk approaches, I search the shores, my eyes keen for any sign of sustenance. Finding none, I return to the cave.

Settling back into my shelter, I fortify it with more dry grass, resigning myself to the relentless hunger that gnaws at me. The berries are my only respite, a small comfort as I slip into a fitful sleep, the day's trials weighing heavily upon me.

Chapter Seven

With the night chill seeping into my cave, I kindle a fire at its entrance using the smouldering fire stick. While offering warmth, the crackling flames carry with them an unintended consequence—a peculiar magnetism that draws the attention of the untamed inhabitants of this rugged shoreline. Wild dogs, the notorious Dingoes, come loping onto the beach, their inquisitive eyes reflecting a fiery glow. Agile creatures, the inquisitive possums, venture above me, adding their curious scrutiny to the nocturnal symphony.

Throughout this harrowing night, I remain entrenched within my rocky refuge, compelled to listen to the horrid howls of the dogs, their eerie cries harmonising with the shrill, childlike wails of others. Each blood-curdling note shatters the silence, rendering my rest fleeting, and my senses are on edge. I cast my gaze into the abyss of the surrounding darkness, seeing naught but the looming silhouettes of boulders and the inky void of the sea beyond, a relentless reminder of my solitude.

As the fire dwindles towards dawn, I don't venture outside to replenish it for fear of the night's lurking dangers. I endure a fitful slumber; my body is weak from the prolonged vigil and provides little solace. Suddenly, a hideous clamour from an overhanging branch near my shelter pierces the crisp morning air, jolting me from my restless dreams. I gaze upward in terrified alertness, witnessing several sombre-looking birds, more prominent than pigeons but with ungainly, robust bodies and disproportionately large heads and beaks.

Their beaks stretch wide in grotesque mockery and emit a series of unearthly chuckles that seize hold of my senses, marking them unmistakably as Kookaburras. These feathered jesters seem to mock and deride me. Before each raucous outburst, they fixate their curious, knowing eyes upon me, their heads slightly cocked as if probing the depths of my very being. These laughing jackasses revel in their fiendish din, an ostentatious overture heralding the imminent dawn, awakening all, be they human or feathered, still nestled in their beds.

My ears are tormented every night by these otherworldly sounds, obliterating any hope of peaceful slumber since their first appearance. Under such relentless assault, even a person of average strength would be utterly spent, incapacitated by exhaustion. However, I persevere, gradually succumbing to mental lethargy yet maintaining a nomadic existence, searching for meagre sustenance in the form of roots, berries, and small shellfish to appease the ceaseless gnawing of my empty belly.

As winter tightens, the climate grows more unforgiving, and the bleak beach becomes a miserable abode. With the rising cold, once-plentiful shellfish become scarce, and I contemplate that I might have depleted all available seasonal nourishment in the vicinity. The unforgiving elements wear my garments to tatters, offering scant protection against the encroaching chill. These relentless hardships severely impact my animal spirit, gradually eroding my stubborn resistance.

Desperation clings to me like a shroud, and I yearn for change, any change that might offer relief from my dire predicament. Thus, like the prodigal son of parable, I resolve to arise and return to my lawful custodians and undertake the arduous trek to the Albany settlement of South-Western Australia. With this determination, I set forth, lamenting that I had not undertaken this journey a month prior when food was more plentiful.

This evening, my weary trudging leads me to a desolate stretch of shoreline on the far side of the cove. The relentless tide pens me against an almost vertical wall of rock, forcing me to scramble into a cavern above the high-water mark. The cavern emanates a pungent odour like rotting fish, leaving me with no choice but to take refuge there for the night. As the tide creeps inward, several seals, or seal elephants, splash and frolic in the vicinity of my shelter.

Locked in my rocky sanctuary until the tide recedes, I excessively watch these slippery intruders converge upon my retreat. Fear surges through me, and I emit a wild, terror-stricken Yell, my voice echoing within the cavern. Frightened and disoriented, the seals clamber over each other, retreating to their watery domain, leaving me victorious and the sole inhabitant of their stony sanctuary. They do not trouble me again that night; I resume my journey with the tide's ebb.

Progress becomes a distant dream as my vitality ebbs. With the last remnants of my strength, I construct a makeshift shelter against the relentless chill, then succumb to restless sleep, my body wracked with fatigue. Dawn's light unveils a startling sight—an earth mound crowned with the remnants of a blackfella's spear. Ignorant of its sacred significance, I claim it to support my weakened frame. Little do I realise that this spear will soon become more than a mere crutch.

My journey degenerates into a desperate crawl. Each movement is an agony, hands and knees dragging my worn body across the unforgiving land. As night descends, I huddle beneath sparse bushes, shivering uncontrollably, the cold seeping into my bones.

In this desolate hour, the mournful howls of distant dingoes pierce the silence, awakening an ancient superstition within me. In Ballarat, it was said that a dog's sorrowful cry portends death. This belief gnaws at me, the dismal cries echoing like an ominous harbinger of my looming demise.

Yet, with the break of dawn, survival instincts flare anew. Hobbling from tree to tree, I scrape at the gum oozing from eucalyptus trunks, my meagre sustenance. But soon, even this effort proves too much, and I collapse under the sheltering boughs of a towering eucalyptus.

There, in the depths of my despair, time becomes a blur. I lay motionless, the spear clutched tightly in my grasp – a final link to life. I drift into a trance-like state, teetering between the living world and the vast unknown.

My plight catches the attention of two Aboriginal Lubras. Their initial curiosity turns to apprehension as they regard my prostrate form. Startled by my feeble motions, they flee, only to return with two wary warriors.

As they approach, their tentative touch stirs me from my stupor. Leveraging the spear, I manage to sit upright, clinging to it as if to life itself. To their eyes, I must seem a spectral figure, a ghostly apparition, perhaps mistaken for a spirit from the world beyond, echoing the sight of their recent burial rites.

Their presence, a mix of concern and wariness, hovers around me. Their gaze reflects my frailty—a man clinging to the last shreds of hope, a solitary soul adrift in a harsh and unforgiving land.

The scene before me is steeped in Aboriginal theology. The natives, believing that a departed soul can reincarnate as a whitefella, view me as a living embodiment of their ancestral creed. Their acceptance is tangible. Their friendly thumps on my chest welcome me to my feet, and their hands blend gentleness and strength.

Guided by their kindness, I shuffle forward, flanked by the women whose sympathetic aid bolsters my every step. Ahead, the men's animated exclamations and extravagant gestures slice through the still morning air, a display that oscillates between jubilation and sorrow. The depth of their emotions is an enigma to me.

Nourishment is offered in the form of a root that tantalises my taste buds, akin to a sweet carrot. Ravenous, I consume it eagerly, my voracious appetite met with nods of approval and quiet satisfaction from my saviours.

With my hunger sated, the tribe convenes around me in a whirlwind of emotions. Their joy at my survival intertwines with sorrow for the trials I've endured. They express their feelings in a ritualistic display – men pounding their heads with wooden waddies, their anguish palpable in each heavy thud. Women's howls pierce the air as they tear at their hair in grief-stricken abandon. The intensity of their self-flagellation crescendos into a dizzying frenzy, leaving many exhausted and injured in the wake of their enthusiasm.

As the ceremony wanes, a sense of calm descends. The tribe disperses, seeking solace in the cool embrace of their mia-mias, their energies spent. They turn to roasted roots to restore their depleted strength, the mood transitioning to one of domestic tranquillity.

I am left to ponder the profound implications of their beliefs, as my comrade Raffaello Carboni from Ballarat once shared with me. He had enlightened me on the Aboriginal creed—a belief in the soul's journey post-mortem to another realm, where transformation into a whitefella occurs before returning to this world anew. In their eyes, I am perceived as one reborn, perhaps a former adversary, now returned in a different guise.

Ingrained in their culture, this perception casts me in an extraordinary light. To them, I am a familiar spirit in an unfamiliar form, a once-known blackfella reborn as a whitefella, returning from a conflict in a new existence. Though steeped in mysticism, their acceptance of me offers a bridge between our worlds, an unexpected but welcome connection in this land of ancient mysteries and timeless beliefs.

Chapter Eight

As the sun dips towards the horizon, the camp, once a haven of tranquillity, transforms into a hive of frenetic activity. My heart races, and sweat beads on my brow as the indigenous inhabitants prepare for an event of grand significance. A chilling thought grips me – could they be planning a savage ritual with me as the unwitting centrepiece? The tales of my youth, spun by my stepfather Bill Brody, haunt me now – stories of whitefella hearts devoured in grim dawn feasts.

The tribe's younger members busily collect wood and bark, constructing a towering pyre. As darkness blankets the camp, the pile is set ablaze, its flames leaping skyward in a primal dance. I retreat to my friend's mia-mia, seeking refuge. Yet, I'm gently coaxed back to the fire by the women, a procession of bare bodies holding fur skins.

The men emerge from the shadows, their bodies adorned with white pipe clay. Some are smeared sporadically, others meticulously covered, creating eerie patterns reminiscent of skeletal apparitions. As they approach, the women, with their fur skins stretched across their knees, create makeshift drums, adding to the night's cacophony.

An elder steps forward, his presence commanding. He leads the assembly in a sonorous chant, the monotone melody of his didgeridoo piercing the air. The men's rhythmic striking of their waddies joins in, creating an overwhelming symphony. To my unaccustomed ears, this musical ensemble is more an overwhelming, horrific racket than a harmonious blend.

With an air of grace and authority, the conductor orchestrates this theatrical performance—a spectacle of dance, drama, and synchronised movement. The zenith of their display is marked by three thunderous shouts echoing into the heavens. Then, they envelop me, their chests thumping in a friendly gesture that bewilders yet comforts me.

Surrounded by these amiable souls, I feel an unexpected safety and gratitude. The tribe disperses, each returning to their mia-mias, and I'm left in the care of my four guardians. They offer me more roots to eat, and after partaking, I retire to a bed of dried twigs and grass, slipping into a deep, rejuvenating slumber.

Morning finds the camp serene, starkly contrasting with the previous night's revelry. I'm greeted with warm regard, and in turn, I strive to reciprocate, engaging in daily chores alongside the women – fetching water, carrying firewood, and digging for roots. My participation in such tasks undoubtedly surprises the camp, perhaps even challenging their initial perception of me.

Meanwhile, in their customary roles, the men focus on hunting, their primary sustenance being possum flesh – a hearty yet unusual diet for me, yet the most fulfilling meals since my arrival.

Observing the creatures they hunt, I note their resemblance to large felines, save for the possums' longer, thicker tails, which they use deftly for grasping branches. In this untamed wilderness, I find sustenance and a newfound sense of belonging, a camaraderie born of shared experiences and mutual respect.

In the nascent light of dawn, the aboriginal warriors ready themselves, their arsenal displaying art and survival. Each weapon, born from hours of laborious craftsmanship, speaks of a deep understanding of their harsh environment and the relentless demands it imposes.

Spears of varying lengths and designs form the backbone of their armament. The meticulous care in their creation is evident – some tipped with jagged shards of flint or bone, affixed securely with tree gum and kangaroo sinew. The notched wooden points, resembling rows of teeth, bear witness to the intricate skill of their makers.

Then there are the waddies, clubs of diverse types and weights, each designed with a singular, brutal purpose – to crack skulls in the throes of combat. Some waddies are masterpieces of carving, while others are more rudimentary, fashioned from young Ti-Tree saplings, their heartwood forming a deadly end. A few sharpened to a point blur the line between club and dagger.

However, in close combat, the curved waddy commands respect. Crafted from solid hardwood, its straight shaft gives way to a sharp curve reminiscent of a wooden pick. In the hands of a skilled warrior, this weapon becomes an extension of their will, a harbinger of doom.

Amidst these traditional weapons, the boomerang stands out in its uniqueness. Crafted from resiliently grained wood, its forms vary – some crescent-shaped, others more angular. Deceptively simple in appearance, its versatility is unmatched. The most common variant, with its uneven thickness and one flat side, is renowned for its return flight, a marvel of aerodynamics.

However, the heavier, battle-ready boomerangs are designed for sheer impact and do not return. These formidable versions, heavier and more substantial, are crafted for war rather than the elegant artistry of the returning kind.

My learned friend from Ballarat, Raffaello Carboni, once mused about the boomerang's enigmatic nature. He described its flight as a dance of physics, a spectacle that defies even the most astute mathematician. "It's an object of singular wonder," he said, "obeying the native's will, tracing intricate paths through the air, only to return to the thrower's feet. This boomerang flight confounds the mind, a true marvel of Aboriginal ingenuity."

Standing among these warriors and witnessing their readiness, I am struck by a profound sense of awe. Their weaponry, so deeply rooted in their culture and land, is not just a means of survival but a testament to their connection with the earth and their mastery over its resources.

Chapter Nine

When food is plentiful, they feast and riot to the limits of their natural hearts, gorging themselves until their abdominal region becomes so expanded as to be decidedly uncomfortable. After they sleep off the effects of their gluttony, some hilarious spirits among them get up a type of entertainment that evokes much merriment.

It is supposed to represent a kangaroo hunt—a kind of pantomime mimicking the stirring events of the day. As with a modern troupe of stage actors, the actors spare no pains to make the representation realistic—to hold the mirror up to nature.

Their preparations include greasing their bodies with the fat of animals and then plentifully daubing themselves with red ochre. Some small branches are fixed to their girdles in imitation of tails, and the fun begins. Those with the tails hop about the camp like a scared herd of kangaroos, the tails sticking out and their peculiar attitudes having a most comical effect. At the same time, those pretending to be the hunters follow closely, hollering and prancing wildly, and pretend to spear them. I am no less amused than my black companions and laugh as loud as any of them.

On this day, I witnessed an altercation between two warriors, one from our tribe against another from a neighbouring tribe. They have the same ardour towards a young girl, but the girl favours the adjacent tribal member, and the conflict needs to be resolved with a traditional fray. Each arm himself with a waddy and wooden shield. They courageously enter the ring of stones, well-matched in size and general strength. They warily advance upon each other with shields and clubs upraised over their heads to form a protecting arch. The deeply set eyes of both men glistened beneath their shaggy brows in a highly vengeful manner, which seemed to me to indicate there would be a fatal termination to their fight.

The antagonists close in, then blow after blow falls with lightning rapidity. Their shields ward off many, but a sickening thud is heard occasionally, indicating they have both been severely wounded on their heads and shoulders. Their hammer-and-tong business cannot last long, and they soon show exhaustion. The blood flows freely from many wounds to the head and torso.

When the tribes consider that each combatant has had enough for one day, they interpose and separate them and lead them to their different camps, each man looking dazed and half-insensible and reeling like drunken men.

That duel reveals to me the tremendous and fantastical thickness of the skull possessed by those I live with. I know any of those blows, showered with so little effect upon their blackheads, would have left my head open and instantly paralysed me.

The injured warrior from our tribe, upon regaining some semblance of health, goes to claim his bride, expecting to find her warm with victory. To his dismay, he discovers her cold and unresponsive. In his frustration, he beats her with his waddy, sending shivers down my spine. However, the rest of the encampment regards this nuptial correction with indifference.

The family with whom I reside looks unsettled. They wander about aimlessly, sometimes on their own and at other times in the company of one or more of the many friendly tribes they encounter. One day, the tribe attempts to bring my bachelor's life to an abrupt end by presenting me with a charming young widow as a wife. Raffaello had informed me about such matters, and I know the widow has not been consulted and has no say in the event. Among the natives, women have no rights; they are considered chattels bought, sold, and exchanged by their parents or guardians.

The customary practice when a man desires a wife is to exchange his sister or daughter for one. A native never marries a woman born in his tribe; instead, he usually seeks a wife from a neighbouring friendly tribe. The older men often have two or three wives, while many young men must content themselves with a bachelor's existence. No old maids appeared among the blacks, as the men generally outnumbered the women by about two to one.

Widows do not mourn their husbands for more than a week at most. They are immediately inherited by their husband's brother or some close relation, who either brings her into their own family or trades her for another woman. Sometimes, she is given as a gift to a bachelor friend if she is considered old and unattractive.

My charming young widow-to-be tests my resolve. I had already experienced such passionate encounters with the bar girls at the Criterion Hotel in Melbourne before I became a fugitive on the run. My loins yearn for a revival of those pleasurable indulgences. Still, after witnessing the detestable reactions of my fellow bachelors to the marriage proposal, I declined, not wanting to jeopardise our friendship.

I have been contemplating my escape, as I am in good physical shape and high in spirits. I plan to head toward the coast, continuing my journey west to Albany or attempting to signal my presence to a passing ship. I deem it prudent not to sew resentment among the younger warriors by accepting the marriage proposal. Moreover, if received, I would bind myself to their tribe in a perceived permanent connection, which might hinder my free departure.

After much wrangling between my companions and the tribal leaders, they yielded to my determination to remain a bachelor. With my limited grasp of their language, I convey my desire to attend a corroboree with other whitefellas, as they do with neighbouring tribes. I explained that these whitefellas would reward me with abundant food for a grand feast and gifts of knives and axes for them if they safely escorted me to the Whitefellas Territory.

They agreed to my journey but insisted that two companions accompany me to ensure my safe passage through the neighbouring tribal districts. During my anticipated five-day trek, their guidance will be indispensable in locating waterholes and the food we need.

However, the warriors do not venture into the territory of the "jumped-up whitefellas", unseen yet conceived ever-present enemies. They will await me patiently in the bush, outside that domain, to receive the items I've mentioned.

Finally, the day arrives for my departure with my two companions. The tribal family expresses their grief through wails and vigorous chest-beating, accompanied by hair-pulling. I am handed a reed basket containing a kangaroo leg and a generous supply of wild roots and tree gum for our journey.

As we journey westward, my two companions become more known. Nulla, a young man of perhaps twenty, stands tall and wiry with matted black curly hair and a light beard. Scars adorn his shoulder and chest from the initiation ceremony, marking his transition into manhood. Jiemba, on the other hand, appears to be around twenty-seven, not as tall, with a lighter build. His black beard is thick and knotted at the end, and he carries scars from similar ceremonies.

During our first afternoon on the road, we paused to construct rudimentary shelters for the night. Lacking a fire stick, I watch Nulla's method intently. He rubs a sharpened stick vigorously between his palms, placing the pointed end in the notch of a sliver of wood. As friction ignites the wood, he adds a clump of dried grass, and within minutes, we have a roaring fire.

We cook the kangaroo leg and pass it around for each of us to gnaw upon. Although I had developed a taste for wombat back at camp, I would turn my nose up at the prospect of the native dog, a favourite dish among my black companions. Apart from this exception, I am an indiscriminate eater, much like the natives. Their culinary repertoire includes witchetty grubs, honey ants, tree gums, snakes, lizards, frogs, and other unsavoury delicacies that pique the curiosity of those with adventurous palates.

A plentiful food supply and the absence of danger contribute to camaraderie within our camp. When circumstances permit, "eat, drink, and be merry" becomes the order of the day, a sentiment that resonates among all Blackfellas.

Living among them has opened my eyes to the harsh reality of the Blackfella's natural provisions and roots rapidly dwindling due to the encroachment of white squatter's sheep back in Ballarat and other settled territories. These settlers have effectively barred the Blackfellas from their hunting grounds while thousands of gold prospectors swarm over their land. It's no wonder the Blackfellas residing near white communities have resorted to begging and sheep theft to survive.

Moreover, I've come to understand the volatile nature of their moods. One day, a Blackfella might exhibit a light-hearted, merry disposition akin to an impulsive boy. The next, as if by some enchantment, he transforms into a vindictive, vengeful, stealthy, and treacherous assassin, sparing neither man, woman, nor child.

These tribes have primitive commercial arrangements with one another, marked by exchanging or bartering unique products from their territories. These exchanges often occur during sizable tribal gatherings. The traded articles may include flints, shells, stones for tomahawks, gum for cement, stalks of the grass tree, clay for body painting, and various types of dietary provisions.

Chapter Ten

Salvation in Albany

Amidst the unforgiving confines of tribal boundaries, the peril of venturing beyond one's domain looms large—a gamble with the very spectre of death. To this end, Nulla, our seasoned messenger, carries a symbol of his office, a sort of passport for our perilous journey. This symbol, a slender stick of roughly six inches in length and an inch in breadth, is a testament to his mission, intricately carved with the primitive hieroglyphics of his people. He adorns it, much like an Irish labourer might tuck a pipe into his hatband, nestled securely within the netted band encircling his head.

Nulla, our trusted messenger, keeps time's relentless march by etching a stripe of clay onto one of his arms for each day that slips through our grasp. Jiemba, my stalwart companion, follows suit, diligently marking the passage of our journey. Upon arriving at the destination of the neighbouring tribe, Nulla fulfils his sacred duty by conveying a message of peace to their most esteemed figurehead.

This tribal leader, with keen interest, lends an ear to the message we bring. Under Nulla's solemn assurance of sharing any gifts forthcoming from the Whitefellas Camp, the leader instructs the tribe's women to prepare a humble meal for our weary souls. Nulla and the tribal leader engage solemnly while Jiemba and I withdraw to a part of the encampment traditionally reserved for unattached men. Nulla maintains a silent vigil, gauging the leader's response, a response that, as it turns out, bears little inclination toward further discourse. Nulla, ever wise, takes this as his cue, recognising that our mission stands accomplished, and with hearts filled with contentment, we depart from their camp.

Our journey onward continues, bereft of notable incidents to recount. As we draw nearer to the outskirts of Albany in Southwestern Australia, the incident leads us to stumble upon a campsite that seems to be the province of woodcutters. Nulla and Jiemba, my loyal black comrades, instinctively halt in response to the rhythmic tempo of wood being hewn. From our concealed vantage point amidst the bushes, we bear witness to the unfolding scene.

The Whitefellas' encampment unfolds an ensemble that includes a substantial white tent. Within its confines, a lone figure tends to a crackling fire, labouring to coax hot water from a billy can. Nearby, two others are engrossed in the laborious task of stacking firewood onto a cart, an aging white gelding tethered to their endeavours. I venture forth, separating from Nulla and Jiemba, motioning for them to remain concealed until my return.

I cautiously approach the trio of woodcutters. Their labour halts abruptly upon my approach, gazes locked upon my dishevelled figure. Long, matted hair obscures my head, and a thick beard drapes my face. My attire is more than tattered remnants of moleskin trousers, crudely severed at the knees, and a Blackfellas' possum skin cloak drapes across my frame. In hand, I clutch a traditional spear, a testament to my peculiar state.

The woodcutters, understandably taken aback, promptly converge around me, their inquiries cascading upon me in a torrent. To their evident astonishment, I respond with only brief, cryptic answers. My demeanour—coupled with the visible signs of weariness and the frailty imposed by my arduous journey and meagre diet of native fare—prompts them to invite me to the fireside. They usher me to a makeshift log seat, their discerning eyes recognising the toll exacted by my odyssey.

A cup of tea and a slice of damper bread, generously slathered with mutton lard, are offered immediately. I partake with a ravenous appetite, savouring each morsel like a delicacy of unmatched grandeur. Observing my voraciousness, the woodcutters cannot help but conclude that I must be on the brink of starvation. They lay several more slices before me, a gesture of benevolence that I accept with raised hands, bearing gratitude in my heart. I rise to my feet, expressing my eagerness to seek the authorities and return to civilisation, relaying my intent. Their camp lies but a scant three miles from Albany Township, and they propose I take respite while they complete loading their cart. Now ready, they assure me they will guide me to my destination.

In the interim, I explain the necessity of consulting with the two Blackfellas from the tribe that rescued me. These two companions remain concealed nearby, their trepidation preventing them from directly following my path. Their resolve, however, is unwavering. They stay in proximity, steadfast in their commitment to await the fulfilment of my promise: the goods I had proffered to the tribe's leaders in return for their guidance to safety.

Returning to Nulla and Jiemba, I tell them I intend to visit the substantial whitefellas camp. I will return within two or three days, though the natives' countenances reflect a noisy mixture of wide-eyed astonishment and agitation. Regrettably, my shrug communicates the stark reality: no alternative exists.

I then summon the two Blackfellas from their place of concealment and present them to the three woodmen who await below; their eyes upturned towards me. This action is paramount; it validates to the authorities that I am indeed accompanied by these indigenous natives precisely as they have been informed.

Subsequently, I am transported to Albany Township by cart, where I find myself in the company of gaol warden James Dunn at the Albany Convict Gaol. Distinct from the convict systems of New South Wales and Tasmania, the Albany convict system espouses the principle of rehabilitation. Convicts are engaged as farm labourers for the benefit of free settlers, and the gaol serves as a hub for hiring skilled and farm convict labourers. This constitutes a marked divergence in the approach from incarceration to rehabilitation.

The goal stands in austere resplendence, constructed of alternating light and dark bricks. Its slate roof, a testament to architectural austerity and pragmatic functionality, slopes steeply. Within its walls, the gaol harbours a cell block, the confines for convicts, and the warden's living quarters, a stark comparison of purpose. At its entrance, two prominent fixtures command attention: the pillory stocks, symbolic of public humiliation, and the ominous whipping post, where the grim reality of cruel retribution finds its sobering embodiment.

I am introduced to Mr Dunn, the warden of this institution. He stands tall, with a slender frame that emphasises his commanding presence. Clad in a goaler's distinctive blue uniform, his attire is topped by a flat, narrow-brimmed jack hat. A full black beard frames his visage, a testament to his dedication to maintaining law and order in these challenging times.

In the austere confines of Albany Gaol, I stand before Mr Dunn, the warden, cloaked in an air of disquiet that clings to me like a shadow. My ragged countenance, with unruly locks and a wild, tangled beard, betrays a man who has endured hardships beyond measure.

Mr Dunn casts his gaze upon me, a curious amalgam of scepticism and concern etched across his countenance. "Well, young man," he begins, his voice resonating with an aura of authority, "what has brought you to this remote corner of the world? You do not resemble our typical traveller."

My eyes cast downwards, seeking refuge in the worn wooden floorboards as I summon the words to respond. "Sir, I hail from Melbourne, Johnny Cartwright by name," I utter, my voice still bearing faint echoes of a city accent. "I found myself aboard a sealing ship, an American vessel, engaged in the dangerous pursuit on these treacherous waters. We embarked to harvest the ocean's riches, but our crew, sir, they mutinied."

The warden's brows arch in genuine astonishment. "A mutinous crew, you say. Pray, do go on."

Summoning a deep breath, I steel myself, fixing my gaze on Mr Dunn, my eyes carrying the weight of the harrowing memories I'm about to unearth. "Indeed, sir. They mutinied without warning or reason. I was but a lowly deckhand, minding my affairs. Yet, they perceived me as a threat or a convenient scapegoat. They held me and unceremoniously cast me into the unforgiving depths."

Mr Dunn's countenance remains stern, but his eyes glimmer with empathy. "Thrown overboard, you say? And how did you find your way here, to Albany?"

I clear my throat, a hint of uncertainty creeping into my voice. "I was fortunate, sir. I managed to swim ashore, and by the grace of Providence, I stumbled upon some kindly natives. They took me under their wing, tended to my wounds, and guided me through this untamed wilderness."

The warden studies me closely, his gaze probing. "Benevolent natives, you claim? Such tales are not commonplace in these wild parts."

I nod fervently, my eyes reflecting earnest sincerity. "It is the truth, sir. They saved my life, and in return, I pledged them gifts to express my gratitude for their kindness. That is why I needed to reach Albany, seek aid, and fulfil my promise. The woodcutters who accompanied me here bear witness to the presence of these natives, who now await their reward at the town's outskirts."

Mr Dunn leans back, his demeanour softening. "Well, young man, your account is quite extraordinary if factual. We must verify your claims, but you are now secure here in Albany. We shall ascertain the veracity of your narrative in due course."

A sigh of relief escapes me, and a swell of gratitude envelops me. "Thank you, sir. I am thankful to be ashore and in the company of civilised folk once more."

As I continue to divulge my tale, Mr Dunn listens intently, and in that moment, a shroud of enigma envelops this fortuitous encounter in the far reaches of Australia. In this Southern land where the line between reality and fiction often blurs, fate has conspired to weave a narrative of perseverance and resilience.

This night, I am afforded food and a bed within the gaol, isolated from direct contact with the convicts. The following day, Mr Dunn, the warden, introduces me to a mysterious native figure named Mokare. A sense of anticipation and intrigue takes hold of me as we clasp hands in greeting.

Mokare stands before me as a commanding presence. Tall and sinewy, his countenance is weathered by a lifetime spent in the rugged Australian wilderness. His deep and penetrating eyes seem to harbour the wisdom of ages, while his stoic demeanour suggests a man who has beheld both the splendours and perils of this untamed land.

"Johnny," Mr Dunn commences, "this is Mokare, a man of great significance within the local Noongar community. He has kindly agreed to aid you in procuring the items you require and throw light on your abrupt arrival here."

I nod in gratitude, striving to convey my appreciation through a heartfelt smile. Mokare's presence instils in me a renewed hope that my plan to retrieve the promised goods for the natives who guided me here might be realised.

"Johnny," Mokare intones in a deep, measured voice, his words conveyed through Warden Dunn's translation as his 'Pigeon English' is difficult to decipher, "I comprehend your predicament, and I am here to offer my assistance. We shall collect the necessary items before reuniting with the waiting natives to deliver their compensation for guiding you safely to Albany."

Guided by Mokare, we embark on our mission. The shining and relentless sun hangs high in the azure sky as we traverse the town's thoroughfares. We pass by the gaol's imposing brick walls and ominous wooden stocks, stark reminders of the consequences met by those who transgress the law.

We arrived at the Government Trading Post, where we assembled the items on my list—Tomahawks, mirrors, beads, flour, sugar, clothing—each meticulously chosen and packed. Mokare's familiarity with the traders and authoritative rapport with them facilitate the process, making it far smoother than I envisaged.

With our valuable cargo, we proceed toward the town's outskirts, where Nulla and Jiemba await compensation. Mokare's presence proves indispensable in ensuring a harmonious and mutually advantageous exchange. The awaiting natives observe us with curiosity and anticipation, their countenances guarded but devoid of hostility.

Mokare steps forward, initiating dialogue in their native tongue. Though I cannot decipher their words, I can perceive the negotiation's subtle ebb and flow. It is a delicate dance, a fragile equilibrium between cultures, and I could not have wished for a more adept partner than Mokare.

After what appears to be hours, though, in reality, mere minutes have passed, an accord is reached. The waiting natives' visages break into radiant smiles as they take possession of the promised wares. It is a moment of shared understanding and cooperation, an affirmation that even in this remote corner of the world, humanity's ability to bridge divides and foster connections can endure.

As the natives gathered their rewards, profound relief washed over me. With Mokare as my guide and the successful culmination of our mission, I have advanced yet another stride toward reclaiming my life in this unfamiliar land. The bonds forged across cultures, the unspoken gratitude and the implicit pledges of future cooperation imbue me with hope for what lies ahead in this strange and arduous odyssey.

Chapter Eleven

Following the successful exchange with Nulla and Jiemba, Mokare, Mr Dunn, and I continued our stroll through the quaint streets of Albany. Reverend Callahan has expressed a keen interest in meeting me, a stranger who has arrived in town under such peculiar circumstances.

The reverend's residence is a modest yet inviting abode, nestled amidst the charming colonial architecture that lines the streets of Albany. Its white-washed walls and well-tended garden exude tranquillity, starkly contrasting my recent trials in the wilderness.

As we enter the reverend's study, a room adorned with shelves of well-worn books and the soft glow of sunlight filtering through lace curtains, I find myself standing before a kindly-faced man, his hair salt-and-pepper, his eyes a testament to the wisdom and compassion he undoubtedly possesses.

Reverend Callahan smiles and says, "Ah, Mr Cartwright, I've been eager to make your acquaintance. Warden Dunn here has apprised me of your unique situation."

I respond gratefully, "I'm much obliged for your hospitality, Reverend. The wilderness has been unrelenting, and your kindness is a balm to my weary soul."

Reverend Callahan replies, resonating with compassion, "We shall help you regain your dignity and present yourself anew, Mr Cartwright. A haircut and a change of attire can restore one's self-esteem. Kindness is the foundation of our community here. I fervently hope we can extend a helping hand to all those in need."

With that, Reverend Callahan unfolds his plan. First, he arranges for a barber to visit me in the coming days, promising to restore some semblance of order to my wild mane of hair and unruly beard. Then, he offered me a fresh set of clothes to replace the tattered native cloak that had been my prime garment since arriving in Albany.

I am humbled by the reverend's offer, my heart brimming with gratitude. It is a rare and precious gift for a man in my situation, a fugitive trying to shed his old life and forge a new path.

Reverend Callahan then calls upon Warden Dunn with a request, spoken in hushed tones. "James, we might utilise your extensive network to assist Mr Cartwright further. Could you help secure his passage on a ship bound for Fremantle Harbour?"

Warden Dunn nods, agreeing, "Reverend, I shall do my utmost. Mr Cartwright's journey here has been fraught with hardship, and we shall facilitate his safe passage to his intended destination."

Their conversation continued as relief washed over me. The path ahead is more transparent with the reverend's kindness and Warden Dunn's resourcefulness. It will lead me away from Albany, away from the shadows of my past, and toward the distant hope of Fremantle Harbour. This harbour promises a fresh start in the town of Perth, an opportunity to rewrite the chapters of my life, and a chance to leave behind the fugitive I once was.

• • • •

THE YEAR IS 1866. ALBANY, Western Australia, is a remote outpost, a coastal sanctuary where the unruly wilderness collides with the unwavering strides of civilisation. As I embark on my expedition through this alien terrain, I find myself immersed in a tableau that merges the splendour of nature with human tenacity.

The salty tang of the ocean breeze entwines with the earthy perfume of eucalyptus trees, enveloping me as I survey Albany's expanse. Cradled amid rolling hills and the serene embrace of Princess Royal Harbour, this coastal hamlet exudes a quiet fortitude—a sense that existence here is both fragile and enduring.

Warden James Dunn, a bastion of authority and discipline in this wilderness, escorts me through the town's slender streets. Cobbled lanes, dust-laden from the passage of carts and horse-drawn carriages, weave their way past unassuming cottages and timbered edifices. The townsfolk diligently perform their daily labours, their countenances etched with tales of unyielding lives in a land that refuses to be tamed.

Warden Dunn introduces me to the place with a sweeping gesture: "This is Albany in all its splendour, Mr Cartwright, our unpretentious township. It may lack the bustle of Sydney or Melbourne, but it possesses a unique charm."

I nod in acknowledgment, replying, "Aye, it's a world apart from what I've known. I've never laid eyes on a place quite like this."

My gaze occasionally falls upon the indigenous Noongar people, who mingle with the settlers as we meander. Their coexistence bears witness to the intricate choreography of cultures on this far-flung frontier.

The harmonious convergence of Noongar and settler life gradually unfolds, with the Noongar generously imparting their knowledge of the land to the newcomers, guiding them through the harsh trials of this unforgiving environment.

Approaching the bustling harbour, a nexus of vibrant activity, I'm greeted by the majestic presence of sailing ships, their masts soaring heavenward. These vessels wear their maritime scars proudly, their timeworn wood bearing witness to encounters with salt and storm. The atmosphere resonates with a sense of adventure and boundless possibilities.

I stand in awe and exclaim, "So, it's here I shall find passage to Perth by the Swan River?"

Warden Dunn nods gravely, replying, "Indeed, Mr Cartwright. But I must forewarn you—your forthcoming journey may prove as treacherous as the one you've left behind by the turbulent storms that thrash the West Coast."

Amidst the eclectic array of ships, one exceptionally rugged schooner captures my attention. Captain Reynolds, a mariner with a grizzled countenance and the indomitable spirit of a seafarer, strides forward to meet us.

Captain Reynolds gruffly inquires, "Warden Dunn, who have we here?"

Warden Dunn introduces me, "Allow me to present Mr John Cartwright. He seeks passage to the Swan River Settlement."

Appraising me with keen eyes, Captain Reynolds states, "Well, lad, if you're willing to pull your weight aboard the 'Wandering Star,' I reckon we can accommodate you."

Determined, I respond, "I shall work, Captain, and earn my passage. Just get me to Fremantle Harbour, and I'll prove my worth."

The trio engages in further deliberations, ironing out the specifics of my journey. Meanwhile, a group of Noongar natives, led by the distinguished figure of Mokare, approaches with their resplendent cloaks, casting a vivid tapestry against the sombre hues of settler attire.

Mokare, via an interpreter, explains, "Warden Dunn, I bring forth gifts for our esteemed guest, Mr Cartwright."

Mokare presents me with an intricately woven basket adorned with vibrant feathers and shells, a finely crafted nulla-nulla stick and a ceremonial kangaroo-tooth necklace.

I express my gratitude, saying, "I am deeply indebted to you, Mokare, for your boundless generosity."

Mokare nods solemnly and responds, "In these lands, the bonds of hospitality are sacred. You are embraced among us."

As these interactions unfold, my path to the Swan River Settlement beyond Fremantle Harbour becomes more defined. Albany's tapestry of cultures interwoven with untamed landscapes has offered me a brief respite. Yet my journey remains far from its conclusion, and the challenges ahead are as unpredictable as the sea's ever-shifting currents.

Chapter Twelve

The following day, beneath a sky streaked with hues of orange and pink, I bid my farewells to Albany's eclectic inhabitants. With their indomitable spirits, the townsfolk showed me warmth and generosity during my brief stay. At the same time, the Noongar people's hospitality served as a humbling testament to the bonds that transcend cultures.

With a heavy heart, I approach the looming silhouette of Captain Reynolds' rugged schooner, the Wandering Star. The vessel stands sentinel over the bustling harbour, her timbers weathered by countless voyages and a testament to the trials of the open sea.

Stepping aboard, the crew acknowledges my presence with curiosity and wariness. I must prove my worth swiftly to gain the crew's trust, for my past as a fugitive cannot stay hidden forever.

Days turn into a week as we sail Northward, the vast expanse of the Indian Ocean stretching endlessly before us. I work alongside the crew, toiling under the scorching sun and enduring the tumultuous swells of the sea. Captain Reynolds, a gruff and seasoned seafarer, keeps a vigilant eye on me, perhaps suspecting that beneath my humble facade lies a secret darker than the ocean's depths.

The inevitable confrontation came one moonless night as we navigated the treacherous waters off the coast. A vicious storm descends upon us, and the ship bucks and groans as she battles the storm's fury. Rain lashes at our faces, and the howling winds drown our shouts.

During the chaotic struggle to secure the sails, one of the crewmen in close adjacency recognises me from a wanted poster showing my profile that has found its way onboard. Panic ripples through the crew as whispers of my true identity spread like wildfire.

Captain Reynolds confronts me, his eyes hard as flint. "Is it true, Mr Cartwright? Are you the wanted murderer, Levi Brody and on the run?"

I have no choice but to admit the truth; my voice is lost in the storm's din. The crew gathers around, with faces a mixture of anger and fear. At that very moment, my fate seemed sealed, to be met with the swift justice of a jury of my peers or perhaps the swifter justice of the sea herself. However, I quickly convey how I was framed by my grandfather, the infamous Jack Riley, who, to my good fortune, is well known to many crew members who, in the past, whilst ashore, had been accosted by the evil that Riley solicited in Melbourne City. His criminal interests had defrauded several crew members aboard. Their shared grievance against my grandfather forges an unexpected bond of empathy.

I'm also fortunate that Mokare, the Noongar elder of Albany, frequently travels by goodwill on ships to the Swan River Colony for aboriginal elder meetings and corroborees with the Whadjuk Nyoongar people on the Maylands Peninsula. Now onboard the Wandering Star, Mokare's generosity again touches my heart. He speaks passionately, pleading for my life, recounting the kindness I have shown him and his people. His interpreted words resonate with the crew, who begin to waver in their determination to deliver me into the hands of the authorities.

Ultimately, it is decided that I will be marooned on the desolate shores of Garden Island, my fate left to the capricious whims of the wild, and free the captain and crew from any Fremantle Authorities inquiries regarding my person and background.

As the ship's longboat carries me toward that lonely island, I look back one last time at the "Wandering Star," her silhouette fading into the horizon. Alone on the desolate shores of Garden Island, I watch the "Wandering Star" sails disappear into the inky blackness of a storm-tossed sea. The wind howls, and the rain beats down, chilling me to the bone. The island's rugged terrain and isolation seem fitting for a man on the run, in exile once again from civilisation.

With nothing but the clothes on my back and the few supplies I managed to grab from the longboat before the crew pushed it back into the stormy sea, I set forth again to survive. The days on Garden Island are harsh and unforgiving, filled with solitude and the constant struggle to find water on this sandy, heavy-wooded, scrub-filled island.

Food is plentiful from a native perspective as I hunt carpet pythons, small tiger snakes, spear tammar wallabies, sea birds and forage for edible plants. The nights are long and lonely; the only sounds are the haunting cries of seabirds and the ceaseless crash of the waves against the shore.

Weeks become months as I eke out my existence on this desolate isle, sleeping within my mia-mia. Each day brings new challenges, from spearing the island's native marsupials for food to finding fresh water sources. I often think of the people I met in Albany, the kindness of the Noongar people, and the brief camaraderie with the crew of the "Wandering Star." But those memories feel like distant echoes in the solitude of my exile.

As the season changes, so does the island. Spring brings a burst of life and colour, with wildflowers painting the landscape in vibrant hues. Then Summer's relentless and unforgiving sun beats down on me, and I've learnt to seek shelter from its punishing rays that burn my already tanned and weathered skin. Autumn arrives with cooler temperatures and a respite from the summer's intensity. During this time, I discover a hidden cave, a sanctuary from the elements, where I can finally find more comfort than my mia-mia affords.

With time, I have become more adept at survival, honing the skills I learned with Nulla and his tribal family and finding solace in nature's rhythms. I cannot remain on Garden Island forever, but the fear of discovery and capture lingers like a shadow over my every move.

One fateful day, as winter is well advanced and the sea churns with the ferocity of an impending storm, I spot a distant ship on the horizon. It is a small vessel, and hope blossoms within me. Desperation drives me to build a makeshift signal fire atop a rocky outcrop, praying that the crew will see my distress and offer me salvation.

As the flames roar to life, I watch with bated breath. As a solitary figure on this lonely shore, the ship draws closer, and I wave my arms frantically. Would this be my deliverance, or has fate conspired again to thwart my escape?

The ship's response is swift, altering its course toward the island. Relief washes over me, but with it comes a flood of apprehension. What lies ahead on this new journey, and will I ever find freedom from the shadow of my past?

The unassuming trading vessel christened the "Sea Serpent" comes to rest not too distant from the rugged fringes of Garden Island. A longboat is gingerly lowered into the shimmering expanse, its crew a testament to the sea's unrelenting demands. As it approaches, I discern the weary etchings upon their faces, the indelible marks of lives endured amidst the ceaseless turmoil of the ocean. They cast upon me a gaze tainted by a curious blend of empathy and intrigue, their unspoken inquiries lingering like a palpable mist upon the salty air.

The ship's commander, a burly figure whose weathered visage sports a formidable beard and resonates with joy, greets with a well-worn hand. "Captain Rafferty's the moniker, and this vessel, my good sir, bears the name 'Sea Serpent.' Might I inquire what unforeseen force led a man to find himself upon this forsaken isle?"

I pause, recognising the precarious equilibrium between revelation and discretion. A fugitive from the long arm of justice cast away on this remote enclave, my only recourse lies in entrusting the goodwill of these unknown benefactors. "Through no fault but mine, Captain, I've become stranded in this desolate locale. A mishap during a turbulent storm led to the capsizing of my small fishing vessel, leaving me adrift.

I find myself in dire need of passage to Fremantle Harbour, the destination I initially set out for."

Captain Rafferty, a shrewd observer of my words and demeanour, studies me closely, his eyes keen as they probe for the veracity within my narrative. "Stranded, you claim? Very well then, Mr...?"

"Johnny, Captain... Johnny Cartwright,"

"Very well, Johnny. The 'Sea Serpent' shall offer you a berth, and Fremantle Harbour stands as our ultimate port of call,"

I am grateful for this fortuitous lifeline and respectfully nod. "Aye, Captain Rafferty. Your benevolence is deeply appreciated. "

As the "Sea Serpent" resumes its odyssey toward Fremantle Harbour, my emotions teeter between gratitude and anxiety. My heart flutters, knowing that the moment of reckoning may loom ever closer. The inadvertent revelation of my presence on Garden Island could occur at any moment, potentially unleashing the explosive consequences of my concealed past.

With a heavy heart and the weight of uncertainty pressing my shoulders, I steel myself for the inevitable. A decision crystallises within my mind—*I must disembark the "Sea Serpent" before Captain Rafferty can exchange words with the port authorities regarding my forlorn tarry. My destiny, fraught with uncertainty, hinges upon my ability to silently slip away, vanishing into the shadows once more as a fugitive, evading the relentless pursuit of the law.*

Chapter Thirteen

On board the "Sea Serpent," Captain Rafferty's kindness knows no bounds. As we continue our journey toward Fremantle Port, he insists on helping me transform my appearance so I may appear more civilised when we finally dock.

Captain Rafferty arranges for a barber among his crew, a gruff but skilled sailor who reluctantly agrees to tame my wild mane and unruly beard. As I sit on a makeshift stool on the deck, the salty breeze ruffling my hair, the barber wields his scissors and razor with expertise. With each snip and stroke, I feel a part of my old life being sheared away, replaced by a newfound sense of respectability.

Once my hair and beard are neatly trimmed, Captain Rafferty offers me a set of clothes from the ship's stores. They are simple but far more suitable than the filthy rags I have worn for so long. I bathe in a bucket of sea wash and change into my new clothes, the fabric crisp and clean against my skin. I feel like a man with purpose and direction for the first time in months.

As the "Sea Serpent" nears Fremantle Port, I am torn between gratitude for Captain Rafferty's help and the fear of facing the authorities once we dock. I realise that I must seize the first opportunity to escape their notice.

The perfect chance presents itself as the crew unloads cargo upon our arrival. While the Captain and his men are preoccupied with their work, I slip ashore, my heart pounding with excitement and trepidation about my escape. The streets of Fremantle bustle with activity, providing ample cover for my departure.

My destination is the Fremantle Sea-Mariners Refuge, a place I have heard about aboard the "Sea Serpent." When I arrive with my improved appearance, I still carry the air of a man who has fallen on hard times. Mr Beasley, the kindly soul who runs the refuge, listens to my fabricated tale of woe.

"Sir, I was once employed on the 'Wandering Star' to work my way from the Port of Melbourne to the Swan River Settlement Town. However, I am now abandoned here without the promised wages. I have been educated in Melbourne at a private school and seek professional work benefitting my educational achievements."

Mr Beasley regards me with sympathy and curiosity, his eyes searching for the truth in my words. I hope my story convinces him to provide me with much-needed aid and accommodation.

I am filled with anticipation and uncertainty as I stand amidst the dimly lit refuge. My journey, it seems, has brought me to a new crossroads. The path forward is unknown, but I am determined to navigate it with whatever means necessary to leave behind the fugitive I once was and embrace the opportunity to start fresh in this distant and unforgiving land.

In the heart of Fremantle, amidst the ebb and flow of life by the bustling port, solace is found in the humble sanctuary of the Sea-Mariners Refuge. Mr Beasley, a man whose kindness knows no bounds, has decided to take me in when I'm at my lowest. His weathered face bears the weight of countless stories, and his eyes hold a compassion that reaches deep into the souls of those he helps.

My room, though Spartan in its furnishings, feels like a haven. It's where I can finally lay down the burdens of my past and begin anew. Each night, I sit by the window, gazing out at the distant lights of the harbour, a shimmering reminder of the world beyond.

One evening, as the sun dips below the horizon, painting the sky in shades of gold and lavender, Mr Beasley approaches me. His footsteps are soft, almost reverent; as he clears his throat, offering a warm, knowing smile, he speaks, "Johnny, you've been with us for some time now, and I've seen the determination in your eyes. You're not just a man seeking refuge; you're a man seeking purpose."

His words strike a chord, and I nod, unable to hold back the emotions welling inside. With gratitude, I reply, "You've given me more than I could have ever hoped for, Mr Beasley. A chance to start anew, to rebuild my life."

Mr Beasley's eyes twinkle with a hint of mischief, like a wise old sage imparting a hidden truth. "Well, Johnny, sometimes life grants us unexpected opportunities. And I believe there might be one such opportunity for you if you're willing to seize it."

With curiosity aroused, I lean forward, eager to hear more. "What is it, Mr Beasley? I'm ready to face whatever lies ahead."

With a knowing nod, Mr Beasley shares his plan. A local barrister, Mr Blackwood, known for his successful business - although cunning and with a devious disposition needs an assistant. He's the man the town's felons turn to when they require legal representation. He will take me on as his clerk, provided I'm ready to learn and work hard. It's an opportunity to put my education to use, albeit in a realm fraught with moral ambiguity.

Mr Beasley encourages, "Mr Blackwood believes in resourcefulness, Johnny. He's willing to give you a chance, knowing you're educated, which is in short supply within the colony. It's a chance to gain employment and prove your worth."

The thought of employment and a fresh journey filled with uncertainties and legal intricacies stirs me deeply. It's as though fate has led me to this crossroads, where my skills and past can be used in ways I've never anticipated.

With renewed purpose, I say, "I'll take that chance, Mr Beasley. Please thank Mr Blackwood and let him know I'm ready to join his office."

As I make this commitment, I can't help but feel a surge of hope and determination. The path ahead, working for a man of dubious reputation, is uncertain and morally complex for me, who has committed evil in moments of weakness but since repented my actions and vowed to my maker to resist the temptations towards sins. But it's a chance to rebuild my life, navigate the maze-like world of law and intrigue, and carve a new destiny for myself in this land of opportunity and moral ambiguity.

The next day, I find myself standing before the imposing entrance of Mr Blackwood's law office on St. Georges Terrace, Perth's main commercial thoroughfare. I straightened my borrowed suit, its fabric itching against my skin, and took a deep breath before pushing open the heavy oak door to this limestone building.

The office is a stark contrast to the tranquillity of the Sea-Mariners Refuge. Dark wood furnishings and shelves lined with leather-bound tomes create an atmosphere of solemnity. A large mahogany desk dominates the room, behind which sits a man who must be Mr Blackwood.

Mr Blackwood is a figure of distinction. His sharp eyes keenly assess my every move. He is of average build, with greying hair meticulously combed to conceal any hints of age. His attire is impeccable, and his countenance exudes an air of calculated authority.

Mr Blackwood appraises me with a calculating smile, "Ah, Mr Cartwright. Please, have a seat."

I nod and take a chair across from him, my nerves masked by a veneer of composure.

I Politely nod, "Thank you, Mr Blackwood."

Mr Blackwood steeples his fingers, regarding me as if trying to discern my true intentions and measures his words, "Mr Beasley spoke highly of your determination and resourcefulness, Mr Cartwright. He mentioned your education."

With a hint of humility, I reply, "Yes, sir, I received my education in Melbourne at the renowned Scotch College."

Mr Blackwood's smile is sly, and he leans back in his chair with a glint, "Education can open doors, Mr Cartwright, but one's adaptability and discretion matter in my work."

His words hang in the air, laden with unspoken implications. I am determined to prove my worth, navigate this world with integrity, and leave behind the fugitive I once was. With all the conviction I can muster, I reply, "I assure you, Mr Blackwood, I am ready to work hard and assist you in any way I can."

Mr Blackwood leans forward, his eyes locking onto mine, appearing satisfied with my reply. "Very well, Mr Cartwright. We shall begin your training and see how you adapt to the intricacies of our profession. You will quickly learn that the law is not always black and white. I will address you informally in-house as John if you are not opposed to my familiarity."

As the conversation progresses, I can't help but feel a mixture of apprehension and determination. This new path, working for a solicitor known for his cunning, will test not only my legal abilities but also my moral compass. Yet, it is a chance to rebuild my life, prove that I can rise above my past, and navigate this uncertain world's complexities with honour and integrity, regardless of Mr Blackwood's moral compass.

Chapter Fourteen

In the days that follow, I immerse myself in the world of Mr Blackwood's law office. The work is relentless, and the intricacies of legal proceedings in Perth are unlike anything I've encountered before. Mr Blackwood is a demanding employer, expecting nothing less than perfection in every document I prepare and every case I assist with.

Despite some of our cases' long hours and morally ambiguous nature, I find a strange sense of satisfaction in the work. The law is indeed a twisting realm, filled with its own rules and strategies. Each day is a new puzzle to solve, a challenge to overcome.

As the weeks turn into months, Mr Blackwood begins to entrust me with more significant responsibilities as his apprentice legal clerk. I can represent clients in court, argue their cases, and negotiate always with Mr Blackwood sitting by my side. It is a heady experience to stand before the judge and jury, defending those who seek our services. I become known among the townspeople as a promising young solicitor in waiting, and my reputation grows.

Yet, with each legal victory, I can't help but wonder about the moral cost. Some of our clients, I feel, are undoubtedly devious in their dealings with the crimes they are accused of, and I defend them with all my skills. This troubling problem keeps me awake at night as I grapple with the weight of my choices.

Today, as I review a case file in my office, Mr Blackwood enters, a cunning glint in his eyes. "John, I have a particularly challenging case for you. One that will test your mettle and your ability to think on your feet."

I react with curiosity, "What is it, sir?"

Dropping a file on my desk, I open it to reveal the case details. It involves a prominent figure in the Port of Fremantle accused of embezzlement and fraud. The evidence against him seems damning, and the townspeople are baying for his blood.

Mr Blackwood, with a knowing look, says, "This, John, is an opportunity. It is an opportunity to prove your legal prowess and secure a victory that will cement your reputation in this town. But remember, the law isn't always about right and wrong. It's about strategy and persuasion."

With those words, he left my office, leaving me to ponder the case before me. As I delve into the details, I wonder what kind of victory awaits me. I also realise that in this world of legal ambiguity, the lines between right and wrong are often blurred, and the pursuit of justice may come at a cost.

The days leading up to the trial are a whirlwind of preparation. I pour over every detail of the case, seeking any loophole or discrepancy that can be exploited in our client's favour. Mr Blackwood guides me through the intricacies of legal strategy, teaching me the art of persuasion and manipulation within the bounds of the law.

As the trial begins, I stand before the judge and jury, facing a formidable prosecutor who presents a compelling case against our client. The evidence is damning, and public sentiment is firmly against us. I can sense the tension in the courtroom, the weight of the impending judgment pressing down on me.

Each day in court is a battle of wits and words. I cross-examine witnesses, present evidence, and make passionate arguments, all while knowing that the truth may not be on our side. The prosecutor is relentless, and I find myself resorting to legal manoeuvres and tactics I never thought I would employ.

As the trial progresses, I am acutely aware of my moral dilemma. While undoubtedly guilty of some document manipulations, our client is also a man with a family who stands to lose everything. The townspeople, hungry for justice, are blind to the complexities of the case.

One evening, as I review my notes in my office, Mr Blackwood enters, a calculating gleam in his eye. He whispers, "John, I've been impressed with your performance in this trial. You have a gift for persuasion, for bending the truth to your advantage."

I hesitate and answer, "But what about the truth, sir? What about justice?"

Mr Blackwood smirks. "Justice, my boy, is a matter of perspective. In this town, it's about who can spin the best narrative and convince the jury of their version of the truth. And that, John, is the essence of our profession."

His words weigh heavily on me as I contemplate my chosen path. I've become a skilled legal practitioner, but at what cost? The lines between right and wrong have blurred, and I am standing at a crossroads.

As the trial nears its conclusion, I must make a decision that will shape my career and my sense of self. Do I continue down this morally ambiguous path or seek a different kind of justice that aligns more closely with my principles? The answer remains elusive as I prepare for the final day in court, where our client's fate hangs in the balance.

The final day of the trial arrives, and tension is palpable in the courtroom. The gallery is packed with townspeople eager to witness the culmination of this high-profile case. I stand before the jury, ready to deliver my closing arguments, my heart pounding with anticipation.

As I begin to speak, weaving my carefully crafted narrative, a commotion erupts in the back of the courtroom. The door swings open, and a dishevelled man bursts in, his eyes wild with desperation. He frantically searched the faces in the room until his gaze fell on our client.

The man shouts, "Stop! Stop this trial!"

The judge pounds his gavel, demanding order in the court, but the man's outburst has already sent shockwaves through the proceedings.

The man begins to plead, "Your Honour, I have crucial evidence to exonerate the accused!"

Whispers ripple through the gallery as everyone turns to see this unexpected interruption. The prosecutor's face contorts with a mix of annoyance and anxiety.

The Judge replies sternly, "Order! Order in the court! Who are you, and what is the nature of this evidence?"

The man takes a deep breath, trying to compose himself before nervously continuing, "My name is Samuel Bligh, and I was with the accused on the night in question. I can testify that he is innocent of the charges brought against him."

The courtroom is filled with gasps, and I exchange a bewildered glance with Mr Blackwood. This sudden turn of events could change everything. Dishevelled and anxious, Samuel Bligh holds the key to our client's fate.

The judge orders Mr Bligh to take the stand, and as he begins to testify, a new truth emerges that casts doubt on the prosecution's case. Each word makes it increasingly clear that our client may indeed be innocent.

As I listen to Samuel Bligh's testimony, I can't help but wonder about the moral complexities of our profession. In this courtroom, where the line between right and wrong is blurred, a new chapter in my legal career unfolds—one that challenges my convictions and reminds me of what Mr Blackwood stated: *that justice, like life itself, is never black and white.*

The courtroom hangs in suspense as Samuel Bligh continues his testimony. His words paint a vivid picture of the night in question, revealing events significantly contradicting the prosecution's narrative. Samuel Bligh addresses the courtroom with unwavering conviction, resonating with authority.

"Your Honor," he begins, "I stand witness to Mr Jenkins's innocence on that fateful night as we occupied the dimly lit corner of a local tavern. The hours slipped away in our company, and I can testify solemnly to his precise whereabouts during the alleged transgression.

He remains a world apart from the crime scene; his character is untainted by the accusations that hang over him like a sinister shroud.

"Having been away on pressing business in the bustling heart of Sydney, I have only recently returned, my arrival coinciding with the revelation of the grave injustice looming over our town's most illustrious figure – the man a symbol of prosperity and accomplishment.

The prosecutor's objections become swift and persistent, but the judge allows Mr Bligh to testify. Doubt permeates the courtroom as the details of his account unfold. It becomes evident that an unbiased witness substantially supports our client's alibi.

In my closing arguments, I passionately emphasise the credibility of Samuel Bligh's testimony: "Ladies and gentlemen of the jury, Mr Bligh's testimony has cast a shadow of doubt over the prosecution's case. You must weigh his words carefully and consider the possibility that our client is innocent. The burden of proof rests with the prosecution, who has failed to provide irrefutable evidence."

The tension in the courtroom is palpable, and the jury's deliberations stretch into the night. As dawn breaks on a new day, we return to the courtroom, awaiting the jury's verdict with bated breath. The foreman stands, his expression inscrutable, as he delivers the verdict firmly, "We, the jury, find the accused, Mr Jenkins, Not Guilty!"

A collective gasp fills the courtroom, followed by murmurs of astonishment. Our client's face breaks into a radiant smile, and tears of relief glisten in his eyes. With authority, the judge intervenes, "Order in the court! This trial is adjourned."

As the courtroom empties and the townsfolk disperse, I exchange a satisfied glance with Mr Blackwood. Our unorthodox alliance had navigated the treacherous waters of justice and emerged victorious.

Mr Blackwood smirks, "Well, John, it seems we've earned our fee today and perhaps a bit of notoriety as well."

I nod, feeling the weight of the past few days finally lift from my shoulders. Reflectively, I reply, "Indeed, Mr Blackwood. We've proven that in the pursuit of justice, unconventional alliances can yield remarkable results."

As I exit the courtroom, the sun's warm rays bathe me in a sense of accomplishment and newfound purpose. My journey in this world of intrigue and moral ambiguity is far from over, but I walk away knowing that, sometimes, justice can prevail against all odds.

Chapter Fifteen

As weeks become months, my reputation as the intelligent legal representative of the cunning barrister Mr Blackwood grows throughout Perth. I become known as a man who can navigate the intricate web of legal matters with finesse, and my services are in high demand. It's a far cry from the desperate fugitive I once was, stranded on a lonely shore.

Mr Blackwood seems pleased with my work, and I continue to learn from the complexities of the law, even as I maintain my moral compass. Each case we take on and each battle we fight brings me one step closer to mastering the art of legal manoeuvring.

One bright morning, as I meticulously prepare documents for an upcoming trial, a commotion in the office disrupts my concentration. I glance up to see Mr Blackwood's perturbed expression as he ushers an elegant young woman into the room as if complying with the young woman's request.

Mr Blackwood looks towards me with a thinly veiled irritation. "Excuse our interruption... this is my daughter, Miss Elizabeth Blackwood. She has returned from Sydney after completing her studies at an exclusive girls' school. Elizabeth, this is John Cartwright, my legal clerk."

I rise to my feet, my heart quickening as I see Elizabeth Blackwood. Her red hair cascades in curls around her shoulders, a vision of grace and beauty. Her eyes sparkle with intelligence and mischief, and her confident demeanour leaves an indelible impression on me. She vividly reminds me of my sweet mother, Alice Brody (nee Riley).

Elizabeth responds with a polite nod and cheeky smile, "Mr Cartwright."

I reply with a nervous tenor, "Miss Blackwood." I extend my hand for a formal greeting, and she accepts it with a graceful handshake. I can't help but feel a sense of inadequacy in her presence, a reminder of our vast differences in backgrounds.

Mr Blackwood briskly says, "Elizabeth, John has been assisting me with various legal matters. He's proven quite resourceful."

Elizabeth's gaze lingers on me momentarily. Her lips curve into a faint, enigmatic smile, and she teasingly says, "Resourceful, you say? Well, Mr Cartwright, I do appreciate resourcefulness." With that, she turns her attention back to her father and discusses her plans and the experiences she has gained in Sydney.

As they speak, I find myself stealing glances at her, captivated by her presence and air of sophistication. My interactions with Miss Elizabeth Blackwood becomes more frequent in the following weeks. She occasionally joins us in the office, taking an interest in her father's legal affairs. As our professional interactions increase, so does my undeniable attraction toward her.

I now stand on the sidelines at the local social gathering this evening to watch Elizabeth glide across the dance floor. Her grace and charm draw the attention of every gentleman in the room. She is well-versed in social etiquette, starkly contrasting my humble upbringing.

Elizabeth's eyes meet mine from across the room as the music plays. She offers a playful smile and a raised eyebrow and extends her arm forward, inviting me to join her on the dance floor. The notion sends a thrill through me, and I can't refuse her silent request.

We dance together, our steps in perfect harmony. The world around us fades, leaving only the two of us in this fleeting moment. As the song ends, Elizabeth leans closer, her voice whispering playfully, "Mr Cartwright, you're quite a mystery. You are a refugee turned legal clerk skilled in the complexities of the law. Tell me, what other secrets do you hold?"

I am intrigued by her question and reply, "Miss Blackwood, perhaps there are more layers to me than meet the eye. But I assure you, they are not all dark and mysterious."

Elizabeth chuckles her laughter like music in the night. She withdraws with a coy smile, leaving me both captivated and perplexed.

In the following weeks, our encounters grow more frequent, and it becomes apparent that Elizabeth likes the mysterious. She enjoys our intellectual debates and seems drawn to the puzzling aspects of my past.

Our attraction deepens, yet Elizabeth maintains an air of intrigue. She engages in a tantalising game of romantic pursuit, supporting and challenging me with a skill that leaves me both frustrated and infatuated.

As I navigate the complexities of the legal world, I find myself equally entangled in the intricacies of my heart, unsure of where this dance of titillation will ultimately lead.

The days turn into weeks, and my courtship with Elizabeth Blackwood is a dance of quandary and attraction. Our interactions at social gatherings and in the office grow more intimate. One crisp autumn afternoon, Elizabeth and I are seated in the garden of her family's elegant home. The fragrant scent of blooming roses fills the air as we engage in a lively conversation about literature, politics, and the complexities of human nature.

Elizabeth says thoughtfully, "Mr Cartwright, you have a way of delving into the depths of human behaviour, understanding the motives behind every action."

I smile, "I've always believed that understanding the human condition is essential, especially in my work."

Elizabeth's gaze turns introspective, lowering her voice as if sharing a secret, "Tell me, Mr Cartwright, what drove you to seek refuge here, to take on such a dangerous and clandestine profession?"

I speak directly and honestly, "Miss Blackwood, there are parts of my past that are best left unspoken. But the desire for redemption and a fresh start brought me to these shores."

Elizabeth's eyes hold a mixture of sympathy and curiosity. She senses that secrets are hidden beneath the surface, and instead of pushing, she chooses to let them lie, respecting the boundaries I have set.

As the days turn into evenings, Elizabeth and I spend more time together, each moment deepening our connection. Our intellectual debates transform into shared laughter and stolen glances. I fell deeper in love with her, captivated by her wit, beauty, and grace surrounding her.

As the sun descended below the horizon one fateful evening, Elizabeth and I began to stroll along Cottesloe Beaches' moonlit shores. The sea whispers its secrets to us, and the gentle breeze carries our laughter into the night.

Elizabeth whispers, " Mr. Cartwright, I haven't yet managed to unravel your complete mystery, but it's only fair that I share something of myself."

Eager and curious, I say, "I would be honoured, Miss Blackwood."

Elizabeth turns to face me, her eyes revealing a vulnerability and sincerity she seldom shows. "I may have employed a strategy of cautious reserve, Mr Cartwright, but I never intended to hide my true feelings. I've come to care for you deeply."

I feel a rush of emotion, my heart pounding. This bewildering woman I've been chasing has finally revealed her feelings. I am completely overwhelmed. "Elizabeth, I..."

Before I can finish my sentence, a loud commotion echoes from a distance. A group of men approaches us, their faces twisted in anger. The lead man angrily vents, "Elizabeth, what are you doing with this *inferior caste of a clerk?*"

Elizabeth replies defiantly, "I will not be judged for my choice of company, nor should Mr Cartwright. We are together of our own accord."

The men continue criticising us, their voices growing louder and more aggressive. They become determined to guide Elizabeth away from me, the man they perceive beneath her standing.

The confrontation on that moonlit beach escalates, and I stand shoulder to shoulder with Elizabeth, facing down her infuriated suitors. My heart races, not out of fear, but out of a burning desire to protect the woman I've grown to care for deeply.

The lead man, who has known Elizabeth since childhood, is angry and red-faced and spitefully replies, "You'll regret this, Elizabeth! Associating with the likes of him will only disgrace you and your family."

Elizabeth is unyielding, "My heart makes its choices, and your prejudice won't sway me."

A nephew of the first chimes in with equal anger, saying, "You've known us all your life, Elizabeth. And now you choose an outsider?"

The confrontation continues for an eternity, with tempers flaring and accusations flying. But Elizabeth's unwavering determination and my resolve to stand by her side in the face of adversity testify to the strength of our connection.

I give the accusers a furious look and ask Elizabeth softly, "Elizabeth, are you all right?"

With relief and gratitude, Elizabeth says, "I am now, thanks to you, Mr Cartwright."

As tensions escalate, I realise that my newfound love for Elizabeth has placed me amid a conflict neither of us had anticipated. That night's events will test the strength of our bond and the depth of our feelings as we face adversity together, determined to defy societal expectations and follow the whispers of our hearts.

The tension of the evening slowly dissipates as the aggressors reluctantly move on, and we continue our walk along the shoreline, hand in hand. The waves lap at our feet as if whispering their approval of our defiance.

I reflect, "This might not be the path we envisioned, but I can't deny that I also feel deeply for you, Elizabeth."

Elizabeth tenderly replies, "And I, Johnny, cannot ignore the depth of my feelings for you. We may face challenges ahead, but I believe we can overcome them."

Our love, forged in the crucible of adversity, grows stronger each day, born from the whispers of our hearts. As we stand together on that moonlit beach, we know that whatever trials lay ahead, we'll face them hand in hand, guided by our love's unwavering compass.

Chapter Sixteen

As the days turn into weeks, Elizabeth and I continue to navigate the complexities of our unconventional relationship. Our love remains a well-guarded secret to most, declared only to a few trusted confidantes. Yet, our clandestine meetings have an undercurrent of excitement and anticipation.

This evening, as we sit in my modest room at Mr Blackwood's office, our fingers entwined, Elizabeth's eyes hold a mischievous glint.

Elizabeth says teasingly, "Johnny, do you ever wonder what the future holds for us? What if we were to defy all expectations and be together openly?"

I reply thoughtfully, "It's a tempting thought, Elizabeth, but we must tread carefully. Society's judgments can be harsh, and your family's reputation—"

Elizabeth interrupts me with determination, "I won't let fear dictate our future. I've made up my mind, Johnny. I want to be with you openly and without reservation."

Her words fill my heart with a mixture of exhilaration and trepidation. I know embracing our love openly will be challenging, but I can't deny the overwhelming desire to be with her.

I say with resolve, "Then, my love, we shall face whatever comes our way together."

Our embrace that night seals our commitment to one another, and we begin to plan for a future where our love will no longer be shrouded in secrecy. Little do we know that fate has more surprises in store for us, and the path ahead will be filled with unexpected twists and turns that will test the depth of our love and resilience.

As Elizabeth and I embrace that fateful night, our love seems unbreakable, our resolve unwavering. The prospect of openly sharing our affection with the world fills our hearts with excitement and trepidation. We discuss our future, laying the foundation for a life together.

But the path to true love is never without its challenges. Though our clandestine relationship is known to only a few trusted confidantes and the disbelieving aggressors at Cottesloe Beach, it remains a well-guarded secret from society's prying eyes. As we soon discover, secrets have a way of unravelling.

One chilly evening, as I sit in my modest room at Mr Blackwood's office, my thoughts are consumed by the woman I love. Elizabeth's radiant smile, intelligence, and the depth of her affection are what I hold most dear. The desire to protect her and cherish our love grows stronger each day. But a knock on my door interrupts my trance, and I open it to find Mr Blackwood himself, his face etched with concern.

Mr Blackwood says gravely, "John, we need to talk."

I usher him in, my heart heavy with apprehension. We sit in the lantern-lit room, the silence between us stretching as he chooses his words carefully. Mr Blackwood hesitates, "John, you must understand the delicate nature of your relationship with Elizabeth. It's become the talk of the town, and some would seek to harm her reputation and both ours."

I feel a chill of dread washes over me. The news of our love has spread beyond our control, and the consequences of our actions are beginning to reveal themselves.

Mr Blackwood continues, "I've tried to protect you and Elizabeth, but you must be prepared for what may come. Society in these parts can be unforgiving, and I fear the association could jeopardise your future career."

His words weigh heavily on my shoulders, and I know he speaks out of concern for us. But my love for Elizabeth is unyielding, and I cannot imagine a life without her.

I am defiant in my reply, "Mr Blackwood, I understand the risks, but my love for Elizabeth is stronger than any adversity we may face. I am willing to endure whatever challenges come our way to be with her."

Mr Blackwood sighs, "I had a feeling you would say that, John. Just promise me that you will protect her, no matter what."

I give him a solemn nod, our unspoken understanding sealing our shared determination to safeguard Elizabeth from the storm that looms on the horizon.

Little do we know that our challenges are far more significant than we could have imagined. Our love is tested as we stand on the precipice of an uncertain future. The whispers of our hearts have brought us together, but our resilience will determine whether we can weather the storm that approaches.

As the days go by, Elizabeth and I continue to cherish the moments we steal together, relishing our love while navigating the perils of society's judgmental gaze. This evening, as Elizabeth and I stroll through Perth's town centre, the setting sun casts a warm glow over the bustling streets, and we encounter a rather unwelcome surprise. A sleek carriage arrives at the corner of William and Murray Streets, and a tall, imposing man steps out, his face contorted in a self-assured smirk.

Elizabeth whispers, "Johnny, it's him whom I spoke of."

The man approaching us is Reginald Thornton, the unwanted suitor pursuing Elizabeth relentlessly before she leaves for Sydney. Reginald hails from a wealthy family in Perth, known for their vast land holdings and ruthless business dealings. Their desire for Elizabeth to marry into their family is no secret, despite their disdain for her father, Mr Blackwood, the barrister who has often clashed with them over legal matters.

Reginald says smugly, "Elizabeth, my dear, I trust you're well?"

Elizabeth replies with a forced smile, "Mr Thornton."

As Reginald approaches, I can sense Elizabeth's discomfort. His arrogance hangs in the air like a foul stench.

Reginald ignores me, "I must say, Elizabeth, you look more radiant than ever. It's been far too long since we last had the chance to catch up."

Elizabeth guarded, "It's been long enough, Mr Thornton."

Reginald's eyes narrow as he finally acknowledges my presence condescendingly, "And who is this, Elizabeth? A new acquaintance, I presume?"

I reply firmly, "I'm John Cartwright, Miss Blackwood's friend and confidant."

Reginald's expression darkens. He looks at me with disdain and jealousy and says Curtly, "Ah, Mr Cartwright, I see. The alien, status-seeking low-life of Blackwood's, I assume?"

Elizabeth replies defensively, "Mr Cartwright is a highly skilled and respected law clerk and has my full trust and confidence."

Reginald insistently, "Elizabeth, you must understand that your father's reputation precedes him, and you deserve better than to be associated with his kind. My family can offer you security and a life of comfort."

Elizabeth's patience with Reginald's persistent advances wears thin, and she finally speaks firmly, "Mr Thornton, I will not be bullied or coerced into a marriage I do not desire. My heart belongs to me alone, and I make my own choices."

Reginald's face is a shade of crimson, his anger barely concealed, in fact fuming, "You will regret this, Elizabeth. I am not accustomed to being denied and will not give up so easily."

With that ominous warning, Reginald Thornton retreats to his waiting carriage, leaving Elizabeth and me standing on the crowded street, our hearts heavy with the knowledge that our love is far from the only obstacle we must overcome.

As we watch the carriage disappear into the distance, I hold Elizabeth close, ready to face whatever challenges lie ahead. The unpredictable path of our journey continues, fraught with both passion and peril, as we dare to defy society's expectations and follow the whispers of our hearts.

Chapter Seventeen

The days that follow Reginald Thornton's ominous warning pass with a sense of unease hanging over us. Elizabeth's unwelcome suitor will refuse to relent in his pursuit, and we are acutely aware of the growing threat to our happiness. Little do we know that another storm is brewing, threatening to shatter the fragile peace we've fought so hard to build.

One crisp morning, a stranger to me returns to Perth as I go about my duties at Mr Blackwood's office. He is a private detective residing in the Port of Fremantle, and his purpose, I discover, is to investigate my background on behalf of the Thornton family. Unbeknownst to us, their family have grown increasingly suspicious of my humble origins and are determined to uncover any secrets I may harbour.

The detective's relentless investigation took him beyond Western Australia's borders to Melbourne. There, he stumbles upon a faded, tattered, wanted poster that has long been buried in the Victoria Police Department's archives.

The poster bears a wanted advertisement for Levi Brody, and a penned sketch shows my profile. The charges listed are haunting: the murder of my grandfather, the infamous Jack Riley. My past, one that I had hoped to leave behind forever, has caught up with me in the most devastating way.

As the detective unearths this damning evidence, he swiftly returns to Fremantle and presents his findings to the Thornton family. Panic sets in as they realise the implications of my hidden past. They waste no time bringing this shocking revelation to the authorities, seeking to have me arrested for the heinous crime I had long since tried to forget.

On the fateful evening, as I return to my modest room at Mr Blackwood's office, I am met with the gut-wrenching sight of two constables waiting outside. They inform me, as my heart sinks, that I am under arrest, charged with the murder of Jack Riley. A crime I had all the intent to commit in Melbourne out of revenge for my family's honour but was denied by my grandfather himself in a twist of fate, taking his own life after setting the scene to appear I was his murderer, which enabled him to take control over my destiny, even in Death.

Elizabeth and Mr Blackwood are devastated by the news, torn between their love for me and the overwhelming evidence against me. The Thornton family watches with vindication as their plan to eliminate me from Elizabeth's life unfolds.

The courtroom becomes a battleground for justice as Mr Blackwood, determined to defend my innocence and prevent my extradition back to Melbourne, takes on the daunting task of representing me in the trial. Elizabeth stands by my side, her unwavering faith in our love tested as she faces the harsh realities of the accusations against me.

As the trial unfolds, the colony of Western Australia watches with bated breath, torn between the desire for justice and the whispers of a love that defies all odds. The shadows of my past loom prominent, threatening to consume my own life and the lives of those I hold most dear.

In this crucible of fate, the strength of our love will be tested like never before, and our choices will determine our future.

• • • •

THE COURTROOM IS A chamber of uncertainty, and the weight of my past crime hangs heavily in the air. I sit there, my heart pounding as the trial unfolds. Mr Blackwood, a staunch defender of justice and my mentor, stands firmly by my side. Elizabeth, the love of my life, watches with hope and trepidation from the gallery.

This day, a letter penned in Jack Riley's hand and given to me as an introduction to Fred Bailey to aid my escape has arrived, and its contents can potentially change the course of my life. It speaks of a cache of gold thrown at me by Riley before his suicide to aid me in running from the Law. A game to ensure, through Riley's madness, it prolongs my agony with the need to look over my shoulder constantly until caught.

Fred Bailey, Jack Riley's business associate and confidant, arrives from Melbourne and is set to testify as the anticipation builds in the courtroom.

Bailey takes the stand, his voice steady as he reads Riley's letter aloud. The words resonate like a lifeline, a beacon of hope amid the storm of accusations. Riley's final wish to see me aided to escape and the dilemma he created is a testament to his twisted mind, cunning and vindictiveness, even from beyond the grave. With his reputation as a standover man, a Melbourne criminal, he is known to have sought revenge through his grandson to get back at his daughter before taking his own life after losing his fortune in a mining venture and with the disgrace of leading other elites of Melbourne to the same fate.

There are also character statements from prominent figures like Mr Lynn, my Ballarat solicitor and an elected Victorian Parliamentary Member whom I helped when he was wounded at the battle of The Eureka Stockade, to add weight to my defence. They speak of my past dedication to public service, selfless actions during the Battle of the Eureka in helping those wounded, and my exemplary work in Perth as a law clerk under Mr Blackwood.

As the trial continues, it becomes evident that the evidence against me is thin. It is built upon the fragile foundation of a past I have long since shed. The prosecution's case unravels, and doubt creeps into the jury's minds.

Then, it is my turn to take the stand. I recount my journey from a troubled youth to a reformed man, grateful for the opportunities that have allowed me to change. I speak of my love for Elizabeth, recent religious transformation, and determination to lead an honest life. My voice trembles with sincerity as I address the jury.

"Members of the jury," I say, "I stand before you now as the real Levi Brody, a man who has sought redemption for his past mistakes. The letter from my grandfather, Jack Riley, is a testament to his belief in my ability to change; even in his madness, he gave me a chance to become a better man than him as a fugitive. I ask you to see not any mistakes of my youth but the person I have become."

The jury deliberates, and the tension in the courtroom is agonising. Hours pass like an eternity, and I watch Elizabeth's eyes find mine, offering a silent reassurance. Finally, the jury returns with a verdict, and the weight of their decision hangs in the balance.

"Not guilty," the foreperson announces, and relief washes over me. The courtroom erupts in applause, and I am overcome with emotion. Elizabeth rushes into my arms, tears of joy streaming down her face.

As we step out into the world, hand in hand, the shadows of Levi Brody's past dissolve into the light of a promising future. Johnny Cartwright's once burdensome moniker fades into memory, leaving behind a reborn man ready to embrace a life of love, hope, and redemption with Elizabeth by his side.

My journey through the crucible of judgement and the labyrinth of my past has forged a new path, lit by the beacon of truth and the strength of a love that transcends all trials. As Levi Brody, I step forward into a dawn of possibilities; a man transformed, a soul unburdened, ready to write the next chapter of a life reclaimed.

The cache of gold, given to me by my grandfather, a symbol of the torment I was to suffer, was cruelly seized by the cunning Purser aboard the SS Britain. Thankfully, through Fred Bailey's benevolence, I now receive the last remnants of Riley's wealth—a fortune that exceeded even my wildest aspirations. It is a business legacy entrusted to Fred Bailey's care by Jack Riley himself, and in my time of need, Bailey generously bestows it upon me.

As Elizabeth and I chart the course of our future together, we make a heartfelt decision regarding the inheritance. We invest it in a modest piece of land on the outskirts of Perth, in Guilford. We envision creating our home, a sanctuary where our dreams can flourish. Our aspirations are simple—to live a life filled with love and simplicity, far removed from the complexities of our past.

Our wedding day dawns, a symphony of joy celebrating the triumph of love over the trials that once beset us. In the embrace of the warm Western Australian sun, surrounded by family and friends, Elizabeth and I stand to exchange our vows. She is a vision of ethereal beauty in her wedding gown, radiating a light that captivates my heart, leaving it brimming with love and profound gratitude.

Elizabeth and I cultivate a life rich with purpose and fulfilment on our sprawling acreage in the ensuing years. Together, we nurture gardens that bloom with vibrant energy, rear livestock that roam the verdant pastures, and bask in our children's laughter—a melodious testament to our enduring love. Once a haven for secrets and shadows, our home transforms into a beacon of hope, a testament to the boundless potential of love that defies societal constraints.

My journey alongside Mr Blackwood continues unabated. I am honing my skills as an indentured lawyer each day. With the wisdom gleaned from my tumultuous past, I dedicate myself to pursuing justice, resolved to leave an indelible mark of positivity upon the world.

The Thornton family, ensnared in their web of vindictive schemes, grapples with the repercussions of their machinations. Elizabeth's former suitor, driven by greed and a sense of entitlement, is deserted by the woman he sought to possess. The Thorntons, thwarted in their attempts to dictate Elizabeth's future, must now face the reality of their actions, a sobering confrontation with the consequences of loss.

Our love story, woven with intricate twists and turns, trials and triumphs, is a narrative of resilience and defiance. It chronicles two souls who dared to transcend the shadows of their pasts, embracing a future illuminated by hope, joy, and unwavering love that knows no bounds.

A story etched into the annals of time, it is an enduring emblem of love's transformative power. It is a beacon to guide those who dare to follow in our footsteps, choosing love over convention, hope over despair.

Chapter Eighteen

O ur farm on the outskirts of Perth becomes a sanctuary for Elizabeth and me, where we nurture our dreams and watch them flourish. The golden fields of our acreage stretch as far as the eye can see, a reminder of the legacy forwarded to me by my confidant, Fred Bailey.

As the years pass, our family grows, and children's laughter fills our home. We raise them with compassion and integrity, believing that one's past should not define one's future. Once filled with secrecy and shadows, our love story becomes a source of inspiration for our children, a testament to the enduring power of love and redemption.

My work alongside Mr Blackwood continues to be a driving force in my life. I have grown from a humble clerk into a respected legal practitioner and am dedicated to seeking justice for those who need it most. My past lessons guide me in pursuing fairness and equality, and I take pride in positively impacting the world, one case at a time.

Elizabeth, too, finds her purpose in advocating for women's rights and education. Her experiences in Sydney have ignited a passion within her, and she has become a vocal proponent of gender equality. Together, we work to create a better future for our children, where societal norms do not limit opportunities.

As our family thrives and the Guildford community grows, we are reminded of the importance of forgiveness and second chances. The Thorntons, once adversaries, have come to regret their vindictive actions. They have seen the happiness that Elizabeth and I have built together and realised the shallowness of their desires.

In a twist of fate, the Thorntons face their own challenges and are forced to confront the consequences of their past business dealings, leading them into bankruptcy. It serves as a reminder that true happiness is not found in the pursuit of power or wealth but in the bonds of love and the richness of a life lived with purpose.

• • • •

THE SUN HANGS LOW IN the Western Australian sky as I survey my field, where our small household toils under the hot sun. The promise of a new beginning has led me to extend my sympathy and offer a chance at redemption to a man named Thomas. Thomas served his sentence in Fremantle Gaol as a transported convict and earned his 'ticket of leave'.

I had seen the spark of remorse in Thomas's eyes, a glimmer of hope for a better life. That spark convinced me to offer him work on our land, hoping that honest labour would help him leave his criminal past behind.

Elizabeth had reservations about my decision, and perhaps she was right to be cautious. Thomas has shown flashes of instability, and His fascination with her, my beloved Elizabeth, is disconcerting. Still, I am determined to give him a second chance.

Thomas works alongside us as the days become weeks, tilling the soil and planting crops. He seems to be trying to turn his life around, and I hold onto the hope that redemption is possible for him.

This evening, as the sun dips below the horizon and the stars illuminate the darkening sky, I discover that some of our supplies have gone missing. I can't ignore the sinking feeling in my chest as I realise we have been stolen from.

My mind races as I confront Thomas, who appears unfazed by my accusation. I speak to him firmly, "Thomas, I trusted you. You were allowed to start anew, and now our supplies are missing. Are you responsible?"

Thomas answers defiantly, "I ain't taken nothin', Mr Brody. Don't go accusin' me without no proof."

I can't deny there is no concrete evidence, but the unease in my gut tells me otherwise. Observing from a distance, Elizabeth approaches with a troubled expression, "Levi, we should be cautious. I've noticed his lingering glances and his fixation on me. It's unsettling."

"I've seen it too, Elizabeth," I say, "I won't tolerate any harm coming to you."

With my resolve to protect Elizabeth in my absence due to my work in Perth and maintain our family's safety, I make a decision and confront Thomas sternly, "Thomas, I cannot have you endangering my family or our community. I offered you a chance, but your actions and unsettling fixation on my wife have left me with no choice. You'll return to the Fremantle authorities."

Thomas's face contorts with anger and desperation, but I know it is the only way to safeguard those I hold dear. Watching him being led away, I wonder if I have made a grave mistake or if there is still hope for his redemption.

The shadows of betrayal and uncertainty cast a pall over our peaceful life in Western Australia, and I fear this is just the beginning of the challenges ahead.

Several days later, a sinister figure emerges as the sun dips below the horizon, casting long shadows over the rugged landscape. After he betrayed my trust, Thomas, the man I once showed compassion for, stalks near my family's property, hidden by the shroud of dusk. He has escaped from a road gang working outside Fremantle Prison.

I stand in the distance, unaware of the impending tragedy that is about to unfold. The day has been ordinary, filled with the routines of life. Elizabeth has just hung the laundry out, and our children play gleefully in the fading light. Little do we know that our world is about to be consumed by flames.

With stealth and determination, Thomas makes his way towards our modest cottage. His steps are silent, his eyes burning with a malevolent fire. He bears a grudge against me, a festering anger for having sent him back to the wretched confines of Fremantle Prison.

As he approaches the cottage, he produces a crude torch; a flickering flame dances ominously at its tip. With a twisted grin, he ignites the dry, wooden walls of our home. The flames catch quickly and greedily consume everything in their path.

Our children's innocent laughter turns into terrified screams inside the cottage as the inferno rages around them. Elizabeth, the love of my life, rushes to their rescue, her heart filled with the fierce protective instinct of a mother. She gathers them in her arms and attempts to guide them to safety.

The chaos inside is mirrored by the mess in my heart as I witness the horror unfolding before me. I sprint towards the burning cottage, my voice hoarse with despair, shouting for my family to escape the flames. But the roaring fire and choking smoke drown out my pleas.

Elizabeth and the children remain trapped inside, the fire's greedy fingers reaching to claim them. Her cries for help pierce the night, tearing through the very fabric of my being. But the blaze is relentless, a merciless force of destruction.

Satisfied with his vengeance, Thomas flees into the wilderness, disappearing into the unforgiving Australian bush. He leaves behind a scene of devastation, a once-happy home reduced to smouldering ruins.

I rush forward, heedless of the searing heat, and plunge into the inferno. The flames lick at my skin, but I am blind to the pain. I reach Elizabeth; her body and my two children are charred and lifeless. In that agonising moment, I realise I have lost everything.

The night sky bears witness to my anguished cries as the flames continue to consume what remains of our home. My world has turned to ashes, and I am left with nothing but the haunting memory of the family I once held dear and a memory of that night permanently etched into the raw, seared flesh of my burnt skin.

Chapter Nineteen

The flames of the inferno not only claimed the lives of my beloved Elizabeth and our three precious children but also exacted a brutal toll on my body. My upper torso bears the searing scars of my futile attempt to rescue them from the relentless blaze. The once-familiar features of my face are now marred and unrecognisable to anyone but those closest to me.

The pain I endure from my burns reminds me of that harrowing night. Still, it pales compared to the agony festering within my soul, like the night I confronted Jack Riley to take his life, but fate denied me the opportunity. The desire for revenge again gnaws at me, threatening to engulf what little remains of my shattered existence.

Mr Blackwood, my dear friend and father-in-law, witnesses the depths of my anguish and the fiery determination that replaces the man he once knew. Instead of attempting to dissuade me from my vengeful path, he stands by my side, offering unwavering support and understanding.

We sit together in the palely candle-lit confines of my makeshift dwelling, where the flickering candlelight casts eerie shadows upon the walls. Mr Blackwood's eyes are profoundly sad, reflecting our immense loss.

Mr Blackwood gravely says, "Levi, my heart aches for the pain you endure and the family we've lost. I wish I had the vigour of youth to join you in your quest for justice. But I know you must do what you believe is right."

I look into his eyes, seeing the grief we share and the unwavering support that has defined our relationship. At this moment, I know that my pursuit of retribution is not just my burden but a solemn promise to honour the memory of those we have lost.

With steely resolve, I reply, "Mr Blackwood, I appreciate your understanding and support. I will do whatever it takes to find Thomas and ensure he faces the consequences of his actions. Justice must prevail."

With each passing day, my injuries begin to heal, leaving behind a tapestry of scars that serve as a constant reminder of the fire that has claimed everything I hold dear. But as my physical wounds mend, the fire within me rages unabated.

I relentlessly pursue Thomas, scouring the known colony for any trace of his presence. The flames may have altered my facial appearance, but my determination remains unshaken. The law no longer constrains me, and my pursuit of justice has become a singular, all-consuming purpose.

As the days turn into weeks and the weeks into months, my quest leads me down a treacherous path filled with danger and moral ambiguity. The once-principled solicitor who has defended the accused in the courtroom has become an avenging force fuelled by a thirst for retribution.

Mr Blackwood watches my transformation with a heavy heart, his aging eyes filled with pride and sorrow. He has come to accept that our paths have diverged and that my pursuit of vengeance reflects the depth of my love and the magnitude of my loss.

In the end, the man who once defended the accused now embodies the justice he sought to uphold. As I venture further into the heart of darkness, I can only hope that my actions will eventually bring closure to the chapter of tragedy that has befallen our lives.

• • • •

AS I STAND ON THE BUSTLING docks of Fremantle Harbour, the salty breeze whips through my hair as I watch the ships come and go. It's been months since the fire that claimed my beloved Elizabeth and our precious children, and the ache in my heart remains as raw as ever. But today, I am here for a different purpose, driven by my unwavering determination to find Thomas, who is responsible for this unspeakable tragedy.

As I scan the workers going about their duties, my eyes lock on a shipping contractor, a burly man with weathered features. He seems to know the ins and outs of the harbour, a man who might have valuable information.

I approach him, my voice steady but filled with urgency, "Excuse me, sir. I'm looking for a man who might have boarded one of these ships. His name is Thomas Moore, though he may use an alias. He's a dangerous man, and I need to find him. This is a penned portrait of his appearance."

The contractor squints at me, taking a moment to assess my sincerity. He scans the portrait and finally nods, realising the gravity of the situation. "I've seen a fair share of faces around here, but your description matches a man who boarded a coal shuttle for Melbourne not too long ago. He's tall, dark-haired, and a bit shifty and goes by an alias, Joshua Peak."

My heart leaps with hope, though I know the road ahead will be far from easy. "That's him. Do you know which ship he was on? Can you tell me more about the shuttle?"

The contractor scratches his head, clearly racking his memory, "It was the SS Phoenix, and it sailed out three days ago for Melbourne's port. The captain sought extra hands, and this fellow seemed eager for the work."

I then pressed him for more details, hoping for any lead to help me track Moore. "Thank you for your help. Can you recall anything else about him? Did he mention his destination or any business in Melbourne?"

The contractor pauses as if dredging up more memories. "He was tight-lipped, but I overheard him talking to one of the crew about needing a fresh start. Said he was done with the past."

I nod as my mind races with possibilities. It's a start, a thread to follow in my relentless pursuit of justice. "Thank you, sir. You've been of great assistance. Please don't hesitate to contact me if you hear or see anything else that might be relevant." I then presented him with my card.

I leave the docks with renewed determination, the image of Thomas Moore, now going by Joshua Peak, firmly etched in my mind. Melbourne awaits, and I will stop at nothing to bring him to account for the pain he has inflicted upon my life.

• • • •

THE SUN DIPS BELOW the horizon as I stand on the bustling Fremantle docks one last time, the weight of my mission pressing upon my shoulders. Mr Blackwood, my dear friend and father-in-law, is by my side, his aged face etched with a mixture of sadness and encouragement.

"Mr Blackwood, it's time for me to depart. I appreciate all you've done, your unwavering support."

Mr Blackwood nods, his eyes reflecting the sorrow that still lingers in our hearts. "Levi, you carry the burden of our collective grief. I can only hope that you find the answers you seek and that justice prevails. Farewell, my friend."

We exchanged a heartfelt embrace, and with that, I made my way to secure passage onboard a ship bound for Melbourne. The voyage was uneventful, and the sea's endless expanse starkly contrasted with the storm within my soul.

Chapter Twenty

As I step onto the bustling streets of Melbourne, memories of this city flood my mind. The weight of my purpose bears down on me, pulling me toward Fred Bailey's dilapidated house on Market Lane. This narrow passage, lined with history, links the vibrant Bourke Street to the heart of Chinatown, where the echoes of the past resonate in every weathered brick.

Market Lane hasn't changed much since I last walked its path, and the familiarity of the worn, red door with its lion-head knocker soothes my restless spirit. With a firm knock, the sound reverberates through the quiet lane, contrasting the lively city beyond—a voice from within demands my purpose, scepticism lacing its tone.

"Who is it? State your purpose."

I answer with determination, my voice conveying the urgency of my mission: "It's Levi Brody. I return to Melbourne with urgent business with Fred Bailey."

The voice, still cautious, commands me to wait. Time stretches thin, and tension hangs like a heavy shroud. Finally, the door creaks open, granting me entry into a densely lit sanctuary. The cold, stone floors whisper stories of countless footsteps, infused with the scent of stale tobacco and the weight of history.

An older man greets me with a knowing smile, his dank grey hair a cascade of memories. He leads me through the dark corridor and into a semi-lit parlour. An oil lamp casts an eerie, dancing glow that reveals antique furniture, each piece a relic from a bygone era. The gilded birdcage, home to a vibrant Corella, still occupies its place, a living testament to the passage of time since my last visit.

Fred Bailey, a man of Continental European heritage, sits in an armchair. His eyes are sharp and discerning. His attire speaks of ancient refinement, and a curved briar-smoking pipe rests between his lips, adding to his air of authority.

"Levi, welcome back to Melbourne. It's been far too long. Sit, please."

I sit, grateful to finally be in the company of someone who might aid me in my quest. Bailey's eyes carry the weight of years and the wisdom they bring. At this moment, I can only hope that he possesses the answers I've been searching for.

"Thank you, Mr Bailey," I begin, my urgency mirrored by the gravity of my situation. "I have urgent matters to discuss, and your assistance is greatly needed."

Bailey's nod is both understanding and welcoming, and I prepare myself to recount the events that have led me to this point; I pray that justice, elusive for so long, may finally find its way into the light. From aiding my escape to standing as a character witness in Guildford, Bailey's role in my past gives me hope that he may hold the key to unravelling the mysteries that have haunted me for far too long.

Bailey's eyes widen as he holds up the lantern sitting beside him to take in my disfigured face, a silent testament to the horrors I've endured since we last crossed paths. He utters a sympathetic murmur, and I can see the questions and concern etched across his features.

"Levi, my dear friend, what has happened to you?"

I recount the tragic events that unfolded on that fateful night, the inferno that robbed me of my beloved Elizabeth and our precious children, and the relentless flames that forever altered my appearance. Bailey listens in solemn silence, absorbing the weight of my words.

"My heart aches for your loss, Levi," he finally says, his voice heavy with sorrow. "I cannot begin to fathom the pain you've endured."

I nod, gratitude welling up within me for his empathy. "Thank you, Mr Bailey. Your understanding means more to me than words can express."

As I share the story of my relentless pursuit of Thomas Moore, now using the alias Joshua Peak, Bailey's eyes sharpen with interest. He leans forward, his demeanour shifting from sympathy to determination. "I will help you find this man, Levi. Such heinous acts cannot go unpunished."

Relief courses through me as Bailey offers his assistance. He's a man of connections and resources, and I know that with him on my side, our chances of tracking down Thomas will significantly improve.

"Thank you, Mr Bailey," I say again, with profound gratitude. "Your support is invaluable to me."

Bailey nods and then waves his hand, calling for his trusted aide, old Alby. Alby appears promptly, and his demeanour is efficient and poised.

"Alby, I have a task for you," Bailey begins, his voice carrying the weight of authority. "Mr Brody seeks justice for a grave injustice. We must help him locate a man named Thomas Moore, who now goes by the name Joshua Peak and has ventured away from Melbourne docks."

Alby nods, his sharp eyes locked onto mine with a sense of purpose. "Consider it done, sir."

Bailey turns back to me, his expression resolute. "Levi, you shall be my guest while Alby continues this pursuit. My home is yours for as long as you need it. We will not rest until we find this man and bring him to justice."

With Bailey's unwavering support and Alby's determination, I finally feel a glimmer of hope on the horizon. Together, we will hunt down the man who took everything from me and ensure justice prevails.

• • • •

MY DEAREST MOTHER,

I hope this letter finds you in the best of health and spirits. It pains me greatly to admit that the reason for my silence all these years has been a matter of grave urgency, one that compelled me to remain hidden from the prying eyes of the law and any who might seek to do me harm, as I'm sure you appreciate.

First, I must emphasise that the charges laid upon me by the Victorian Police have been cleared, but the circumstances surrounding the matter are still dangerous. You see, while I was acquitted of the murder of Jack Riley in Perth, the shadow of suspicion still hovers over my name. I am vulnerable to arrest should my whereabouts and current position become known in Melbourne or Ballarat.

In brief, after my escape, I was cast overboard from a ship bound for Perth, left to the mercy of the treacherous sea. Fate, however, saw fit to intervene, and I was rescued by a friendly tribe of Aborigines who showed me kindness and compassion. They guided me to the distant convict settlement in Albany, where I managed to secure passage to the Swan River Colony.

In Perth, I embarked on a new path, trained as a lawyer and eventually married a woman of exceptional beauty and intelligence who, in many ways, reminds me of you, my dear mother. She then blessed me with three precious children, a son and two daughters, all as beautiful as they were spirited.

But tragedy, as it so often does, struck swiftly and mercilessly. A deliberately lit, devastating fire claimed the lives of my beloved wife and our darling children. The same inferno marred my face, rendering me unrecognisable to all but those closest to me.

This altered visage provides me with the anonymity I desperately require, allowing me to navigate Melbourne without fear of immediate apprehension. Still, I remain cautious, for I am uncertain if the Victorian Courts have annulled my arrest warrant.

Be assured, my dearest mother, that once these matters are sorted and the threat to my freedom is entirely dispelled, I shall return to Ballarat without delay. I long to see your face and that of our dear friend Pol, to embrace you both and recount the full details of my journey and trials.

Until then, please hold me in your thoughts and prayers, and know that I carry your love and wisdom with me through every twist and turn of this arduous path.

With all my love,
Levi.

Chapter Twenty-One

As Alby returns from his inquiries down by the Melbourne docks, I can see the sombre expression etched on his face, reflecting the grave news he carries. In the dimly lit parlour, Fred Bailey and I turn our attention to him, our hearts heavy with anticipation, hungering for answers.

Alby begins to speak, taking a deep breath, his voice laden with the weight of his findings. "I found him, Levi—this Thomas Moore, the man responsible for the fire that claimed your family. He's hiding under the protection of a gang down on the docks led by a rather unsavoury character named Billy Johnson."

My fists clench involuntarily, and anger and frustration surge at the thought of the man who robbed me of everything I hold dear. Fred Bailey, ever composed, leans forward, his gaze locked on Alby. "Please, Alby, share all that you've learned," Bailey implores, his voice steady but brimming with determination.

Alby details the extent of Thomas Moore's involvement with the gang and the layers of protection surrounding him from the law. This is a difficult situation that demands immediate action if justice is to prevail.

I turn to Bailey, my resolve unwavering. "Mr Bailey, we must confront this Billy Johnson and make him understand the gravity of Moore's crimes. We need his cooperation to bring Thomas Moore to justice."

Bailey nods in agreement, his commitment to the cause unwavering. "Very well, Levi. I shall accompany you when we meet with Johnson. Together, we will impress upon him the urgency and significance of our pursuit."

With our plan set in motion, we embark on the search for Billy Johnson, a man known for his ruthless cunning and extensive connections. Our journey leads us to a candle-lit, smoke-filled room within an inn, a sanctuary for whispered alliances and covert dealings.

Seated in a shadowy corner, Billy Johnson regards us with cautious curiosity. He embodies the rugged, street-smart demeanour of a man who's seen it all. His appearance is imposing, with a tall, broad-shouldered frame that commands attention. Billy's weathered face bears the scars of countless physical and metaphorical battles, etching his history onto his skin. His dark hair, streaked with hints of grey, falls untamed over his piercing eyes, which seem to hold a lifetime of secrets and a steely resolve.

His tattered yet well-worn attire reflects his life on the gritty waterfront. A worn leather jacket, patched trousers, and scuffed boots are his armour as he navigates the perilous world of the docks. Around his neck, a weathered pendant, a cherished memento from his past, dangles like a talisman.

With a blend of sternness and desperation, Fred Bailey and I recount the heart-wrenching story of the fire that consumed my family. As the tale unfolds, I watch Billy Johnson's demeanour shift from indifference to reluctant sympathy. He can see the torment in my eyes and deformed face, the unwavering determination resonating in Bailey's words.

Finally, he speaks, his voice gruff but tinged with begrudging empathy. "Very well, I'll assist you, not for Fred Bailey or any reconciliation between us, but for you, young man. But let it be known, Bailey, that I'll call upon this favour you owe me one day."

Bailey nods solemnly, acknowledging the uncertainty of the future. Our shared goal is clear for now—to pursue justice for tragically lost lives. With Billy Johnson's reluctant cooperation secured, we depart the dimly lit room; our hearts kindled with a renewed sense of hope. The path to justice may be treacherous, but our determination to see it through burns brighter than ever, driven by the memory of my beloved family and the promise of closure that justice will bring.

• • • •

AS THOMAS MOORE STANDS before us, roughly delivered into our custody, his eyes darting nervously between Fred Bailey and me. The weight of his murderous deed hangs heavily in the air, and he knows there's no escaping the reckoning he now faces.

Bailey wastes no time, his voice cold and unwavering. "Moore, you will tell us everything. Confess to the crime you committed in Guildford."

Moore glances from Bailey to me again, his eyes darting with uncertainty. He knows that the walls are closing in, that the time for deceit is over. With a heavy sigh, he hangs his head and finally relents. "All right, I confess. I set that fire in Guildford, hoping to exact my revenge on Brody's property. But I never intended for anyone else to get hurt."

Still shaken from the abrupt turn of events, Moore hesitates for a moment before he begins to recount the night of the fire that consumed my family. His voice trembles as he describes his malevolent satisfaction from setting the cottage ablaze, believing he was only exacting revenge upon my property.

Bailey listens intently, his gaze never leaving Moore's face. He knows that this confession is essential for the justice we seek.

Once Moore has laid bare the details of his crime, Bailey turns to me, his eyes betraying the anguish he knows I carry. But he also understands that this moment requires a level of pragmatism that transcends our grief.

"Levi," Bailey says, "we can't hand Moore over to the Victoria police. The crime happened in West Australia, and doing so would jeopardise your identity and activate the previous warrant for your arrest."

His words hang in the air, heavy with the weight of the truth. We're in a precarious situation that demands a unique form of punishment, a reckoning that fits the crime.

Bailey considers various options, even to the point of contemplating torture and death by hanging. But as Moore pleads for his life, a glimmer of compassion flickers within me. The heart that regales against my genuine desire and hunger for raging revenge to match the ferocity of hurt and pain carried so long like a wicked curse.

I slowly console my frayed nerves, "Justice and repentance are possible, even for a man like Moore," I assert, my voice steady despite the turmoil within me.

Bailey, always the strategist, ponders this new perspective for a moment. He then reveals a plan that, while unconventional, offers a form of retribution and redemption.

"Alby," Bailey instructs, turning to his loyal ally, "find a ship heading through the Pacific Seas to the Americas. We need a captain known for mistreating his crew who will welcome taking Moore onboard as a galley slave. Let Moore toil in the harshest conditions until they reach some desolate foreign southern shore of the Americas, where he'll be cast ashore to fend for himself."

Moore's face contorts with fear and despair, but he realises this is his only chance at survival. He nods, his voice trembling, and agrees to this fate.

And so, the wheels of justice turn in our makeshift court of retribution. Moore's life takes a dark and uncertain turn, but it's a chance for redemption and his soul to find its way back from the abyss of his own making.

The plan is both poetic and a way for Moore to experience the torment he caused others and, perhaps, find his path to redemption. It's a form of punishment that reflects the severity of his crime while leaving room for a change of heart.

As Moore's fate is sealed, I can't help but feel a sense of closure wash over me and, in some small way, the beginnings of healing. My pursuit of justice has been served and taken an unexpected turn, not by cruelty or vengeance with death, but with the hope that even the darkest souls can one day find their way back to the light.

• • • •

I FIND MYSELF AT A crossroads, with Thomas Moore's justice served unconventionally. The weight of my grief and the pursuit of vengeance have given way to a sense of closure, albeit one tinged with sadness and regret.

After Bailey makes inquiries to a connection, a police sergeant, he receives the news that the Victorian Police have annulled the warrant for my arrest. The evidence Bailey presented to his connection and the finding of not guilty of murder in Western Australia has subsequently cleared my name in Melbourne.

With my newfound freedom, I decided to take a coach to Ballarat and return to my mother and dear friend Pol. It's been far too long since I've seen them, and I owe them a full explanation for my prolonged absence.

Fred Bailey, the architect of my unorthodox form of justice, has been instrumental in this journey. As I prepare to leave, I turn to him, my gratitude evident. "Mr Bailey, I can't thank you enough for your help. You've shown me a path to resolution I couldn't have imagined."

Bailey nods, his face bearing the marks of the burdens he carries. "Levi, it's been an honour to assist you in seeking justice. I hope you find some peace on your path forward."

With our parting words, I leave Bailey's company, knowing that justice has been served and my quest for vengeance has ended. It's time to move forward and rebuild what remains of my life.

As I step onto the coach, leaving Melbourne's tumultuous events behind, I feel hope for the future. The scars of the past remain, but they remind me of the journey I've undertaken, the justice I've sought, and the strength I've discovered within myself. The road ahead may be uncertain, but I face it with a renewed spirit, ready to embrace challenges and joys.

Chapter twenty-Two

Ballarat 1868

The coach ride to Ballarat feels like a journey through time, bringing me back to where my heart truly belongs. As I approach Doveton Street North in a hackney carriage, my anticipation grows, and I can hardly contain my excitement.

Finally, I arrive at that familiar cottage and step down from the carriage with a mixture of nerves and joy. The door before me seems to hold a world of memories, both joyful and painful, and I can't wait to step inside.

I knock, and the door opens slowly, revealing the warm and welcoming interior. Standing in the doorway, her eyes widening in disbelief, is my dear mother, Alice Brody. Her once-youthful face bears the lines of time, but her eyes still hold the same loving sparkle I remember from my youth.

"Levi?" she gasps, her voice quivering with emotion.

I can't hold back my tears any longer. "Mother," I whisper, and we rush into each other's arms. The years apart melt away instantly as we cling to each other, overwhelmed by the joy of our reunion.

As we embrace, another familiar figure steps into the room. It's my dear friend, Pol, whose infectious laughter and unwavering support in the past had been a constant.

Polly's eyes start to well up with tears as she joins our embrace, forming a small circle of love and reunion. We hold onto each other; afraid this moment might slip away like a dream.

"Levi, you're back," Pol murmurs, her voice filled with happiness.

I pull away just enough to look them both in the eye, my heart overflowing with gratitude. "Yes, I'm finally back, and I'm home."

We spend hours catching up, sharing stories of the years that have passed and the trials we've endured. My mother listens with rapt attention, her eyes shining with pride and love. Pol's laughter fills the room, reminding me of the laughter that had been a balm to my soul during our darkest days, recorded in the manuscript, 'The Gravel Pits' – (revisited in 'Golden Bloodline 1.')

As the day turns to evening, I feel a deep sense of contentment settle over me. I'm home, surrounded by the people who mean the most to me, and the wounds of the past finally have a chance to heal.

In this moment, I know that the future holds endless possibilities. With my mother's love and Pol's friendship by my side, I'm ready to face whatever challenges lie ahead. The scars of the past will always be a part of me, but they no longer define me.

I feel a profound sense of peace as I drift asleep that night. The road has been long and arduous, but it has led me back to where I belong—home, in the loving embrace of family and dear friends.

• • • •

BALLARAT HAS SHED ITS wild, lawless image from the earlier 1850s alluvial gold rush days. It's now a bustling and vibrant borough with deep gold mining as its current industry, a far cry from the chaotic and disorderly place it used to be around fourteen years ago, the time of the 'Eureka Stockade Rebellion,' which saw a battle between the *Gold Diggers* and the Victorian government's *Blue and Red Coats forces* set upon them. Twenty-two Diggers and one woman died, and five soldiers alongside scores of poorly wounded on both sides.

The streets are still dusty but lined with wooden planked boardwalks and well-constructed timber and bluestone buildings that now line Sturt Street on the upper plateau, a testament to the town's growth and evolution. In the evenings, lantern posts cast a warm glow, illuminating the path for the townsfolk going about their business between Main Road, Bridge and Sturt Streets.

As I stroll through these streets, I can't help but marvel at Ballarat's transformation from a small shanty town to a Borough filled with life and promise. Soon, it will be named a city where people from all walks of life converge, each with their dreams and ambitions. The clattering of horse-drawn carriages raising dust on the streets mingles with the lively chatter of the townsfolk.

My former mentor, Mr Crockett, under whom I was apprenticed as a tent maker, and his family left Ballarat several years ago when tents were no longer in demand. They were enticed by the allure of a new goldfield outside of Rockhampton in Queensland, hoping for prosperous times again through the high demand for their tents. I often wonder about their fate and whether their gamble has paid off.

Today, I am drawn to Snake Gully, a place steeped in memories from my youth. It's where I used to frequent when I needed respite from the abuse of my drunken stepfather, Bill Brody. I previously hid there, a Rowland's branded ginger beer bottle, filled to the brim with gold dust and tiny gold specimens I prospected for on weekends and after school—a secret treasure I intended to collect later when I returned from the Melbourne Learning Academy as a teenager. It was my nest egg, my ticket to a brighter future.

But as I arrive at Snake Gully, I'm met with a disheartening sight. The creek and its surroundings have undergone a dramatic transformation. Gold prospectors have scoured the area, sluicing, digging, and panning for the rich alluvial gold hidden beneath the earth and in its creek.

The familiar landscape I once knew has been altered beyond recognition. Gorse and wild, prickly blackberry bushes have taken over, obscuring the creek banks and their former beauty. My heart sinks as I realise that finding where I buried my treasure may be impossible.

I spend hours searching, my hands scratched, and my determination unwavering. But no matter how hard I look, the elusive ginger beer bottle remains hidden, swallowed by Snake Gully's ever-changing landscape.

As I finally give up the search and make my way back to town, I feel a profound sense of loss. The gold I had hoped for is forever buried in the past, just like the town's tumultuous history. This is a poignant reminder that some treasures are meant to remain hidden beneath the layers of time and memory until a portal opens for discovery.

On this day, I make my way through the familiar streets of Ballarat, the memories of my youth flooding back with every step. That old grey-rendered building on Basalt foundations I remember from the past stands proudly on Lydiard Street, and I find myself before it—that solicitor's office of Mr Lynn.

The years have taken their toll, as evidenced by Mr Lynn's appearance. His once-vibrant countenance is now etched with the marks of time, and I can see the weariness in his eyes. Retirement seems to be on the horizon for the man who had served as a trustee for my anonymous benefactor who financed my education at the renowned 'Melbourne Academy of Learning' – later Scotch College. Only to find out in the end that my benefactor was none other than the very man I despised most – Jack Riley.

As I step into Mr Lynn's office, I am greeted by the scent of aged books and well-worn leather furniture. Mr Lynn looks up from his desk, his expression a mixture of surprise and recognition. "Levi Brody," he exclaims, "Is that you? You've grown into a pleasing young gentleman."

I offer a warm smile, conscious of his kind remark towards my appearance when my scarred face is anything but pleasing. "Indeed, it is I, Mr Lynn. It's been many years, hasn't it?"

We exchange pleasantries, catching up on the years leading up to my recent trauma; I explain my journey, training, and success as a renowned lawyer in Perth, Western Australia. Mr Lynn listens intently, his curiosity piqued by the twists and turns of my life.

Finally, I reach into my pouch to retrieve a letter of recommendation written by my father-in-law, Mr Blackwood, the barrister I trained under and worked for in Perth. The letter speaks to my exemplary character, skills, and dedication to the legal profession.

I hand the letter to Mr Lynn, who reads it thoughtfully. When he finishes, he looks up at me with hope. "Levi," he says, "I'm encouraged by your accomplishments and the kind words in this letter. I'm considering retirement. I have often considered whether I should entrust my practice to someone capable."

His words hang in the air, unspoken but heavy with meaning. The offer is clear: I would take on a partnership in his business, thus allowing him to retire as a silent partner and allowing me to continue his practice's legacy.

I take a moment to reflect on the proposition. It's a chance to establish myself further in Ballarat and become a respected lawyer here. "Mr Lynn," I finally say, "I am deeply grateful for this opportunity and will consider it carefully. I promise to let you know directly once I've decided."

As I leave his office, the weight of the decision ahead lingers. This unexpected opportunity could alter the course of my life once more, and I must tread carefully as I navigate the path that lies before me.

Chapter Twenty-Three

The decision weighs heavily on my mind as I once again stand before the grey stone building on Lydiard Street, Mr Lynn's solicitor's office. His opportunity could redefine my future, which I don't take lightly. After careful consideration, I accept Mr Lynn's offer to take over his practice as he retires as long as he continues to serve as my mentor.

As I enter the office, I'm again greeted by the comforting scent of aged books and polished mahogany. The well-worn leather furniture whispers stories of cases long past, and I can't help but feel reverence for Mr Lynn's legacy.

The days that follow are a whirlwind of learning and preparation. Mr Lynn, with his vast experience and wisdom, has become my guiding light. He introduced me to the intricacies of the legal profession practised in Victoria, sharing insights into the nuances of Ballarat's legal landscape.

But it's not all confined to the walls of the office. This evening, Mr Lynn invites me to join him at the Unicorn Hotel on Sturt Street. The hotel is a grand testament to Victorian-Era architecture, with its ornate façade adorned above with intricate details and a broad-fronted verandah.

Inside the Unicorn Hotel, the scene is lively. The dimly lit space is abuzz with gentlemen in their finest attire engaging in hushed conversations. Servers bustle about, delivering drinks and food to patrons seated at rustic tables. Secrets are whispered, alliances are formed, and the powerful and influential gather to discuss public and private matters.

As I step inside, Mr Lynn's warm smile is welcoming. He is a season patron of the establishment, and it's clear that he's a respected figure in these circles. As we settle at a corner table, Mr Lynn discreetly points out various gentlemen, offering brief descriptions of their roles and influence. "Do you see the gentleman by the fireplace, Levi?" he asks, indicating a distinguished-looking man with salt-and-pepper hair. "That's Sir Charles Abernathy. He's a prominent barrister known for his brilliant courtroom tactics. You may find yourself opposing him in court one day."

As I approach the scene, my gaze follows Mr Lynn's direction. It's a complex web of relationships and power dynamics, and I understand I have much to learn quickly. These connections and faces will become integral to my success in the Ballarat legal world.

As the evening unfolds, Mr Lynn imparts invaluable knowledge and advice, offering guidance on navigating this world's delicate balance. It's a crash course in understanding the intricacies of Ballarat's legal and social elite, and I soak in every word.

With each passing moment, I realise this new chapter will test my legal understanding, ability to forge alliances, and strategic decision-making skills. The Unicorn Hotel, with all its secrets and whispers, becomes a symbol of the challenges and opportunities that lie ahead.

I gaze toward a little man with a black beard who enters. His frock coat and dignified demeanour catch my attention. Mr Lynn does introduce me to J B Humffray, a name I have heard whispered in Ballarat's political circles.

Mr Humffray's eyes, though showing signs of age, still carry a spark of vitality that hints at the firebrand leader he once was - helping to establish the 'Miner's Charter' of The Ballarat Reform League towards improvements to the miner's conditions under the strict goldfield regulations. However, the Victorian Government ignored the Ballarat Miner's Charter, leading to the Eureka Stockade Rebellion.

"Good afternoon, Mr Humffray," Mr Lynn respectfully greets as he passes.

"One of the Parliamentary members now," Mr Lynn explains.

I can't help but raise an eyebrow in response. "Good Lord, how many constituencies does this town have?" I ask, genuinely curious about the intricate political landscape of Ballarat now.

Mr Lynn chuckles softly before responding, "It is more than a town, Levi. Soon to become a city, I might mention. To answer your question—several. For example, Peter Lalor's been... let me see... Member for Ballarat, South Grant, and North Grenville, and elected to both houses - largely unopposed."

I take a moment to absorb this information, realising that Ballarat's political arena is a complex web of shifting loyalties and ambitious figures. It's a testament to the growing importance of this place, now on the cusp of becoming a city.

As I continue to observe the scene at the Unicorn Hotel, I understand that my journey as a lawyer in this thriving town is just beginning. The connections I make here, both legal and political, will play a pivotal role in my future endeavours. With Mr Lynn's guidance and the knowledge I'm gaining, I am determined to navigate this intricate world and make a name for myself.

As Peter Lalor, the leader of the 'Eureka Stockade rebellion', enters the Unicorn Hotel, a reverent hush suddenly settles over the bar. He's a striking figure, tall and immaculately dressed despite the conspicuous absence of his left arm, which was amputated due to his wounds at the battle - the empty sleeve tucked tidily into the side pocket of his coat. His beard is meticulously groomed, and his grey eyes hold a piercing steadiness that commands respect. Nods of acknowledgment and muted greetings ripple through the room, marking his entrance with an air of authority.

Mr Lynn's face lights up with delight at Lalor's approach. "Mr Lalor," he begins, his voice laced with deference, "we are honoured by your presence."

Lalor, a man of few words, nods in acknowledgment. "Mr Lynn," he replies curtly, his tone businesslike. "Will you give our friend Sigmund a message from me?"

Mr Lynn, eager to assist, responds, "I shall be delighted, sir."

"Thank you," Lalor continues. "If you would kindly tell him that a meeting has been called for ten in the morning. I don't expect to see him before then."

"Of course, sir," Mr Lynn assures him. "Allow me to present my replacement now that I'm retiring, Mr Levi Brody. He's recently returned to Ballarat and will take on my practice. You may be familiar with his name from the past with his help to the wounded after the Stockade Battle, and he assisted your rescuers in getting you to safety, away from the clutches of the military to Father Smyth's Manse after your wounding."

Lalor regards me with a dry, almost dismissive tone. "I'm sure you're now in good hands, my man," he remarks, his words leaving a chill in the air.

Mr Lynn, sensing the tone's implication, attempts to smooth things over. "May I offer you a drink, sir?"

Lalor declines graciously, "Thank you, some other time, my friend. I have an appointment with Mr Humffray. You won't forget the message?"

"Certainly not, sir!" Mr Lynn assures him, as Lalor moves away, his two admirers already forgotten, and joins his fellow parliamentarian at the other end of the bar.

Mr Lynn leans closer; his voice lowered conspiratorially. "There is no love lost between those two," he confides.

"OH!" I reply, sensing the underlying tension.

"When the rebels went into the Stockade," Mr Lynn explains, "Humffray bolted for cover and didn't come out until it was over. He's now some Democrat. He and Peter Lalor cross swords regularly in the House."

"I suppose they're discussing the present miner's strike that's taking place?" I inquire.

"I shouldn't be surprised," Mr Lynn agrees, a mischievous twinkle in his eye. "The cream of the whole joke," he adds, chuckling and setting down his drink, "is that the man leading the striking miners was fighting in the Stockade with Peter!"

• • • •

AS I SETTLE INTO MANAGING Mr Lynn's solicitor's office, my days become a whirlwind of legal matters and paperwork. The task is demanding, but I embrace it with vigour, determined to make my mark in this esteemed profession. Ballarat's transformation is the perfect stage for my resurgence.

Over time, I earned a reputation as an excellent advocator. My clients, from miners to landowners, trust my judgment and dedication. But it isn't just my legal acumen that sets me apart; it's the moniker they bestow upon me, which carries affection and respect: *The Phoenix*.

The name has a poetic resonance, symbolising rebirth and renewal along with my facial scars. It captures my journey from the ashes of my past to the confident man I have become. The title resonates within Ballarat's influential and parliamentary elite, a testament to my ability to rise above adversity.

With each successful case, my confidence grows, and my legal prowess becomes a force to be reckoned with. I navigate complex land disputes, draft intricate contracts, and defend the rights of those who seek justice.

The gold rush has brought prosperity and the need for laws and regulations to govern this burgeoning community whose future rides on the back of share trade speculations taken against the numerous deep leads and deep mines scattered even within central streets of Ballarat besides its surrounding districts. As one of its legal architects, I play a pivotal role in shaping the legal framework of this thriving city.

Amid my professional ascent, I often find myself in the company of influential figures other than J B Humffray and Peter Lalor, with whom I once crossed paths as a lad during the tumultuous days of the Eureka Stockade. Our interactions blend camaraderie and rivalry as we debate and discuss the day's issues.

Sitting with Mr Lynn one evening at the Unicorn Hotel, sipping a glass of whisky, I muse, "I suppose Lalor's too much of a popular hero for any opposition to be worthwhile."

Lynn chuckles and replies, "Well, our Peter's not as popular as he once was, especially among the lower orders. He's disappointed some early supporters by not pushing for more democratic reforms."

I can't help but note the irony in Lalor's trajectory from a rebel leader with a price on his head to a politician who resists significant changes to the electoral system. Like me, he seems to have his path to follow.

Amidst political discussions, I continue to handle legal matters with diligence and care, earning the trust and admiration of my Clients. I have been affectionately and respectfully bestowed the nickname 'The Phoenix', and I have indeed emerged from the ashes. I am determined to make the most of this new chapter in my life.

Chapter Twenty-four

I n the legal circles of Ballarat, even though they call me The Phoenix, that moniker I've earned through relentless perseverance. Beneath this veneer of success, I am perpetually shadowed by the scars that mar my face – a cruel reminder of the inferno that ravaged my family and left its indelible mark on me. The notion of love, of being seen beyond these scars, is a distant dream, locked away in the recesses of my heart.

Days meld into nights as I lose myself in the complexities of land disputes and legal intricacies. Solitude becomes my solace, my refuge in the realm of law where emotions hold no sway. But life, ever unpredictable, ushers in an unexpected chapter on an otherwise mundane day. During a routine legal consultation, I first saw her – Isabella Montgomery. She enters with the grace of a swan, her beauty transcending the ordinary, captivating my world-weary heart.

Her hair, dark as the midnight sky, flows in gentle waves, framing a face of ethereal beauty. Her skin, a canvas of purity, glows with vitality, while her eyes – pools of celestial light – draw me into their depths, holding me captive. Her presence ignites a warmth in the sterile confines of my office, her natural allure challenging the shadows of my self-doubt.

Despite the enchantment she weaves, I barricade my heart, convinced a man scarred by life's cruel flames could never aspire to hold such a woman's affection.

Yet, as if guided by a hand of fate, our paths intertwine beyond the confines of professional etiquette. Casual conversations evolve into shared moments at social events, her interest in me seemingly genuine. She sees beyond the attorney, beyond The Phoenix, reaching for the man shrouded in scars.

Initially, I dismissed her attention as mere politeness, a social grace bestowed upon a respected figure in the community. But her laughter rings true, her gestures sincere, and against the walls I've built, I find myself succumbing to her charm.

Our love is a silent song, its melody sweet yet laced with the pain of my insecurities. Her presence in my life defies the logic of suitable matches, igniting a battle between my past scars and the promise of a love-filled future.

In her gaze, my scars are not the marks of tragedy but symbols of resilience and strength. With Isabella, I dare envision a life where love transcends the physical, and the phoenix within me can soar above all else.

Isabella, a beacon in Ballarat's elite circles, brings more than beauty to my world. Her intellect matches her grace, and her conversations blend literature, the arts, and philosophy. In her, I find a Lover and a kindred spirit, a companion who shares my passion for knowledge and depth.

Yet, the shadows of my past cling stubbornly, and my disfigurement is a constant reminder of loss and unworthiness. Despite this, Isabella's affection remains steadfast, and her eyes see the essence of who I am beyond the scars.

As our bond deepens, I stand at a crossroads, grappling with a choice between yielding to love or remaining shackled by the remnants of my past traumas. The heart, it seems, holds wisdom that defies reason, urging me to embrace a future illuminated by love and acceptance.

In Isabella Montgomery, I find an embodiment of beauty, privilege, and a soul that resonates with empathy and understanding. Our journey together challenges the confines of my self-imposed limitations, urging me to rise, not just as The Phoenix from tragedy, but as a man reborn from the ashes of doubt into the light of love and hope.

In the warm embrace of the cottage on Doveton Street South, this night finds me seated with two of the most influential women in my life: my mother, Alice, and my dear friend Polly, whom I affectionately call Pol. I feel the strength to share a part of my recent blossoming life in their presence.

"Mother, Pol," I start, my voice quivering slightly with nervousness and excitement, "I've met someone. Her name is Isabella Montgomery, and she's... well, she's remarkable."

Alice's eyes light up with a mother's intuition and warmth. "Levi, tell us more," she prompts gently, her smile inviting and encouraging.

With each word about Isabella, I paint a vivid picture of her: her grace, intelligence, and the unexpected connection we've forged. My mother's eyes glisten with joy, but I can't miss the shadow of surprise and a tinge of sorrow that crosses Pol's face. Pol, whose father's tragic end left her life intertwined with mine, clearly harbours feelings that go beyond friendship.

Alice, ever perceptive, senses the complexity of emotions in the room. She rests her hand on Pol's shoulder, her voice soothing yet candid. "Love is a mysterious journey, Levi. It takes us down paths we never expected. What matters is your happiness."

Pol, masking her inner turmoil with a brave front, echoes Alice's sentiment. "Your happiness is all I could ever wish for, Levi."

In that moment, with the unwavering support of these two remarkable women, I feel gratitude and clarity. Isabella Montgomery has indeed entered my life, igniting the possibility of a love I had not dared to dream of again. It seems that the phoenix within me might still soar higher.

Isabella's parents heighten the complexity of our budding relationship. Her father, Alexander Montgomery, a pillar of Ballarat's society, recognises and appreciates my past struggles and aspirations. He sees in me qualities he deems worthy of his daughter's partner: determination, intellect, and a shared passion for learning.

Conversely, Lady Evelyn Montgomery, Isabella's mother, views the world through the lens of social prestige and appearances. To her, my disfigurement and the scars of my past are blemishes that could mar

Isabella's prospects in their elite social circle—her obsession with maintaining a pristine social image clashes with her husband's more progressive outlook.

Caught amid this familial divide, Isabella and I tread a path fraught with societal expectations and her parents' judgments. Our growing affection is a testament to the heart's resilience against the rigid confines of class and appearance.

As we navigate these tumultuous waters, the question looms large: Can our love, as pure and profound as it is, withstand the relentless pressures of social conformity and the scrutiny of a society that prizes appearances above all else? Can our bond endure these challenges, or will it be quelled by the harsh realities of our differing worlds?

Our story unfolds in the heart of Ballarat, a city on the cusp of transformation. It is a tale of love and resilience, a testament that the heart has the power to conquer social convention barriers. This narrative promises to challenge, inspire, and redefine the very essence of love and acceptance—one I have had to endure in the past.

As my affection for Isabella grows more robust, I can no longer deny the depth of my feelings. It's a love that transcends the boundaries of my disfigured face, and I know I can't keep it hidden any longer. With a heart full of hope and trepidation, I seek permission from Alexander Montgomery to ask for his daughter's hand in marriage.

Alexander, a wise and understanding man, recognises my sincerity and intentions. With an air of authority that leaves no room for dissent, he grants his blessing for our union, setting aside his wife's objections.

On the other hand, Lady Evelyn Montgomery remains resolute in her determination to thwart our marriage. In the privacy of her thoughts, she vows to use every means at her disposal to ensure that our union will not last. Her obsession with appearances and social standing has blinded her to the depth of our love, and she is determined to preserve her image at all costs.

Chapter Twenty-Five

O ur wedding day is a lavish affair that befits the grandeur of the Montgomery family. It takes place at the illustrious Craig's Royal Hotel, an icon of the goldfields since 1867 when Queen Victoria's son, Prince Alfred, the Duke of Edinburgh, graced its halls. Alexander and Lady Evelyn personally met Prince Alfred during his visit, a moment they cherish as a highlight of their social standing.

The hotel's opulent interiors are the perfect backdrop for our weddings. The ceremony is held in the grand ballroom, adorned with crystal chandeliers and fresh flowers. A sense of history and prestige permeates the air as if the hotel's very walls whisper secrets of past grandeur.

Guests from far and wide gather to witness our union, a blend of Ballarat's elite and influential figures. Isabella, radiant in her wedding gown, walks down the aisle with grace and poise, her beauty rivalling that of a fairytale princess. I stand tall and resolute, my scars a testament to the trials I have endured and the love that has brought me to this moment.

A prominent clergyman officiates the ceremony, and our vows are exchanged amidst applause and admiration. As we seal our love with a kiss, I can't help but feel a sense of triumph, knowing that our love has overcome the obstacles of societal expectations and prejudice.

The reception that follows is a grand celebration of love and unity. The ballroom is transformed into a banquet hall, where guests dine on exquisite cuisine and dance the night away to the melodies of a live orchestra. Floral arrangements and fine china adorn the tables, and the atmosphere is joyful and filled with merriment.

As I look into Isabella's eyes this night, I know our love has conquered the odds. Despite our challenges and opposition, we've found our way to each other, and nothing can dim the radiance of our passion. Alexander Montgomery himself paid for our marriage, which is a testament to the power of love in the face of adversity and the enduring strength of the human heart.

My mother and Pol, my dear companions who have been by my side through the trials of life, are present at the wedding, their joy palpable as they witness the union between Isabella and me. They've seen the evolution of my love for her, the blossoming of affection that defies the disfigurement on my face, and they couldn't be happier for us.

As the night progresses, the atmosphere is filled with laughter and music. Pol twirls around the dance floor in the arms of a handsome cousin of Isabella's with a smile that lights up the room while my mother watches with pride and contentment. It's a joyous occasion, one that should be without blemish.

However, Lady Evelyn approaches my mother and Pol, dampening our enjoyment. Her displeasure with the nuptial arrangement is evident, and she makes no effort to conceal her objections. Her words, with their cutting edge, leave no room for misunderstanding.

"I hope you understand, Mrs Brody, Miss Pol," Lady Evelyn begins, her tone laced with condescension, "that should this marriage not stand the test of time, I will ensure, by whatever means necessary, that Mr Levi Brody receives not a single penny in any divorce settlement."

The weight of her words hangs in the air, casting a shadow over the merriment. Though taken aback, my mother and Pol maintain their composure, their expressions a mixture of surprise and disappointment.

Despite the disappointment of hearing about Lady Evelyn's warning, Isabella and I retire to the towered apartment for our wedding night. The apartment is a sanctuary of romance, tucked away in the upper floors of Craig's Royal Hotel. The walls are adorned with rich tapestries, and a grand four-poster bed takes centre stage in the opulent chamber.

Moonlight streams through the ornate windows, casting a soft glow over the room. Roses, a gift from one of our well-wishers, delicately scent the air. Candles flicker on the bedside tables, and warm, inviting light adds to the room's intimacy.

As I look into Isabella's eyes, I can't help but feel a rush of emotion. Despite the challenges and obstacles ahead, I know our love is a force to be reckoned with. In the quiet of that towered apartment, we begin our journey as husband and wife, ready to face whatever trials the future might hold, armed with the strength of our love and the unwavering support of those who believe in us.

• • • •

THE MORNING AFTER OUR wedding, Isabella and I awake to a world imbued with enchantment. Sunlight filters through the lace curtains, casting intricate patterns of light and shadow on the walls of our towered apartment. The air is filled with the sweet fragrance of those freshly arranged roses within the room, and the soft chirping of birds provides a musical backdrop to the start of our new life together.

Our hands often find each other's, silently reassurances of our deep and abiding love as we dress and prepare for the day. Our wedding was a lavish affair, and the memories of that night still dance in our hearts. But now, the promise of our future beckons, and we are eager to explore what it holds for us.

Soon, hooves clip-clopping and carriage wheels rumbling reach our ears. We exchange excited glances, knowing that Mr Montgomery's gig carriage has arrived to collect us. Isabella's eyes sparkle with anticipation, and I can't help but smile, feeling a surge of joy.

We descend the grand staircase, hand in hand, and are greeted by our friends and family who have gathered for the occasion. Pol, who has been like a sister to me, offers her congratulations and a knowing wink. My mother, Elizabeth, radiates happiness, her eyes filled with pride and love for her son. The towered apartment has been the perfect place to spend our first night as a married couple, and we have left it filled with cherished memories.

As we step outside, the gig carriage stands before us, a vision of elegance and craftsmanship. Mr Montgomery, in his usual dignified manner, greets us with a gracious smile. His presence conveys authority and warmth, and I know he has something special in store for us.

"Good morning, my dear children," he says, his voice carrying the weight of wisdom and affection. "I trust you had a restful night?"

Isabella and I exchange glances, our hearts filled with love and gratitude. "Yes, Father," she replies, her voice filled with happiness. "It was a magical night."

I nod in agreement, unable to find words that adequately express my heart's joy.

Mr Montgomery gestures toward the awaiting carriage. "Then, if you would be so kind as to join me, there is a place I would like to show you."

We climb into the carriage, the soft cushions providing a comfortable seat for our journey. Pol waves to us from the doorstep, her eyes glistening with tears of joy. I can't help but feel a pang of emotion, knowing how deeply she cares for me.

As we set off, the carriage glides smoothly along the dusty streets of Ballarat. I look at Isabella, her beauty illuminated by the soft morning light. She leans against my shoulder, and I gently kiss her forehead. It's a moment of pure contentment, a sense that our love will withstand the tests of time.

We venture beyond the bustling inner city streets into a tranquil outer suburb. The landscape is a patchwork of colourful cottages and rolling hills, a picturesque backdrop to our journey. I marvel at the beauty of the world around us and am grateful for the love that has brought us to this point.

Finally, the carriage stops as we arrive at our destination—a quaint and cozy cottage atop a hill in Mount Pleasant. Smoke curls from the chimney and vibrant flowers adorn the garden, creating an aura of serenity.

Mr Montgomery helps us out of the carriage, his eyes filled with paternal pride. "Welcome, my dear children, to your new home," he says warmly.

Isabella and I exchange glances, our hearts overflowing with gratitude. The cottage is more than we imagined, symbolising our new beginning as husband and wife.

"Thank you, Father," Isabella says, her voice trembling. I nod in agreement, but my voice is too choked with feelings to speak.

Mr Montgomery looks at us with profound satisfaction. "I'm delighted that you both appreciate it. Consider it a wedding gift and a symbol of my hopes for your future."

Isabella and I can't contain our gratitude. We embrace Mr Montgomery, our hearts full of love and affection for the man who has made our dreams a reality.

As we step into our new home, I can't help but think of the remarkable journey that has led me here, from the ashes of my past to the promise of a future filled with love and happiness. The cottage is a testament to our enduring love and the support of those who believe in us.

With Mr Montgomery's generosity and our unwavering love, our journey has only just begun. The cottage, nestled in the embrace of nature, is where we will build our life together, and I can't wait to see what adventures await us in this new chapter of our story.

Chapter Twenty-Six

O ur new cottage, nestled in the hills surrounding Ballarat, is a sanctuary of tranquillity and a symbol of our love's endurance. Isabella and I spend our days discovering the beauty of the countryside, the rolling hills, and the hidden trails that wind through the landscape. Our love seems boundless, and with each passing day, it only grows stronger.

Yet, as the weeks turn into months, subtle hints of trouble appear on the horizon. Mr Montgomery, though generous in gifting us the cottage, alludes to tensions within the Montgomery family. Lady Evelyn Montgomery, ever vain and concerned about her social standing, still does not take kindly to our union.

Her disapproval is evident in her icy demeanour whenever we cross paths, and her gaze holds a malevolence that sends shivers down my spine. Isabella tries to mend fences with her mother, but Lady Evelyn seems determined to have her grudge.

As we settle into our new life, the shadow of Lady Evelyn's disapproval looms over us, casting a pall over our happiness. Isabella remains resolute, determined to find a way to bridge the gap between her mother and herself.

On this fateful evening, just as the sun dips below the horizon and the cottage is bathed in lamplight, Isabella shares her concerns with me. "Levi," she says, her voice tinged with worry, "I fear my Mother's disapproval is more than just a family dispute. She has been acting strangely, and I've overheard her speaking with a man several times, whispering in hushed tones about matters she refuses to discuss with me."

I furrow my brow, concerned by Isabella's revelation. "What do you think she could be involved in?"

Isabella shakes her head, her expression troubled. "I can't be certain, but it has me deeply worried. My mother has always been concerned with appearances and social standing, but this seems different, more sinister."

We can't shake the feeling that something is amiss as the days pass. There are mysterious visitors to the Montgomery estate when Mr Montgomery is absent, whispered conversations in the dead of night, and a sense of foreboding that hangs like a dark cloud.

A sudden commotion outside catches our attention as Isabella and I enjoy a quiet dinner in our cottage this evening. We rush to the window to witness a scene sending chills down our spines. Lady Evelyn is embroiled in a heated argument with a tall, shadowy figure whose features are obscured by the darkness.

Their voices carry on the wind, and though we can't make out the words, the tension in the air is palpable. Lady Evelyn's gestures are frantic, and the mysterious figure seems to be demanding something of her and moving towards our cottage door. Still, Lady Evelyn appears to restrain his arm, appealing to him to leave.

Isabella turns to me, her eyes wide with fear. "We need to find out what's going on. My mother's safety may be at risk."

I nod, my heart pounding with apprehension. "Agreed. We'll be discreet, but we can't longer ignore this."

Little do we know that our pursuit of the truth will plunge us into a world of intrigue, deception, and danger. Lady Evelyn's mystery will lead us down a treacherous path that will test the strength of our love and family bonds.

The following day, Isabella and I decided to discreetly investigate the mysterious events unfolding around Lady Evelyn. Secrecy is paramount, for the danger lurking in the shadows is real and unpredictable.

Our first step is to follow Lady Evelyn, hoping to learn more about her interactions with the shadowy figure from the previous evening. We observe her discreetly as she leaves the Montgomery estate alone at dusk in a gig carriage and enters the heart of Ballarat.

She moves with an uncommon urgency, and whatever she is involved in weighs heavily on her mind. Isabella and I keep our distance, careful not to arouse any suspicion.

Lady Evelyn's journey leads her to a run-down warehouse on the city's outskirts, a place that seems incongruent with her usual refined tastes. She disappears inside, and we wait anxiously, wondering what could transpire behind those weathered walls.

As the hour passes and the sun dips below the horizon, Lady Evelyn emerges from the warehouse, her face pale and her demeanour anxious. In a hurry by her behaviour, and without a second thought, we follow her back to the Montgomery estate.

As we sneak into the shadows outside the manor, we notice Lady Evelyn is not alone. Another mysterious figure is with her as they stand outside the mansion. Their conversation is heated, and though we strain our ears, we can't make out the words. They are engaged in something that goes far beyond a family dispute.

We watch as Lady Evelyn hands a small package to the shadowy figure, who then disappears into the darkness. It is a moment that sends a shiver through us, for it hints at clandestine dealings and a web of secrets that stretches beyond our comprehension.

Once Lady Evelyn is alone, Isabella and I approach cautiously. Her eyes widened in surprise, and she did not expect to see us. "Mother," Isabella says, trembling with concern and frustration, "what is happening? Who is that man, and what are you involved in?"

Lady Evelyn's face contorts with mixed emotions, including fear and guilt. She hesitates for a moment before finally speaking. "Isabella, Levi, there are things you cannot understand. I am doing what I believe is necessary to protect our family."

Her cryptic words only deepen our curiosity and concern. We press her for answers, but she remains elusive and refuses to divulge more information.

Our minds race with questions and possibilities as we leave her standing in the moonlight. Lady Evelyn is entangled in a dangerous web threatening her and our entire family.

Isabella and I return to our cottage, our hearts heavy with the weight of our uncovered mysteries. We know we are embarking on a perilous journey that will test the limits of our love and loyalty.

As we enter uncertain days, danger, deceit, and an unwavering pursuit of the truth define our resolve. We remain steadfast in our determination to unearth the secrets that ensnare Lady Evelyn and shield our family from the looming threat. Yet, little do we comprehend that our relentless quest for answers will lead us into a realm of intrigue. Here, alliances will shift, loyalties will be tested, and the past will converge with the present in ways none of us could have foreseen.

• • • •

IN THE DAYS THAT FOLLOW our unsettling encounter with Lady Evelyn, Isabella and I can't shake the feeling that we are caught amid a grand conspiracy. The mysterious figures she has been meeting, the clandestine exchanges, and her cryptic words ignite our determination to uncover the truth.

Our first action is to investigate the warehouse where Lady Evelyn had discreetly met the enigmatic man. We know that returning to the exchange scene might yield valuable clues, so we venture there under the cover of darkness, shrouded by the secrecy of night.

The warehouse appears abandoned and forlorn, its wooden doors creaking in the wind. The air is thick with the scent of dampness and decay, and our lantern's flickering light casts eerie shadows on the dilapidated walls.

As we cautiously enter the building, mustiness and the lingering scent of burnt candles assault our senses. We comb the area meticulously, hoping to find traces of what has transpired here.

Amidst the debris and disarray, we discover a sprinkling of fresh mortar dust on the floor below an interior brick wall. After removing two loose bricks, we are attracted to a hidden compartment. Inside, we find a series of letters used in correspondence that shed light on the nature of Lady Evelyn's involvement. She has been providing bribed payments and receiving instructions for their delivery from an anonymous source using the cryptic alias "Molly Maguires."

The letters hint at a dangerous game of intrigue, with Lady Evelyn acting as a pawn in a much larger scheme. The contents are vague, but whatever the 'Maguires' involvement, it extends far beyond our comprehension.

We know that we need to uncover the identity of this mysterious society, for it is evident that Lady Evelyn is being manipulated for purposes unknown. With the newfound evidence, Isabella and I confront her to demand the truth.

Our meeting with Lady Evelyn is fraught with tension. We present the letters we have found, leaving no room for denial or evasion. Isabella's voice quivers with anger and concern as she implores her mother to come clean.

"Mother, we know about the Molly Maguires and the payments," Isabella says, her eyes pleading. "Who is behind all of this, and what are you involved in?"

Lady Evelyn's face contorted with the mixed emotions of guilt and fear. Once again, she seems torn between protecting her family and keeping her secrets hidden. Finally, she speaks, her voice trembling. "You must understand, Isabella," she says, "I did this out of love for our family. But there are things I cannot reveal for your safety – you must trust me."

Her words are frustratingly cryptic, and we still miss a crucial puzzle. Yet, Lady Evelyn's vulnerability and genuine concern for our well-being tug at our hearts, leaving us torn between our quest for the truth and our compassion for her.

As we leave her that evening, we are no closer to unravelling the full extent of the conspiracy that has ensnared our lives. The days ahead promise more peril and uncertainty, but Isabella and I are resolved to face whatever challenges come our way. We are determined to unveil the identities behind the Molly Maguires and uncover the truth behind the shadows that have cast a sinister pall over our lives.

Chapter Twenty-Seven

Following our unsettling encounter with Lady Evelyn and her connection with the Maguires, Isabella and I are thrust into a labyrinth of intrigue and danger. This odd, shadowy society's enigmatic presence continues to cast an ominous cloud over our lives, enveloping us in a shroud of uncertainty and foreboding.

Our investigation into the Maguires becomes more urgent as we endeavour to unveil this elusive adversary's identity. We meticulously comb through the documents we discovered in the abandoned warehouse, painstakingly searching for clues that may lead us closer to the truth.

We decipher obscure messages and coded references within the cryptic letters and correspondences. One statement stands out, bearing the emblem of the Maguires— the parchment's edges are blackened by burnt cork, a symbol that seems to hold the key to unlocking the Molly Maguires' secret society. It references an impending meeting, a vital piece in the puzzle that beckons us forward.

With a sense of urgency coursing through our veins, Isabella and I decided to attend the forthcoming meeting in place of Lady Evelyn. Confronting the Maguire's associate face-to-face represents our best chance at prying the truth from their secretive grasp and halting the shadowy machinations threatening our family.

The clandestine rendezvous unfolds in the same abandoned warehouse on the outskirts of Ballarat, which seems to serve as the recurring backdrop for these covert dealings. Isabella and I arrive ahead of schedule, concealed within the shadows. Our hearts are resolute but filled with a potent mixture of fear and determination.

As we linger in tense anticipation, the dilapidated warehouse door creaks open, and a tall, enigmatic figure steps inside. The Maguires' associate is cloaked in sombre black attire, their face obscured, blackened by burnt cork, a haunting emblem of their clandestine identity. The atmosphere becomes almost palpable as we confront this orchestrator of our family's torment.

Isabella's voice remains unwavering as she demands answers. "Who are you, and what is your intent concerning our family?"

The Maguire hesitates briefly before responding, his voice masked and distorted. "You should not have ventured into realms beyond your understanding, Isabella Montgomery."

Those words send a shiver down our spines, leaving us with a disturbing awareness that the Maguires possess an intimate knowledge of our family. Before the Maguire can divulge more, an unforeseen commotion erupts outside the warehouse, dramatically disrupting our encounter. It becomes evident that we have fallen into a meticulously orchestrated trap. Panic sets in, compelling the Maguire to vanish through a side window into the enveloping darkness, leaving many unanswered questions.

As we emerge from the warehouse, we are greeted by a tableau of chaos. Lady Evelyn and Mr Montgomery, accompanied by two constables, have arrived in furious bewilderment. They believe we are in grave danger and are determined to rescue us from our perceived peril.

Amidst the confusion, Lady Evelyn finally admits to her association with the Maguires. She maintains that her actions were driven by desperation to safeguard the family's wealth and reputation. It becomes painfully evident that the Maguires wield damning information capable of tarnishing our family's name, that Lady Evelyn is still reluctant to divulge even now.

Despite our differences, we share a concern for the family's well-being. We agree to work together to uncover the Maguires' true identities and the extent of their influence. Our quest for the truth has led us down a perilous path, and we know that our journey is far from over.

The Molly Maguires' enigmatic figures remain elusive, and their motives are mysterious. But with determination and unity, we are resolved to face whatever dangers lie ahead and protect our family from the looming threat that has infiltrated our lives.

After our confrontation with the Maguire representative and Lady Evelyn's confession, our lives have turned sharply into intrigue and uncertainty. The revelation of Lady Evelyn's involvement has shaken us, and her motives are more complex than they appear, but she is determined to enlighten us.

We convene in the dimly lit drawing room of Montgomery Manor, the ancestral home that has witnessed two generations of Montgomerys. The atmosphere is tense as Lady Evelyn recounts her version of events, her voice trembling with guilt and desperation.

"I never meant for any of this to happen," Lady Evelyn admits, her eyes brimming with tears. "The pressure to protect the family's reputation and wealth drove me to make decisions I now deeply regret."

Isabella and I exchange glances between our sympathy for Lady Evelyn and the need to uncover the truth about the Maguires and their vendetta against our family.

Mr Montgomery, though initially furious with our actions, has calmed considerably. He looks at Lady Evelyn with a mixture of concern and understanding. "Evelyn, you should have confided in me. We could have found another way to protect our interests without resorting to these shadowy dealings."

Lady Evelyn nods, her remorse palpable. "I know, Alexander and I'm truly sorry for my choices. But the Maguires threaten to reveal secrets that could ruin us and another prominent member of Ballarat society. I acted out of fear."

I can't help but wonder about the nature of these secrets that Maguire holds over Lady Evelyn and, by all accounts, Mr Montgomery, who is also being evasive as if he is acquainted with Lady Evelyn's dilemma. The Maguire's knowledge seems far-reaching and insidious, and we must uncover the extent of their influence.

As we discuss our next steps, we are interrupted by the arrival of Mr Charles Montgomery, a cousin of Alexander Montgomery's and the family's trusted legal advisor. He has been made aware of our recent troubles and has devised a proposal that could potentially unravel the mystery surrounding the Molly Maguires.

"Isabella, Levi, Lady Evelyn, Alexander," Charles Montgomery begins, "I believe I may have found a lead that could shed light on the Molly Maguires' identity. Rumours have been circulating about a secretive society operating in Ballarat as a breakaway group from Ballarat's Ancient Order of Druids... those characters who wear white linen gowns with high cowls and long false white beards. The Maguires, I am told, wear black linen gowns with high cowls and blacken their faces. They deal in clandestine information and covert operations alongside an associated group called 'The Whispering Shadows.'

The name sends shivers down my spine, for I have heard whispers of this enigmatic group during my time in Ballarat. They are said to be a network of spies and informants, their motives shrouded in secrecy. Mr Charles Montgomery continues, "I have contacts within the legal fraternity who may be able to provide us with more information. But we must proceed with caution. 'The Whispering Shadows' are known for their brutality and ability to protect themselves."

We agree to pursue this lead, knowing it is a difficult path fraught with danger. Our family's reputation and future are at stake, and we are resolved to uncover the truth behind the Maguires and its connection to this other shadowy organisation.

As we embark on this new investigation chapter, I feel foreboding. The road ahead is treacherous, and the secrets we are about to unearth will test the bonds of our family and the limits of our courage. But we are determined to face whatever challenges lay ahead, for the honour of the Montgomery name and the safety of our loved ones depend on it.

Chapter-Twenty-Eight

Our investigation into the Molly Maguires and their connection to the Whispering Shadows takes us down a labyrinthine path of intrigue and danger. Our trusted advisor, Mr. Charles Montgomery, proves to be an invaluable ally in navigating the shadowy world of secret societies and clandestine information networks.

In the following weeks, Charles Montgomery discreetly contacts his contacts within the legal fraternity, probing for further information regarding the Whispering Shadows. He is met with hushed conversations and furtive glances for even discussing this enigmatic group that seems perilous.

One evening, as Isabella, Charles, and I are gathered in Montgomery Manor's lantern-lit study, our advisor brings forth a sealed envelope. It bears the mark of a wax seal imprinted with a coiled serpent—a symbol associated with the Whispering Shadows.

"Levi, Isabella," Charles begins, his voice grave, "I've received a message from a reliable source within the legal fraternity. It appears that the Whispering Shadows have taken notice of our inquiries."

With a sense of foreboding, I break the seal and unfold the letter. Its contents are cryptic, written in an elegant script that conceals as much as it reveals. The message hints at a clandestine meeting, a rendezvous with a mysterious contact who claims to have purchasable vital information regarding the Molly Maguires and their involvement with the Whispering Shadows.

Isabella looks at me, her eyes filled with determination and trepidation. "Levi, we must pursue this lead. We cannot let fear deter us from uncovering the truth."

I nod in agreement, my heart heavy with the weight of our mission. "You're right, Isabella. We've come too far to turn back now. But we must proceed cautiously."

Charles Montgomery also advises caution: "I will arrange the meeting, but we must take every precaution to ensure your safety. The Whispering Shadows are not to be underestimated."

We prepare for the meeting with our mysterious contact as the days pass. It will occur remotely—at a dilapidated house on Talbot Street South. The air is thick with tension as we arrive at the appointed hour, our hearts pounding with anticipation and dread.

The house is dimly lit, the shadows dancing eerily on the cracked wooden floor. Our contact remains hidden in the shadows, their identity concealed by a hooded cloak. The only sound is the distant hum of the wind, whispering secrets we cannot decipher.

"I have information about the Maguires and their ties to the Whispering Shadows," the cloaked figure speaks, their voice a mere whisper. "But this knowledge comes at a price. If you agree, you will be informed of my demands later."

Isabella steps forward, her resolve unwavering. "Name your price. We will pay for it."

The figure hesitates momentarily without revealing our next meeting. This task will take us deeper into the web of intrigue and danger than we have ever imagined. This dangerous mission will test our courage and resolve to the fullest.

As we leave the derelict house this night, our hearts heavy with the weight of our new mission, I can't help but wonder what other secrets the Whispering Shadows hold. Our pursuit of the truth has brought us on a steep journey that will challenge our beliefs and lead us to the darkest corners of Ballarat's hidden underworld.

Still, we are determined to press forward for our family's honour, our loved ones' safety, and the pursuit of justice. The shadows may conceal the truth, but we are determined to bring it to light, no matter the cost.

The following days are consumed by our efforts to unearth the hidden truth. Charles Montgomery is as dedicated as ever, tirelessly delving into legal records and covertly consulting with his network of contacts. Isabella and I, too, conduct our investigations, visiting the Mechanic Institute's archives and discreetly interviewing those who might hold the missing puzzle pieces.

Our breakthrough came when I stumbled upon an old newspaper article tucked away in the archived depths of the 'Ballarat Star Newspaper'. The headline, "A Lady's Secret Scandal: A Whispered Whiff of Betrayal," catches our attention, dated September 18th, 1853. As we read the article, the puzzle pieces fall into place.

The story recounts a society scandal that shook Ballarat years ago. Even then, Lady Evelyn Montgomery was a prominent high society figure known for her beauty, charm, and social grace. But the article reveals a darker side—a passionate affair with an unnamed, eminent married man whilst betrothed to Alexander. The liaison brought disgrace to her and the good name of her family. Alexander Montgomery was aware of the scandal but married Evelyn regardless out of love and forgiveness, and over time, the scandal disappeared into obscurity.

The identity of Lady Evelyn's paramour remains hidden in the shadows, a well-kept secret buried beneath layers of discretion and wealth even by the editor of the Star Newspaper. But our mysterious secret society has uncovered the identity behind that prominent high-society figure, her paramour, and uses it to leverage Lady Evelyn for monetary gain.

They are willing to resurrect the scandal, which now promises a more significant effect on Montgomery's business interests and the ruin of the high society figure who is now a distinguished State Parliamentary Member and, if named as Lady Evelyn's past paramour, will ruin any chance of re-election.

As we piece together the details, it becomes clear that besides the Maguires, the Whispering Shadows also have a vested interest in this scandal. Lady Evelyn has become a pawn in their game, forced to carry out their bidding to protect her family and others.

But what is Molly Maguire's goal? Is it just for financial gain, and we are still ignorant about how their actions tie in with the Whispering Shadows - the shadowy organisation with supposable interests in a parliamentary member's re-election?

With newfound determination, we are determined to confront Lady Evelyn with our uncovered knowledge. It's a delicate matter, for we understand the potential consequences of exposing her secret. But the need for the truth and our pursuit of justice outweighs our reservations.

The evening air vibrates with tension in Montgomery Manor's opulent drawing room. Adorned with lavish tapestries and aglow with the soft candlelight from a crystal chandelier, the room becomes the backdrop for a pivotal confrontation.

We present the damning evidence to Lady Evelyn. Her composure, usually unshakeable, crumbles under the weight of our revelations. She sinks into an armchair, her aristocratic poise melting into vulnerability. Her confession, tinged with fear and regret, reveals her entrapment in the Maguires' web.

"I had no choice," she whispers, her voice a ghost of its usual confidence. "The threat to Alexander's business and the honour of a respected Ballarat figure I vowed to protect was overwhelming. The potential shame and dishonour unbearable."

With her inherent strength, Isabella comforts her mother. "Mother, we understand your predicament. We must join forces to expose these hidden networks and unmask the villains behind them."

With Lady Evelyn's reluctant cooperation, we brace ourselves for what lies ahead. Our united front will test the Maguires' grip on the city's secrets. We are resolute in bringing their deceitful reign to light, no matter the personal cost.

As we leave Montgomery Manor's grandeur, Isabella and I are entangled in a web of thoughts and plans. We return to our cottage, our hearts heavy with the weight of our discovery and the enormity of our task. We underestimate that our pursuit of truth will lead us into a maze of political intrigue, where alliances are fleeting and the ghosts of the past intertwine with the present.

Over the coming weeks, our investigation takes us deeper into the twisted aims of the Maguires. We uncover the extent of their influence, which has infiltrated Ballarat's high society like a silent, insidious force.

Yet, we tread a dangerous path with each step toward unravelling their dark network. The Maguires are formidable, wielding their secrets as a powerful weapon. Our quest for justice teeters on a precipice, overlooking revelations that could forever change our lives and the destiny of Ballarat.

In this dance of intrigue and deception, where friends and foes blur, Isabella and I stand together, ready to face the unknown. Our journey has evolved into more than a quest for truth; it's a testament to our commitment to justice and the unbreakable bond of love that sustains us through the darkest times.

Chapter Twenty-Nine

T he waning sunlight yields to the encroaching dusk, casting elongated shadows across my study where we assemble. The gravity of our task, a labyrinthine investigation into the Maguires' underworld, looms over us. As the city's lamps pierce the gathering gloom, our table, bathed in the amber radiance of an oil lamp, becomes an island of clarity in a sea of mystery.

His visage etched with resolve, Charles Montgomery breaks the silence enveloping us. "Our inquiries reveal a staggering truth," he declares, his voice unwavering yet tinged with unease. "The Maguires' tendrils of influence are entwined in the fabric of Ballarat's echelons of power. Their clandestine and formidable network ensnares the corruptible in government and key figures in commerce and high society."

Isabella's steely and unwavering gaze contributes to the discourse: "Their ambitions are mired in a thirst for dominion, yet the extent of their machinations and ties to the Whispering Shadows still elude us. They are central players in a grand, insidious design."

Lady Evelyn's countenance, a blend of apprehension and grit, is cautionary. "Our approach must be meticulously calculated. The Maguires wield secrets as their arsenal—a double-edged sword that could devastate reputations besides ours if wielded with evil intent."

The puzzle coalesces piece by piece, unveiling a disturbing reality. The Maguires and the enigmatic Whispering Shadows conspire to orchestrate a silent coup. Their goal is a sinister reformation of Ballarat's power structure, bending the city's future to their will through manipulation, coercion, and the exploitation of secrets.

Yet, in this high-stakes chess game of shadows and deceit, we refuse to be relegated to the role of mere pawns. Our resolve is steeled to thwart the Maguires' nefarious scheme, to cast light upon their dark ambitions. The future of Ballarat teeters precariously at the edge of a knife.

• • • •

AS WEEKS TURN INTO months, and our pursuit of the Maguires continues unabated, each day brings new revelations and challenges. The shadowy organisation remains a step ahead, veiled in secrecy and cunning. We know that to uncover the truth, we must delve even deeper into the heart of the conspiracy.

Our investigations take us to the darkest corners of Ballarat, where alliances are forged and secrets exchanged in hushed tones. We frequent the dimly lit taverns and backrooms, seeking information from those who have glimpsed the Maguires' influence.

One evening, as Lady Evelyn, Isabella, and I are gathered around the same mahogany table in the manor, I can't help but feel a growing sense of frustration. The Maguires' web of intrigue seems impenetrable, and our efforts have yielded only fragmented clues.

"We must find a way to expose them," I declare, my voice filled with determination. "They have manipulated the city for too long, and their secrets have caused enough harm."

Isabella nods in agreement, her eyes reflecting the same resolve that has drawn me to her. "But we must also be cautious," she warns. "We know the Maguires' power is extensive, and they will stop at nothing to protect their interests—even committing murder!"

Lady Evelyn, always the voice of reason, adds, "We need irrefutable evidence, something that will expose and name them to the public without a shadow of a doubt."

Our discussions turn to the possibilities of our insider within the Whispering Shadows ranks—one person who can provide us with the information we need. This proposition carries the risk of their betrayal and danger for the informant we await to divulge the information we seek.

Days turn into nights, and our breakthrough comes when we least expect it. Upon receiving the call to deliver a payment demand, we have the chance for another clandestine meeting and rendezvous with our mysterious contact wearing the hooded cloak at the dilapidated house on Talbot Street South. The Whispering Shadows' associate claims vital information about the Maguires and their involvement with the Whispering Shadows. After growing disillusioned with both organisations, he is willing to share his knowledge.

With bated breath, we listen as he reveals the Whispering Shadows' ultimate plan, assisted by the Maguires, that will shake Ballarat to its core. Our informant's voice is filled with determination as he speaks, "The Molly Maguires is a conspiracy affiliated not only with Ballarat's 'Ancient Order of Druids' but more directly with the clandestine 'Fenian Brotherhood,'" he says, "a much-feared society created in America in1858 to fight for the independence of Ireland. Members arrived here in the late 1850s, attracted by Ballarat's gold rush, and their members formed their local secret society.

"With the announcement of Prince Albert's visit to our borough to see first-hand the working of our deep gold mining, the Molly Maguires conspired with the Whispering Shadows organisation, also consisting of sympathetic Irish Catholics from Melbourne, to assassinate the prince whilst the opportunity was available on his visit here to Ballarat. They orchestrated the conspiracy with a society assailant to shoot Prince Alfred in their attack on the British Monarchy.

"Still, they aborted the attempt due to the increased military presence during the prince's visit and a lack of opportunity. They then went on with their attempt, as we now know, in Melbourne with the crime committed by Henry O'Farrell on 12 March 1868, when he shot and injured the visiting prince at the Clontarf picnic grounds during a function. With the help of the Whispering Shadows, they intend to manipulate the local candidates for the upcoming council and state elections, ensuring their chosen candidates rise to power and control our city from within.

This informant's revelation sends shockwaves through our small group, and we know that time is of the essence. We must act quickly to expose the Maguires' plot before it can be set into motion.

As we prepare to confront the shadows that have haunted Ballarat for so long, I can't help but feel a sense of unease. The stakes have never been higher, and the city's future hangs in the balance. But we're determined to see this through, to shine a light on the darkest corners of Ballarat and bring the Maguires and Whispering Shadows to justice. Our journey is far from over, and the final chapter is yet to be written.

The days leading up to our confrontation with both organisations are filled with tension and anticipation. As we know, exposing their nefarious plot to manipulate the elections won't be easy.

Our informant, the disillusioned former member of the Whispering Shadows, has provided valuable information about both organisation's inner workings. Armed with this knowledge, we plan to expose their machinations and bring their leaders to justice.

Isabella, Lady Evelyn, and I spent countless hours strategising in my study, pouring over maps and documents, and coordinating with our trusted allies. We must be meticulous and precise, leaving no room for error.

The day of reckoning arrives, and we gather our evidence and prepare to present it to the authorities and the public. We know timing is critical, and we can't afford any delays. As we set out to unveil the truth, I feel both trepidation and determination.

This evening, a chilling letter arrives, and we pore over the documents in my study. It bears the Molly Maguires' burnt cork parchment with its smudged edges, a sinister reminder of the shadowy organisation we are up against. The message is clear: *"We know of your plans and will stop at Nothing to silence you!"*

Isabella's face pales as she reads the words aloud, and Lady Evelyn's eyes flash with fear and determination. We have come too far to back down now. Our resolve is unshaken, and we must confront the Maguires head-on.

The town of Ballarat teeters on the edge of transformation, poised to attain city status. The Maguires, steadfast in their grip on power, face an impending challenge. The battle for supremacy looms, and the destiny of our cherished city hangs in precarious balance.

As days unfold, it becomes increasingly apparent that the Maguires will not relinquish control without a fierce struggle. Threats and warnings rain upon Isabella, Lady Evelyn, and me. In this perilous game, Alexander Montgomery maintains a deliberate distance, ensuring our revelations concerning the enigmatic societies are not perceived as devious maneuvers to further his business or political interests.

The secret societies, driven by a relentless thirst for retribution, leave us in constant jeopardy. We employ every precautionary measure available to shield ourselves from their nefarious designs. Our lives become a strategic dance of heightened security, ever-changing routines, and a vigilant eye on the shadows to evade becoming easy prey.

Our journey of revelation begins with a rendezvous at the office of T.D. Wanliss, the reputable editor of 'The Star Newspaper,' is known for his unwavering commitment to uncovering the unvarnished truth. Here, we unveil our trove of evidence, and Wanliss, recognising the gravity of our cause, pledges to publish our exposé, laying bare the sinister plot of the Molly Maguires. The potent influence of the press becomes our ally in this unfolding battle.

Our next move takes us into the heart of law enforcement, where we rendezvous with a sympathetic figure in the local police hierarchy—someone we believe we can trust to act decisively. Within the confines of his office, we hand over our cache of evidence, urging him to initiate an immediate investigation into the activities of the Maguires. It's a dangerous gambit, for we remain uncertain which members of the police force might be under the sinister sway of the Maguires' or Whispering Shadows' influence.

Ballarat is thrown into a frenzy as the news breaks in the papers, and the investigation begins. The Maguires' carefully laid plans unravel before their eyes, and panic spreads among the local Whispering Shadows' ranks. We know they'll fight back, and we must be prepared for whatever they unleash.

Amid this chaos, Isabella and Lady Evelyn remain steadfast by my side. Their unwavering support gives me the strength to continue, even as the pressure mounts.

In the following days, the truth slowly emerges, the public's outrage grows, and the Maguires and the Whispering Shadows' plots are exposed. Although individuals are not named for the lack of concrete evidence, their grip on the city begins to slip as their supporters get cold feet. The State elections approach and their local candidates will face a significant backlash if exposed.

But the Whispering Shadows aren't defeated yet. They fight with cunning and desperation, using underhanded tactics to salvage their plans. Threats are made, alliances are forged, and we find ourselves in a dangerous game of cat and mouse.

Amid the turmoil, our small group remains resolute, determined to see this battle come to its conclusion. We've uncovered the Maguires' secrets, but the final chapter has yet to be written.

As we prepare for the ultimate showdown with the Maguires, I can't help but wonder if our efforts will be enough to bring about justice and restore the city's integrity. The tension in Ballarat continues to escalate as our battle with the Maguires climaxes. The town is divided, with whispers of conspiracy and betrayal filling the air. The elections are drawing nearer, and the Whispering Shadows' candidates are desperate to regain their foothold in the political arena.

Chapter Thirty

I n a bold move, the Maguires unleash a salvo through the pages of 'The Star Newspaper', unveiling a letter to the public. They attempt to cast doubt on our motivations within its lines, alleging that a concealed past scandal drives our actions—one they possess knowledge of and threatened to reveal. Their narrative unveils the once-forgotten but now resurrected account of the scandal entangling Lady Evelyn and the prominent State Politician.

The politician's identity now revealed as Mr James Caton MLA adds a layer of complexity to the unfolding drama. At the time of the affair, Mr Caton was wedded, and his dalliance with Alexander Montgomery's betrothed, Lady Evelyn, again casts shadows on the Montgomery family. The revelation is a double-edged sword, which could cause considerable upheaval for Mr Caton, who is on the brink of re-election in the impending state election and threatens to tarnish the reputation of Montgomery's business interests.

However, a silver lining emerges amidst the turmoil. With the exposure of this scandal, the Maguires lose their leverage over Lady Evelyn, and the news released on the newspaper's back pages is minuscule in its damage as our crusade against the secret societies gains renewed potency.

Isabella, Lady Evelyn, and I gather in a close-knit circle, aware that our mission to expose the dark secrets of these clandestine groups and prevent harm to Ballarat's community will eventually eclipse the impact of the scandal and its involved parties.

Our unwavering allies within the police force and the press stand firmly by our side, but the Maguires' reach extends far and wide, casting a shadow over every move we make. As danger lurks around every corner, we remain vigilant, for the battle is far from over.

As election day looms, we intensify our efforts to gather evidence of the Maguires' wrongdoing and to name the individual conspirators. We comb through financial records, interview witnesses, and follow every lead. It's a race against time, and the stakes could not be higher. With the evidence we have gathered, we call a public meeting to expose and name the secret societies' leaders. It's a risky move, as we know it will put further targets on our backs, but it's the only way to rally public opinion against them.

In the heart of Ballarat, under a sky heavy with the promise of change, we convene a critical public meeting. The air crackles with anticipation as the town hall, a grand edifice echoing the city's gold-rush prosperity, fills to the brim. Reporters, their pens poised like swords, and citizens, their eyes wide with fear and fervour, gather to hear the truths we've unearthed.

Beside me stand Isabella and Lady Evelyn, their presence a bastion of strength. The room falls into a hushed expectancy as I step forward, the weight of our mission anchoring my resolve. With a steady voice, I unravel the tapestry of deceit woven by the Maguires and the Whispering Shadows. Naming—John Smith, Richard Davis, David Clementine—once names shrouded in secrecy, now echoing through the hall, the resonance a clarion call for action.

The evidence is irrefutable, and the implications are staggering. I then expose Frank Burley, the hidden hand guiding the Maguires, his tendrils entwined within the city's burgeoning political landscape. The revelation sends a ripple of shock and anger through the crowd. His name, synonymous with manipulation and power, symbolises the corruption festering at Ballarat's core.

"Our beloved Ballarat stands on the precipice of a new era," I proclaim, my voice rising above the murmurs. "We cannot let these shadowy figures dictate our future. It's time for transparency, for justice, for change!"

The crowd responds fervently, a sea of determined faces ready to reclaim their city. The clamour for a thorough investigation and accountability fills the hall, a chorus of unity against the darkness.

But the Maguires and their allies are not easily vanquished. Frank Burley, a master of the political game, will no doubt launch a counterattack, his resources vast and his resolve unyielding. The shadows of retribution loom over us, yet our collective spirit remains unbroken.

As the meeting concludes, the citizens of Ballarat disperse into the night, their voices carrying the message of our revelations. The battle lines are drawn, and the fight for Ballarat's soul is just beginning.

Isabella, her eyes ablaze with a fiery determination, grasps my hand. "We've started a revolution, Levi. There's no turning back now."

Lady Evelyn, her usual composure laced with a newfound zeal, adds, "This city deserves better than to be a puppet in the hands of the corrupt. We'll see this through, no matter the cost."

As we step out into the cool night air, the city's lamps casting long shadows on the dusty streets, I realise this is more than a fight against corruption. It's a battle for the heart and soul of Ballarat to preserve the integrity of a city born from the hopes and dreams of those Diggers who sought fortune in its golden soil with a similar political injustice they resolved at 'The Battle of Eureka'.

In the waning light of a day fraught with tension, we, a trio bound by a common cause, hasten toward a handsome cab waiting for us. Suddenly, our path is barred by a group of the Maguires' enforcers, their grim determination etched in their steely gazes. They descend upon us with a ferocity that belies their human form, wielding batons with ruthless efficiency. Their blows rain down upon me, each strike a brutal testament to the lengths they will go to protect their nefarious empire.

Resplendent in her fortitude, Isabella faces the onslaught with a bravery that belies her delicate frame. With her parasol transformed into a weapon of defiance, she parries and thrusts, her spirit unyielding. Lady Evelyn, her usual grace under siege, withstands her verbal abusers with a stoicism that is nothing short of heroic. Their strength is a beacon of hope amidst the chaos.

Our struggle, though valiant, leaves us bruised and battered, but our resolve remains unbroken. The enforcers retreat into the shadows from whence they came, leaving us to lick our wounds and steel ourselves for the battles yet to come.

Ballarat becomes a divided city in the following days, a microcosm of tension and suspicion. The Maguires and their Shadowy allies cling desperately to their crumbling edifice of influence. The public, now awakened to their duplicity, clamours for justice.

Within the sanctum of our cottage, Isabella, Lady Evelyn, and I find solace in our unity. Our love and shared purpose form an unbreakable bond, a bulwark against the storm outside. We stand together still, an unyielding trio against the barrage of corruption and deceit.

As the day of reckoning approaches, the town buzzes with anticipation. The streets teem with fervent supporters, their cries a cacophony of hope and defiance. The Maguires' stronghold on the city's soul wavers, and the winds of change sweep through Ballarat's storied avenues.

On the eve of the election, our final gathering in the lantern-lit cottage is a conclave of strategy and resolve. We pore over the evidence, each document a piece of the puzzle we've painstakingly assembled. A letter slipped beneath the door reveals a traitor within our associates' midst, its words a chilling reminder of the Maguires' reach.

Election day dawns, a day that will define Ballarat's future. The streets buzz with the clamour of democracy in action. We venture forth, our hearts laden with hope and trepidation. The polling station at 'The Alfred Hall' is a hive of activity, a testament to the city's awakened conscience.

As the votes are tallied, the atmosphere is electric, charged with the collective will of a people yearning for change. When the results are announced, they spark joy and relief. Ballarat has spoken; the reign of the Maguires and their Shadowy cohorts is over.

In the aftermath, justice is meted out with a firm hand. The guilty are summoned before the courts and brought to account, their misdeeds laid bare for all to see. Ballarat, reborn from the ashes of corruption, steps into the light of a new dawn.

And so, our journey, fraught with peril and steeped in the pursuit of justice, draws to a close. But the story of our bond—Isabella, Lady Evelyn, and I—remains. In the crucible of our struggle, we have forged a connection that transcends the ordinary, a testament to the enduring power of love and righteousness.

The sunsets over Ballarat, once a harbinger of darkness, now blaze with the glory of our triumph. In their fiery embrace, Isabella and I find a love that defies convention, a love that has weathered the storm and emerged stronger and brighter. Once shrouded in uncertainty, our future stretches before us, bathed in the golden light of hope and promise.

• • • •

ON A SERENE EVENING, as twilight casts its gentle glow over our cottage, Isabella and I stand on the porch, enveloped in the tranquillity of our little haven. She gazes at me, her eyes reflecting the twilight stars, and her hands rest gently and gracefully on her swollen belly. She remarks softly, "Life is full of unexpected twists, isn't it?" Her voice is a tender melody in the hush of dusk.

I smile, feeling the pulsating rhythm of our shared excitement. "Absolutely," I agree, my voice brimming with anticipation. "And I relish every surprise it brings." Leaning in, I seal my vow with a tender yet fervent kiss upon Isabella's lips.

With the birth of our son, Samuel, our life takes a vibrant leap forward. His infectious laughter echoes through the corridors of our home, infusing our days with pure joy and love. Each sunrise heralds his growth, a testament to our enduring love.

One crisp morning, I cradle Samuel and gaze into his bright, curious eyes. "You, my boy, are the living testament to the strength of our love," I murmur to him, my voice thick with emotion. He gurgles in response, his tiny hands clutching at mine, symbolising our unbreakable bond.

My reputation as an attorney soars in my professional realm, reaching unprecedented heights. The once-turbulent waters of the Maguires conspiracy and Lady Evelyn's scandal have receded into the annals of history. I stand as Ballarat's most esteemed lawyer, lauded for my tenacious pursuit of justice. Isabella's brilliance and beauty serve as a beacon by my side, amplifying the impact of my legal endeavours.

Our home, a sanctuary in the storm, now resonates with the vibrant pulse of our family's love. Samuel's wonderment at the world unfurls under our nurturing guidance. Isabella and I are united in our resolve to instil in him the virtues of integrity and compassion, ensuring that he becomes a beacon of hope and a bearer of our legacy. Our love story, once tempest-tossed, now blossoms in the calm, a testament to the enduring power of love and the triumph of the human spirit.

Chapter Thirty-One
Sixteen Years Later in Ballarat City:

As the late 19th century unfolds, the city of Ballarat stirs to life under a canvas of golden sunrise. Nestled in the thriving heart of this emerging Australian metropolis, I stand — Samual Brody, a young man on the cusp of adulthood, regarded as both brilliant and full of promise.

I now use the pen to chronicle my family's continuing saga in these defining moments of history. Bearing the weight of our esteemed legacy, I wander the corridors of our quaint cottage, now expanded to accommodate a burgeoning family and the heavy legal volumes that speak of my father's profession. The love that once ignited the Ballarat sunsets flickers passionately within me, casting complex, intriguing shadows on the path of my destiny.

Ballarat, a city sculpted by wealth and furore, has become a canvas of dreams and tribulations for the Riley-Brody lineage. My parents are pillars of unwavering principles in this community. My father, Levi Brody, commands respect as a discerning attorney-at-law. Alongside him stands my mother, Isabella, a woman of keen intellect and immeasurable compassion, his equal in life and legal endeavours.

Together, their triumphs and values resonate down the still-dusty, vibrant streets of Ballarat. Years ago, the malignant whispers of the Molly Maguires threatened to engulf the spirit of our town, but my parents, Levi and Isabella, stood as beacons against the storm of fear and corruption. They peeled back layers of deceit in the council chambers, revealing a nefarious network of political blackmail masterminded by a figure shrouded in mystery, known only as the "Whispering Shadows."

Back then, I was merely a glint in the eye of hope in my parents' vision, oblivious to the danger that loomed over Ballarat. However, as the walls of secrecy crumbled, I understood their unwavering commitment to justice, absorbing the tales of their past exploits, recounted to me by my late grandmother, Alice Brody (nee Riley). Now, as I edge into adulthood, the legacy of their past triumphs casts a formidable shadow over my path.

The burden of expectations melds with the enthralling tapestry of our family's history, presenting me with choices that challenge the very essence of my character. I'm acknowledged as a beacon of academic excellence in our growing city, and my scholarly achievements shine brightly, projecting a future brimming with potential.

Yet, the expectation to tread in my father's legal footsteps weighs heavily on me. The future beckons me to embrace the legal profession and to continue our family's legacy of honour and integrity. However, as I delve deeper into my studies, a creeping sense of self-doubt undermines my confidence.

My parents, Levi and Isabella, observe with pride and concern as I wrestle with these internal struggles. They wish me to find a path that resonates with my talents and passions. Nevertheless, the weight of a generational legacy of respectability, coupled with my ancestors' silent convictions, press down upon me relentlessly like shrouded ghosts of the past.

My journey is a precarious dance between upholding my family's esteemed heritage and carving out my own discoverable identity. As each day in Ballarat ends with the sun dipping below the horizon, I ponder whether I will muster the strength to forge my own destiny or if the long shadows of the Riley legacy will forever dictate my journey.

• • • •

NOW, STILL IN THE FINAL throes of my teenage years, I find myself at a pivotal juncture, my heart and intellect entangled in the lofty expectations accompanying the Brody name. The corridors of our once quaint cottage, replete with volumes of legal lore and ancestral relics, echo the stories of my forebears. I diligently study my father's written chronicles, tracing back to the criminal undertakings of my great-grandfather, the infamous Jack Riley.

Jack Riley casts a long shadow, a figure shrouded in enigma. He is known for his illicit gambling enterprises, sly grog shops, and more sinister dealings. His notorious reputation starkly contrasts the Dignified legacy my father has crafted for us. I grapple with this legacy, finding my way through its complexities as I approach the threshold of adulthood.

Secluded in the attic, my private refuge, I delve into the concealed archives of my lineage, uncovering secrets that now steer my fate. Tales of my great-grandfather's bold escapades lure me toward a realm of dissent and intrigue, seducing me with whispers of power and riches far from the bounds of decency.

In the bustling heart of Ballarat, I navigate a life vastly different from the shelter I've known. It's not a conscious choice; instead, destiny seems to guide me into the arms of these new enigmatic acquaintances.

Or, more precisely, they find me during my extensive strolls from Lydiard Street north to the notorious Main Road of Ballarat East—a gritty, vibrant quarter of the city. Here, amidst the working-class citizens, the Chinese miners and gardeners frequent opium dens and Joss Houses - where you will find sly grog shops, brothels, Jewish moneylenders, and thirty-two hotels hosting weary miners - where I discover a side of Ballarat that's starkly different from my upbringing.

This contrast is striking. While the more respectable denizens favour the stretch from Little Bridge Street to Sturt Street's central district, I find myself irresistibly drawn to the captivating life on Main Road.

My intrigue with Main Road stems from its chronicling in my family's history, a narrative I've only recently uncovered. My father's stories have kindled a curiosity, propelling me to explore the more sordid aspects of life that their chronicles reveal. This newfound knowledge, coupled with an innate desire to break free from the shackles of my sheltered existence, beckons me deeper into the realm of Main Road.

On this pivotal night, as I wander under the dim glow of a streetlamp at the intersection of Victoria and Humffray Streets, my path veers into the unknown. There, a motley crew of larrikins, four youths and a daring girl, all around my age, hold court. Adorned in cabbage tree hats, snug vests, and checkered trousers as tight as drainpipes, a lanky youth leads them with a piercing gaze.

"Hey, Toff! Where do you think you're off to?" the leader calls out sharply.

"I'm merely enjoying a stroll down Main Road... and the name's Samuel, Sam for short," I respond, my naivety bare.

"Oh, is that so?" he sneers. "You're on 'Cabbage Tree Mob' territory. A toll is due for passage here. We're not fond of trespassers, especially ones who don't pay their dues. A bob, that's your price, Toff."

A surge of fear races through me, and the thought of fleeing crosses my mind for a fleeting moment. But quickly, I dismiss it; they're like a pack of feral hounds, certain to pursue with even grimmer consequences. Reluctantly, I hand over a shilling from my fob pocket, hoping to quell any further confrontation.

But the situation escalates unexpectedly. The girl, with a magpie's nest of a haircut, steps forward with a threatening air. She grabs me cruelly around my groin, eliciting such pain that I'm forced onto my toes, tears brimming in my eyes. The mob erupts in laughter as I grimace.

"This toff's hiding something. Hand over the rest of your stash, or I'll squeeze tighter!" she threatens.

Gasping in agony, I yield, digging out the rest of my money. As she releases her grip, I collapse to my knees, gasping for air. The gang's leader then offers a hand, helping me to my feet, my body throbbing from the ordeal.

"I apologise for intruding," I say, "but now that I've made payment, may I proceed with my walk?"

"That depends on your destination on Main Road," the leader muses. "We might join you if it's to the Theatre Royal or Empire Bowling Saloon."

"I've no more money for such pursuits," I confess. "I just wish to observe. My life's been confined to the front yard... I'm now eager to see what lies beyond."

"The Toff's a philosopher, eh?" he chuckles. "Just here to witness the risks of this part of town? No coin for fun, you say—why not join us? We make our own amusement."

Torn between the safety of home and the allure of the unknown, I hesitate. Yet, this is my chance to delve into their world, an opportunity too rare. I resolve not to let it slip away.

Chapter Thirty-Two

A s we set off toward Main Road, I am enveloped in the vibrant energy of my new acquaintances. Their vitality is contagious, filling the night air with a sense of adventure. The slender youth leading us strides with a swagger, his male counterparts matching his confidence, while the spirited young woman moves with a buoyancy that defies the earth's pull.

We navigate the boardwalk, crossing the intersection of Humffray and Victoria Street, where the city's raw underbelly reveals itself. Discarded papers and fruit peels are strewn about, remnants of the day's frantic life.

Our path leads us by a draper's shop, its window a tableau of contemporary fashion: high masher collars and ample trousers for the discerning gentleman. Next door, a craftsman diligently stuffs a large sofa with horsehair, his skill apparent in every movement.

next, we arrive at a liquor store marked by the licensee's name, "August Thetaz." The owner, a Swiss gentleman with a commanding black moustache, stands guard, leisurely smoking his briar pipe, adding a layer of intrigue to our expedition.

"Andrew Blackman," August Thetaz addresses our leader. "If it's spirits you seek, I'll need your father's presence."

Andrew's bravado retorts, "My old man's not fit for such errands. If Constable Gribble collars me, I'll take a small hipflask of whiskey home, unnoticeable in my pocket."

"If you expect credit," Thetaz counters sternly, "tell your father his account's closed until settled."

Andrew presents my two shillings, "He'll square up next week. This is for today's purchase."

Thetaz returns with the flask and hands it over. Andrew quips, "Thanks, and just so you know, you're now on notice for serving minors. This whiskey happens to be for our use; Ha, har!"

Thetaz's fury is palpable as he snarls, "Get lost, you idle 'Currency' juveniles, and find some honest exertions!"

Andrew responds defiantly, "Better a 'Currency lad' than a foreigner exploiting our homeland!"

Thetaz retreats into his shop, and we continue. A blacksmith's rhythmic hammering fills the air as we pass, followed by a watchmaker's window. The watchmaker is engrossed in his delicate task, oblivious to our passing.

As I journey with this brazen crew, the contrasting worlds of Ballarat unfold before me, each step further immersing me in the city's multifaceted existence.

Our journey takes us next to the London Chartered Bank, a distinguished structure and the only one of its kind in Ballarat East. It is located on the corner of the future site of the Post Office. We cross Humffray Street, the sharp whirring of saws being sharpened cutting through the evening's hush.

We find temporary shelter under the verandah of Phillips and Chamberland's Potato Depot. We secretly listen to Joe Phillips and J N Dunn's conversations, their words mingling with the rich scent of their cigars. I crouch alongside my newfound companions, conscious of remaining unseen, aware that my father would disapprove of this foray into the unknown.

Our path leads us to Fred Montgomery's barbershop, an inviting place offering three-penny haircuts even at this late hour. Fred, a relative of my grandfather, runs the shop in Ballarat's oldest brick building.

As we advance, the imposing mullock heap of the Sulieman Pasha Mine looms, a stark reminder of the region's abundant gold history. I catch sight of Mr Jackson, the manager, deep in conversation with Mr Watson, M.L.A., who also serves as the mine's Chairman. Notably, my father holds shares in this prosperous venture.

Continuing, we pass the tinsmith's shop, where artisans skillfully create shiny dippers and buckets under dim torchlight. Next, we observe John Phillips Cooper's workshop, a hub of meticulous craftsmanship where barrels are made for local breweries.

Finally, our expedition brings us further along bustling Main Road, passing an array of hotels, a Chinese market garden, and a Joss House until we reach Eureka Street. Here, we quietly maneuver behind 'The Beehive Hotel' and soon stand before an old miner's cottage, its years of neglect evident in its façade. Overgrown grass dominates the front yard, and a well-worn path leads us to a once-sturdy door, now barely hanging on its hinges.

As we navigate through the narrow opening to the leaning door, the cottage's interior unfurls before us, steeped in the echoes of its storied past. The room, dimly illuminated by the scant moonlight filtering through tattered curtains, is a mosaic of forgotten days and neglect. Our steps across the creaking wooden floor seem to stir echoes of the past; each groans a whispered tale from another time.

To our left, a forlorn fireplace stands, a once-crucial hearth now surrendered to dust and cobwebs that hang from the ceiling like spectral tapestries. The air is thick with the mustiness of disuse, and a poignant, almost ghostly nostalgia permeates these time-worn walls as if awaiting discovery.

Andy moves to claim an aged armchair, its pattern faded by years of use, while the others find places on a grimy, threadbare Persian rug. They sit with an easy familiarity, legs crossed, as Andy adopts a regal posture. He gestures for me to join the others, and I take my place on the dusty floorboards beside the carpet.

Once settled, Andy begins to introduce his crew. "This here's me lot," he says with a hint of pride. "And Sis, she's as sharp and tough as any of us, no question about that."

The introductions reveal the simplicity behind their nicknames. 'Shorty' is aptly named for his compact, stout build, his unruly hair tamed only by liberal grease applications. 'Red' is distinguished by his fiery hair and flushed complexion, while 'Stretch' appears almost comical, his limbs awkwardly protruding from clothes he has outgrown.

Andy, or Andrew as he's properly known, is the only one who goes by his actual name. Unrelated to Andy, Sis stands apart with her hermaphroditic toughness. Her robust features starkly contrast Andy's rugged charm. Despite her masculine demeanour, there's an undeniable handsomeness about her, different yet complementary to Andy's leadership presence.

Observing the Cabbage Tree Mob under the flickering candlelight, I realise that contrary to their rough exterior and Andy's hard-edged rhetoric, they resemble a social club more closely. This starkly contrasts the Ballarat Mashers of the upper town, known for their coarse language, aversion to honest work, and disdain for those who pursue it. The Cabbage Tree Mob, however, still live with their families and attend to their education, challenging the stereotype of shiftless youths engaged in petty crime and scornful of the straight path.

After the informal introductions, Andy shifts the conversation to more serious matters. "Firstly, let's all thank Samuel, now known as Sam, for his unintentional yet valuable contribution to our cause," he begins, a sly grin playing on his lips. "Tonight, part of his half-crown has procured us a bottle of Thetaz's fine whiskey. It's only right that we initiate Sam into the mysteries of our side of Ballarat, courtesy of the Cabbage Tree Mob. A toast, everyone... to our new mate Sammy!"

With a flourish, Andy uncorks the flask and hoists it high. "To good times and Sammy! May he continue to bless us with his presence and, perhaps, his generosity—Ha, har!" He takes a generous gulp and passes the bottle along the circle.

The bottle makes its way to me, and I hesitate. The thought of sharing the same bottle with everyone and my aversion to its taste and legality makes me uneasy.

"I appreciate it, Andy, but I'm not fond of whiskey."

"Ah, come on, Sammy," Andy prods. "If you're going to roll with us, you've got to be a bit daring. This is part of the deal. It'll put hairs on your chest!"

Sis joins the teasing, "You didn't warn me about that, Andy!"

"That's because you've already got chest hair to prove it, Sis!" Andy retorts, and they all burst into laughter.

Sis counters, half-jokingly, "And how would you know, Andy? Have you been peeking through my bedroom window again?"

Andy, now slightly flustered, tries to regain control. "Enough, Sis! You're embarrassing me in front of Sam. Come on, Sammy, it's just a bit of fun, part of your initiation."

"I'm sorry, Andy. I didn't mean any offence. I'm just a visitor, not a member of your gang."

Andy's tone turns serious. "Well, Sam, you're now privy to our hideout and know our faces. You're in this, like it or not, unless you fancy a roughing up to keep our secret safe. So, what's it going to be?"

I quickly realise the gravity of the situation. "In that case, I'm honoured to be an honorary member of your esteemed group, Andy."

"That's the spirit, Sammy!" Andy approves. "Now, let's discuss the Leary Gang Treasure. With your education and connections, you could be the key to finding it. Imagine us, rich and famous!"

As the conversation turns to tales of treasure and grandeur, I feel a mixture of excitement and apprehension. This night's encounter plunges me into a world far removed from my familiar life, opening doors to adventures and dangers I have never imagined.

Chapter Thirty-Three

I n the following days, my newfound friends drew me deeper into a world that echoed Jack Riley's bygone days. We traversed the lively thoroughfares of Main Road, sneaking peeks into clandestine gambling houses and obscure trade networks. This enigmatic underworld, thriving beneath Ballarat's facade, is rife with danger and allure, as described in my ancestors' historical records.

Our escapades soon involve observing two enigmatic and respected societies in Ballarat. The first is the 'Druids of the Two Oaks' of the Ballarat Order, who meet among the oak trees in the Botanical Gardens. They believe in the soul's immortality, transferring from one being to another at death. One of these sacred oaks stands behind the Lindsay Gordon Cottage, while the other anchors the garden's southern end. As they convene around these ancient trees at dawn or dusk, performing their rituals, we hide in the foliage, emitting ghostly sounds and adding an eerie undertone to their solemn proceedings.

On other nights, our mischief leads us to the Odd Fellows lodge, where we pelt their tin roof with stones, fleeing into the darkness, our laughter reverberating through the night.

This clandestine life slowly widens the chasm between my father and me. He, a paragon of virtue, watches in despair as I edge closer to the destiny he struggled to keep our family away from.

In public, I remain the esteemed Samuel Brody. Still, beneath this guise, I walk a perilous path that mirrors my great-grandfather's notorious past and threatens to dismantle the Brody legacy's carefully constructed respectability.

My decisions now weigh on whether to uphold our family's pride or lead me down a path fraught with danger and disappointment. As the sun sets over Ballarat, casting long shadows, my family's legacy looms, shaping an uncertain future.

In the secluded confines off Main Road, Andy and our crew possess a relic that is both a treasure and a burden: an ancient map, its edges worn and yellowed with age. This map, a silent witness to a tumultuous gold heist of the 1860s, holds the key to a forgotten fortune.

We gather in the dimly lit backroom of our ramshackle hideout, the air thick with anticipation. As the map is unfurled across an old table, a world of hidden riches and untold stories unfolds before us, igniting our imaginations and fuelling our quest for adventure.

The tale of the map we now hold traces its roots deep into Ballarat's storied past, back to the fevered days of the gold rush in the early 1860s. Then, a gold escort, heavily laden on its journey to Melbourne, fell prey to the infamous 'Leary Gang', shrouded by the notorious figurehead known only as 'The Phantom'. That fateful night, gunfire shattered the stillness, heralding a fierce confrontation. When the tumult subsided, the gang emerged victorious, laden with a fortune in gold, and vanished into a sprawling mining tunnel beneath Ballarat.

However, their victory was fleeting. The heist, marked by the cold-blooded murder of police troopers, drew the swift and unforgiving hand of the law. The gang members were apprehended and met their fate at the gallows of Pentridge Prison, leaving their plundered treasure unclaimed.

The map, a relic of their audacious escapade, was left in the care of a brothel madam. Over time, it transformed into a legend whispered in the underbelly of society, its very existence a tantalising myth.

This enigmatic artifact resurfaces in our time, unearthed beneath the decaying floorboards of our hideout's backroom. The discovery is accidental, revealed when Andy's foot crashes through rotten wood, unveiling the map wrapped in aged leather. Its surface, etched with arcane symbols and faded lines, whispers of a hidden bounty deep within Ballarat's subterranean labyrinth.

Andy and the others become feverishly obsessed as we pore over the map. They concoct a daring scheme to trace the map's elusive trail and plunge into the dark, neglected tunnels that veil the lost gold. The lure of untold riches and the thrill of emulating our forebears' boldness beckon us to embark on a perilous quest.

But as we navigate in our minds the serpentine underground maze depicted on the map, our journey becomes more than a treasure hunt. We find ourselves wrestling with the haunting legacy of the Leary Gang—the violence and the relentless quest for justice that led to their demise. With each step we take into uncovering the map's secrets, it dawns upon us that the treasure we seek might exact a price too steep, challenging our bonds, moral compass, and the core of who we are.

• • • •

AS WE, THE CABBAGE Tree Mob, immerse ourselves further into the map's enigmas, our fixation on unearthing the long-lost gold intensifies. Nightly, we gather, the map spread before us on the worn table. Our conversations and strategising are vibrant with the fire of youthful audacity, dreams of incalculable riches, and a thirst for fame.

We try to unravel the map's cryptic symbols daily, diligently piecing together the forgotten pathways and abandoned mine shafts that have shielded this treasure through the ages. The call to resurrect the daring spirit of our forebears, to revive a legend lost in the annals of time, is an enticement we cannot resist.

Yet, unknown to us, danger is brewing closer than we perceive. Stretch, swayed by familial bonds, confides in a cousin entangled with a notorious Melbourne criminal syndicate. Soon, the map's existence will no longer be a secret in our circle; it will become a whisper of intrigue in the murky depths of the criminal underworld.

On a night cloaked in the moon's ghostly light, our decrepit hideout is invaded by a menacing envoy from this Melbourne gang. Shrouded in shadow, their identity concealed, their voice drips with dangerous intent. The air is tense, teetering on the edge of imminent violence, as they demand the relinquishment of our treasure map.

Fear tightens its grip around us. The threat of a hardened criminal looms over us, a storm ready to quash our aspirations and existence unless we yield the treasure map.

Yet, in this moment of dire threat, we find an unbreakable unity. Confronted with a harrowing decision - to forsake our dreams and the map or to summon our most bottomless courage and confront our adversary - we choose the latter.

With resolve hardened like forged steel and a blaze of defiance in our souls, we refuse to bow. We rise to defend not only the legacy of Ballarat but also the dreams we've dared to nurture. This criminal associate departs, thwarted and vowing retribution by his leader, Blackjack and their gang, oblivious to the indomitable spirit ignited within us, a heart that will not be quenched, come what may.

Chapter Thirty-Four

In the flickering candlelight of our now vulnerable hideout, tucked away in the East District of Main Road, we, the Cabbage Tree Mob, huddle together. The air is thick with anticipation and a hint of fear. Our refuge, an old, derelict miner's cottage, has become the bastion of our survival as we brace ourselves to defend the treasured map, our gateway to a forgotten fortune.

Andy, our de facto leader, stands tall amidst our makeshift war room. His eyes, alight with the fire of youth and the grit of determination, scan over our assembled group. We have collectively crafted a daring strategy to safeguard the map from the ruthless criminals claiming it.

Sis, the sole female among us, yet fierce as any, unfolds her plan across the weathered table. The creak of the floorboards under our feet punctuates the tense atmosphere as we lean in, absorbing her every word.

"We can't just let them storm in and claim what's ours," Sis asserts in an unwavering voice. "We need traps and ambush points. This cottage must be our fortress."

The room nods in agreement; we believe in Sis's tactical acumen. We quickly set to work, repurposing items from around the cottage into defensive tools.

Stretch, lanky and nimble; he becomes busy setting up tripwires and concealed pitfalls near the entryway. He cleverly attaches salvaged bells to signal any intrusion.

With his fiery hair and inventive mind, Red crafts slingshots and stone projectiles, envisioning a salvo of surprise attacks to disorient any assailants.

It is shorty, compact, and ingenious, who reinforces the windows and doors. He scrounges for wood and nails, transforming our entry points into impenetrable barriers. I lend my hands to each task, driven by our collective resolve to protect our map.

Andy, ever the leader, orchestrates our efforts with a keen eye, ensuring precision and efficacy in our preparations. He watches as fear and adrenaline are channelled into fortifying our hideout, morphing it from a mere shelter into a strategic stronghold.

As the night deepens, we pause, a moment of unity strengthening our resolve. We are acutely aware of the looming threat, but our determination is unwavering. Our fortifications are complete, and we step back to survey our work. The decrepit cottage now stands as a testament to our resolve, a fortress crafted by our hands, poised to defend a map and the dream it represents.

The air crackles with unspoken understanding as we exchange glances. We are ready to face whatever challenges lie ahead. Within these walls lies not just a piece of history but our destiny, intertwined with the legacy of a treasure that has beckoned us to become its new guardians.

Our audacious plan has been set into motion. The stage is prepared to confront those seeking to usurp our claim. In this standoff, we are the rightful heirs to a legacy of adventure and mystery.

• • • •

IN THE CLOAK OF NIGHT, under a star-strewn sky, the showdown between the Cabbage Tree Mob and Blackjack's hardened criminals unfolds with tense and scary intensity. Blackjack, leading his nefarious crew, mistakenly believes our youthful band will easily succumb to their seasoned ruthlessness. Yet, unbeknownst to them, our cottage hideout is a labyrinth of cunning traps and ambushes.

The first sign of our preparedness jolts the air as a tripwire triggers a racket from a rusty bell, startling the advancing criminals into a tense pause. After a moment of wary glances, they press on, only for a criminal gang member to yelp in agony as he ensnares his foot in a concealed rabbit trap, adding to the escalating chaos.

With calculated precision, Red and I begin unleashing a barrage of metal ball bearings and stones from slingshots from our hidden perches. This forces the criminals into panicked cover, and their arrogance dissolves into confusion.

Fortunately, our stalwart defender has transformed the doors and windows into formidable barriers. As the intruders attempt to breach them, they're met with unwavering resistance. Shorty, his face set with fierce determination, thwarted their efforts, striking at their clawing fingers with a hammer whenever they dared to tear down our boarded obstructions.

Meanwhile, lithe and quick Stretch moves through the cottage's tight spaces like a ghost, emerging unexpectedly to assail the invaders with his barrage of slingshot projectiles.

Panic takes hold of the criminals as they respond with wild gunfire, their shots piercing the night. Their growing desperation is compounded by the fear that their gunshots might attract unwanted attention from nearby residents, potentially drawing the law to our violent clash.

In a fury, Blackjack realises too late that our well-laid trap has ensnared them. Our meticulous planning and unity have transformed our modest refuge into an unassailable fortress.

As the confrontation continues, the criminals' initial threats dissolve into desperate pleas. Outnumbered and outmanoeuvred, they recognise their predicament and the urgency of their escape before any constabulary arrives.

Andy senses our advantage and knows the tide has turned in our favour. The traps and ambushes have decisively defeated and humiliated our adversaries.

In a last-ditch effort to salvage some semblance of victory, Blackjack, battered but cunning, approaches with a proposition, waving a white neckerchief. "You've won this round," he barks, "but we won't leave empty-handed. Hand over the map or face the destruction of your hideaway by fire and the potential loss of lives."

Andy clutches the decoy map we had prepared and recognises the opportunity to end the confrontation without bloodshed. With strategic reluctance, he hands over the fake map and watches the criminals depart, duped into believing they've claimed their prize.

As they urgently disappear into the night, smug in their false triumph, Andy declares with quiet conviction, "You underestimated us, Blackjack. This map, our legacy, will always remain ours."

Triumphant yet vigilant, we, the Cabbage Tree Mob, stand united. Our hideout remains our stronghold, and the legacy of Ballarat's rich history is safe within our care. But our journey is far from over. As we steel ourselves for the next phase, we realise time is crucial. We must locate the treasure before Blackjack and his gang discover our ruse.

Carrying the weight of history and the daring spirit of our forebears, we are ready to step into the labyrinth beneath Ballarat, Their legacy will guide us. With each step, we will delve deeper into the city's secrets, drawing ever closer to the elusive treasure that has evaded discovery for generations.

Our adventure is only beginning, with mysteries yet to be uncovered. But as the Cabbage Tree Mob, united in our quest, we stand ready to face whatever lies ahead in our relentless pursuit of the audacious dreams of those who came before us.

Chapter Thirty-Five

As we delve deeper into the quest for the hidden treasure, our journey intertwines with the rich tapestry of Ballarat's history. The town's legends of fortune, daring exploits, and tragic ends guide our path. We hope these tales, passed down through generations, will reveal the elusive starting point and unlock the cryptic clue to the Leary Gang's hiding place.

Our exploration into the past commences with visits to Ballarat's elderly residents, the guardians of the town's collective memory. We listen, spellbound, to their narratives of a time when gold was plentiful and fortunes were made and lost in moments.

We gather around an aged map in the peaceful confines of our dimly lit sanctuary, a place steeped in history and whispered secrets. Its creased surface, adorned with cryptic symbols and faded lines, holds the promise of an adventure akin to old fables. The legend of "Old Jack" — a figure shrouded in the mists of Ballarat's past — captivates our imaginations.

A decade after the notorious Leary Gang's heist, tales of Old Jack discovering a treasure trove reminiscent of Aladdin's cave had ignited the town with fervent whispers of hidden riches. His remarkable find, evidenced by a small bag brimming with glinting gold nuggets, had become an irresistible beacon for fortune-seekers. Yet, Old Jack's decision to shroud the location in secrecy, leaving behind only mysterious verbal clues and riddles, fueling our relentless pursuit.

Andy, the natural leader of our motley crew, his eyes alight with the fire of ambition, postulates that this map might guide us to Old Jack's find, a prospector of fame who may have found a rich vein of gold, a fortune beyond our wildest dreams. This fortune could irrevocably alter the course of our lives. His words hang in the air, a tantalising possibility that beckons us to the unknown.

Sis, with her mind always strategising, suggests a tantalising possibility. Perhaps this map was made by Old Jack, as Andy means, not leading to the infamous Leary Gang's hidden spoils, but Old Jack's fabled rich gold reef, which, if found, would become our legal find to keep. Her theory adds a twist to our quest, deepening the enigma.

Red, whose heart thrums with the thrill of adventure, argues with a glint in his eye that the map is a breadcrumb trail left by the Leary Gang, leading to their long-lost treasure. His adventurous spirit sees the map as a gateway to untold escapades.

Stretch, the thinker among us, ponders aloud, his voice steady with reason. Could it be that Old Jack's legendary find is, in fact, the Leary Gang's stolen loot? His analytical mind seeks to bridge the gap between legend and reality.

Shorty, ever the pragmatist, voices a simple truth: regardless of its origins, this map is an artifact of Ballarat's rich and tumultuous history, a piece of our collective past that we are duty-bound to explore.

With a sense of revelation, I add a crucial piece to this historical puzzle. According to my father's enquiries, our clubhouse was once a den of illicit pleasures - a brothel later purchased by Old Jack, which might hold the key to this mystery. Could it be that Old Jack, before meeting an untimely and mysterious end, discovered this map leading him to the location of the Leary gang's stolen gold? The map he hid again, which has come into our hands as his unintended legacy?

United in our resolve, Andy announces our grand plan: we will decipher the map's arcane clues and follow the shadowed path, whether leading to Old Jack's gold vein or the Leary gang's loot. Our determination is unwavering; we will uncover the hidden truth at the end of this enigmatic trail. The legend of Old Jack, intertwined with the lore of the Leary Gang, is more than just a tale; it's a path to discovery, and we are its chosen seekers.

Sis leads the map's deciphering, scrutinising each symbol against known landmarks and historical references in Ballarat's archives.

Stretch suggests the characters may form a navigational pattern or sequence, while Red speculates they could indicate a specific mine shaft's cryptic name and location.

Shorty reminds us of the value of revisiting the town's elders for additional insights that may align with locations on the map. If this treasure has eluded discovery for so long, it could be hidden in a secret mine not found in official records.

Andy concludes with a plan of action. We will utilise all available resources—local legends, historical records, elder wisdom—and divide the map among us for exploration. We will reconvene regularly to share findings.

We set out with sections of the map and a renewed sense of purpose. The path ahead is uncertain but driven by the legend of Old Jack's discovery and the lure of the Leary gang's hidden treasure within Ballarat's rich history. We are committed to unravelling the secrets of the past to secure our future.

· · · ·

AS A WEEK TURNS TO a month, our quest to decipher the cryptic map becomes an all-consuming endeavour. Each symbol, each faded line, is etched into our consciousness. We delved into historical records, seeking insights into Ballarat's rich past. I even cautiously approached my father, Levi Brody, for guidance, noting his growing suspicions about my inquiries. Repeatedly, we sought out the elderly residents of Ballarat, piecing together their memories associated with our puzzle.

This night, the air in our hideaway is heavy and tired. We've encountered numerous dead ends, chased down misleading leads, and grappled with frustration, yet our resolve remains steadfast.

With her strategic insight, Sis breaks the silence. "We need to rethink our strategy. Perhaps we've been interpreting this map mistakenly."

Stretch ponders her words and suggests, "The symbols might not be literal. They could represent hidden meanings towards discovering the real landmarks or features."

Red recalls the legends surrounding Old Jack's cryptic verbal clues. "What if Old Jack's spoken riddles align with these symbols? We need to find out if anyone documented his words."

Shorty, ever grounded, offers a practical approach. "We should consider Old Jack's mining habits. He was known to prospect in old mine shafts around Ballarat East. We need to explore which sites were most significant to him."

I interject, thinking about the legend of Old Jack's Aladdin Cave. "Perhaps the cave isn't a place but a metaphor, a clue to the nature of the treasure itself."

Andy, absorbing our collective insights, decides it's time to reevaluate our approach. "Let's view the map through this new lens."

We spread the map on the table once more. Our fresh perspectives transform the once enigmatic symbols into a coherent narrative. It's as if the map gradually reveals its secrets, guiding us on this journey.

Sis traces a route across the map, her expression one of revelation. "These symbols, I believe, outline a journey Old Jack took, beginning at his starting symbol, which could be this cottage. This path appears to lead to a waterway, and if it's in Ballarat East as Shorty suggests, it has to be Yarrowee Creek leading eastward towards the treasure."

Stretch aligns the symbols with known landmarks in Ballarat. "They seem to be waypoints, significant spots Old Jack or the Leary Gang might have referenced, leaving behind clues leading to each location along the way."

Red proposes an intriguing theory. "What if Aladdin's Cave is symbolic, representing a type of gold mine? Like in the fabled story, one with multiple branches leading to a large cavern."

Short, practical, and direct, he concludes, "If we follow this path as indicating Yarrowee Creek, it should lead us to logical places on our eastward journey that align with the map symbols."

Andy's eyes are full of determination as he scans the map. "We've broken the code. I believe the treasure is finally within our grasp."

Chapter Thirty-Five

A s the pieces fall into place, our excitement mounts. The weight of East Ballarat's history and Old Jack's and the Leary Gang's legacy propels us forward. With this newfound clarity and a sense of purpose that burns within us, we embark on the next phase of our journey. The map's symbols have led us beside Yarrowee Creek, a place steeped in the history of Ballarat East. It's a location where the waters once teemed with gold, dreams were forged, and fortunes were won and lost.

Standing on the creek's banks, the sun casting long shadows in the late afternoon, we are filled with anticipation and trepidation. The clues on the map have brought us to this historic waterway that played a vital role in the gold rush era.

Sis, our strategist, takes the lead once more. "If, according to the map, this is where Old Jack or the Leary Gang journeyed, we need to follow the course of Yarrowee Creek and see where these symbols take us."

Red adds, "We should watch for anything unusual or out of place. The compiler of the map is known for his cunning."

Shorty, practical as ever, suggests, "And let's stay alert. We don't know who else might be searching for this treasure."

I nod in agreement as we set off along the banks of Yarrowee Creek, the map clutched tightly in Sis's hands. The waterway meanders through the landscape, its history intertwined with the dreams of countless miners who once sought their fortunes here, prospecting by taking soil samples from the creek's banks and panning them off in the water to find a new source of payable gold.

Our journey takes us into the old mining district of Brown Hill, where the earth holds secrets untold. This district is steeped in history, where generations of miners made their fortune. The remnants of their efforts—abandoned mineshafts, rusted machinery, and crumbling ruins—serve as silent witnesses to the past.

As we explore this historic hilly landscape, we can't help but feel a connection to those who came before us. We envision the miners of yesteryears with their cabbage-tree hats, wearing colourful twilled shirts and moleskin trousers tucked into high boots, with their hopes, dreams, and relentless determination. We understand that our quest is not just about wealth but honouring the legacy of those who once walked these paths before us.

Our journey along Yarrowee Creek finally leads to a specific location marked as the end by a distinctive rock formation that matches the final symbol on the map. This is a moment of validation, a confirmation that we are on the right track.

We gather around this symbolic pinnacle of rock, our hearts pounding with anticipation. Andy, our steadfast leader, speaks, "This is it, mates. We've followed the clues, deciphered the map, and now we stand at the threshold of discovery."

With reverence, we clear the overgrown greenery at the front of the rock and start digging around, our hands and shovels breaking the earth's surface through soil fill that now seals what was once the entrance to a mine shaft blasted through the rockface. The soil yields to our efforts, revealing the shaft's opening—a tunnel leading down into the earth's depths.

As we enter the shaft, our flaming lamp illuminates the surroundings, revealing the length of a long passage that winds beneath Brown Hill. It's a labyrinthine maze, a testament to the miners' ingenuity and determination.

We follow the map, navigating the twists and turns inside numerous side tunnels. Along the way, we encounter obstacles—a collapsed passage, a flooded chamber—but we press on, driven by the promise of the treasure that awaits.

Hours of discovery turn into days, and we return home and back again when the time within our daily routines permits. We need to explore a maze of tunnels to their full depths, and as we delve deeper into the labyrinthine tunnels beneath Brown Hill, the weight of history and the promise of treasure fuel us on. The map's symbols continue to guide us towards the correct route within the maze, but deciphering their meaning is a complex puzzle.

We finally reach a point where the symbols diverge, leading in five directions. It's uncertain, and we gather to examine the map again. With her tactical acumen, Sis scrutinises the characters and points to one that stands out—a tiny mark resembling a crossed pickaxe and shovel. "This symbol," she says, "signifies hard work and perseverance. It must be the key to finding the treasure."

With newfound resolve, we tread the path marked by the crossed pickaxe and shovel. The tunnel constricts around us, and the air thickens, almost tangible in its oppression. Yet our determination is unshaken, fuelled by the nearness of our elusive goal.

At length, the tunnel yields to a chamber, grand and cavernous, just as the ancient map had promised. Here, nature's artistry is on full display – stalactites glitter like jewels in our lamplight, each flicker unveiling the chamber's majesty.

A stunning reality unfolds before us as our eyes adjust to the erratic dance of flame. Not the vein of gold we supposed Old Jack had chased, but something far more significant – the fabled bounty of the Leary Gang's notorious gold escort heist, lost since the fevered days of the 1850s gold rush. The treasure, unguarded and resplendent, sprawls before us. One strongbox lies agape, its innards a chaotic glimmer of bags of gold dust and ungainly nuggets – a silent testament to Old Jack's rudimentary discovery method of this treasure.

Within us, a tempest brews: exhilaration entwined with a creeping dread. This is no ordinary find; it's a storied hoard, tainted with blood and betrayal, elusive through history, and now, improbably, within our grasp.

In the chamber's depths, we stand transfixed by the golden allure, but our dreamlike state shatters with the distant echo of footsteps. Fear clenches our hearts – we are not alone in this underground world. The thought of pursuit, until now unconsidered, strikes us cold.

Abruptly, a shadow detaches from the darkness: Blackjack, the notorious leader of his gang, his presence menacing, his gang members, a grim group behind him, have followed our lamp's light.

Blackjack's eyes rove over the treasure, wide with greed and surprise. "Well, what do we have 'ere?" he sneers, his tone venomous. "Looks like you lads have found something big."

Andy, his expression a bastion of defiance, steps up. "This treasure is Ballarat's Blackjack. Not yours."

Blackjack's response is a chilling grin, his teeth a yellowed snarl. "Oh, but I will take it. There's nothing you can do to stop me."

Control shifts swiftly. The gang members, weapons in hand, close in, corralling us towards the treasure. Andy and Stretch are pressed into service, grappling with one strongbox, while the gang tends to the others.

I catch a fleeting chance in the tense atmosphere, forming a silent strategy among us. "Drop everything and run at my signal," I murmur. "Follow me. The treasure must not fall into their hands."

As we edge towards the tunnel proper, our steps hasten, stretching the distance between us and our captors. The moment is ripe; at a juncture where the shaft forks, I whisper our cue: "Now!"

Chaos reigns. We abandon our burden and dash towards salvation, clutching the map tightly. Our extinguished lamp leaves our pursuers blind in the enveloping darkness, as our map reveals that the tunnel is straightforward to travel blind for the next one hundred yards.

Fleeing through the tunnel's labyrinthine length, we come to a corner. We finally pause to relight our lamp, and the sounds of the disoriented and floundering Blackjack Gang fade into the depths. Blackjack's futile and distant orders echo in the stale air.

Our flight is desperate, guided by the map's retreating symbols. "The surface," I pant. "We must collapse the entrance before they can follow."

Gasping for air, we emerge into the daylight, the mine's gaping maw behind us. With frantic urgency, we set towards sealing it, our shovels casting dirt and stone as a barrier against pursuit. The gravity of our choice is palpable—we have entombed both the treasure and our foes.

In the silence of our labour, reflections haunt us. The gold, once a beacon of hope and a testament to Ballarat's rich history, now lies buried, a prize beyond reach. We trek back to our hideaway, our thoughts heavy with the treasure's fate. It feels like a dream lost, confined forever to the mine's depths.

After spirited discussion, our path becomes clear – we must reveal everything to the Ballarat Police. Our story will be laid bare, beginning with the old cryptic map and leading to the uncovered treasure, now claimed by criminals.

Resolved, we wait until the following daylight to stride towards Camp Street Police Station, with the map as our damning evidence, ready to expose the truth of the treasure beneath Brown Hill.

Chapter Thirty-Seven

The next day dawns, sombre and heavy with the weight of our profound discovery beneath Brown Hill. Clutching the tattered map that guided us to the hidden depths of Ballarat's past, we stand before the imposing facade of the Camp Street Police Station. Our hearts beat with apprehension and resolve as we prepare to unveil the truth about the treasure that now lies forever out of reach, buried in the earth's embrace.

Inside the station, the stark reality of the law contrasts sharply with the shadowy tunnels we left behind. The sterile white walls and the crisp blue uniforms of the officers present a world far removed from our clandestine adventures. We are a motley crew bound together by a shared secret that could alter the course of Ballarat's history.

Andy, our fearless leader, steps forward. His firm, steady voice breaks the silence, "We've unearthed a secret about a treasure hidden in an old mine shaft at Brown Hill. We need your help to verify its existence."

Although our story was initially met with scepticism, it captivated the officers. We recounted our journey, from discovering Old Jack had the map to the Leary Gang's hidden treasure from their gold escort heist to our harrowing encounter with Blackjack's Gang in the labyrinthine tunnels. Gradually, scepticism turned to intrigue, and soon, a team of officers accompanied us back to Brown Hill's mine entrance.

With shovels clutched tightly, we reopen the sealed passage, its dark maw beckoning us again into its depths. As we descend, a tableau of despair and desperation unfolds. The Gang, led by the infamous Blackjack, huddles in defeat, their hands bloodied from their futile effort to dig their way out. Nearby, three strongboxes, laden with gold dust and nuggets, bear silent witness to their avarice.

The police move with swift precision, securing the gang and the treasure. The legacy of greed that once haunted these tunnels is finally brought to justice, a victory wrought by our unwavering resolve.

The news of our discovery spreads like wildfire. The Ballarat Star Newspaper headlines our story, immortalising us as the "Cabbage Tree Mob." While the gold's wealth is not ours to claim, our place in history is firmly established.

We later learn of the Victorian Government's longstanding reward—six hundred pounds for information leading to the recovery of the stolen gold. In a unanimous decision, we agree to share the reward equally, a testament to the camaraderie and unity that have sustained us through this incredible journey.

Standing outside the police station, we feel the weight of history upon our shoulders. The legacy of Old Jack and the Leary Gang, the allure of the hidden treasure, and the protection of Ballarat's rich heritage have left an indelible mark upon our lives. Our quest may not have concluded as we initially hoped, but it has forged bonds of friendship and adventure that will endure a lifetime.

As we part ways, the future remains uncertain. Still, one thing is clear: the Cabbage Tree Mob's daring endeavour will forever be etched in the annals of Ballarat's history, a chapter replete with courage, solidarity, and the indomitable spirit of adventure.

· · · ·

AS I SIT IN THE CONFINES of our family home, the walls close around me, each tick of the clock a reminder of my fall from grace. Once the pride of my parents, Levi and Isabella Brody, I, Samuel Brody, now bear the weight of their disappointment. My adventures with the Cabbage Tree Mob, while thrilling and heroic in the eyes of Ballarat, have cast a shadow over the legacy of the Brody name.

The revelation of my double life splashed across the pages of the newspaper has shamed my family. My father, a paragon of the legal community, finds it hard to reconcile the son he thought he knew with the adventurous spirit that led me down such a dangerous path. My mother, always the gentle soul, looks at me now with sorrowful eyes, her heart torn between love and disbelief.

The irony of my situation is not lost on me. As a top Clarendon College student, my academic excellence was never questioned. Mathematics, history, and every subject came naturally to me, allowing me to maintain the facade of a dedicated scholar while I roamed the streets with my comrades. But now, the truth is out, and the freedom I once cherished has been snatched away.

I'm relegated to a life of quiet study and familial duty, and my every move is watched with hawk-like scrutiny. The brief moments I steal with the Cabbage Tree Mob are fleeting and urgent. We speak in hushed tones, our conversations a mixture of nostalgia and plans for a future we know may never come to pass.

In the stillness of my room, I ponder my next move. The thrill of adventure and the lure of the unknown call to me, yet the weight of my family's expectations holds me back. The path ahead is fraught with uncertainty, and I find myself torn between two worlds – the rigid structure of my family's aspirations and the untamed freedom of the streets of Ballarat.

As days turn into weeks, I grapple with my identity. Am I Samuel Brody, the educated son destined to follow in his father's footsteps, or am I the daring adventurer who helped solve one of Ballarat's greatest mysteries? The internal struggle is relentless, a battle to find where my true loyalties lie daily.

In the golden hues of a Ballarat afternoon, I find myself wandering the familiar Sturt Street, the echoes of my recent adventures with the Cabbage Tree Mob in East Ballarat still ringing in my ears. My parents, Levi and Isabella Brody, confine me, yet fate intervenes most unexpectedly during one of these reflective strolls.

I chance upon a quaint bookshop nestled between the grand towers of the town. Its window displays an array of volumes that speak of distant lands and daring exploits. Compelled by an invisible force, I push open the door, the bell chiming softly, announcing my entry into a world of forgotten tales and hidden truths.

Inside, amidst the labyrinth of shelves and the scent of aged paper, I encounter her – Eleanor. She stands in a shaft of sunlight that filters through the dusty air, her eyes intently scanning the pages of a book. Her hair, the colour of autumn leaves, cascades in gentle waves down her back, and her presence radiates an aura of quiet intelligence.

Our eyes meet, and in that moment, a connection forms, as tangible as the books surrounding us. She looks up, her gaze curious and penetrating. "Can I help you find something?" she asks, her voice a melody that resonates with my soul.

I stutter a reply, caught off-guard by her presence. "I-I was just browsing," I manage, my usual confidence faltering under her scrutiny.

Eleanor smiles, a gesture that lights up the room. "Well, feel free to explore. There's much to discover here," she says, returning to her book.

As I meander through the aisles, I can't help but steal glances at her. There's a grace in her movements, a serenity that contrasts starkly with the chaotic world I've known. I find myself drawn to her, a moth to a flame.

Eventually, our conversation begins – a tentative exchange about literature and life that soon blossoms into a deep, intellectual connection. Eleanor, I learn, is a student of history, and her mind is a treasure trove of knowledge about the world beyond Ballarat. She speaks of ancient civilisations and great explorers with a passion that ignites my thirst for adventure.

In the days that followed, our meetings at the bookshop became regular. Each conversation revealed more of her character—her wit, compassion, and understanding of life's complexities. She becomes my confidante, the one person who sees the real me—not just the obedient son or the daring member of the Cabbage Tree Mob but Samuel Brody in his entirety.

With Eleanor, I find a balance between the two worlds that tug at my soul. She encourages my academic pursuits while understanding the restless spirit that drives my thirst for adventure. In her, I find a kindred spirit, someone who believes in the potential of what I can become.

As our relationship deepens, Eleanor becomes more than just a friend; she becomes the beacon guiding me toward a future where I Can embrace all facets of my identity. With her by my side, I envision a life where I can be true to myself, unburdened by others' expectations.

The path ahead is still uncertain, but with Eleanor, I find the courage to face whatever may come. Together, we stand at the precipice of a new chapter that promises a journey filled with discovery, growth, and the unfettered pursuit of our dreams. I have found a companion and partner in life's grand adventure in her.

Chapter Thirty-Eight
Three years Hence.

Three years have woven their intricate tapestry since my escapades with the Cabbage Tree Mob, and I, Samuel Brody, now stand at the cusp of another monumental chapter. My journey at Clarendon College concludes with distinctions, culminating in an academic odyssey that has earned my parents, Levi and Isabella Brody, both pride and expectation. Yet, within me, the embers of adventure refuse to be extinguished.

My father, envisioning a future for me in the realms of law learned through Melbourne University, is to be surprised. With a heart yearning for uncharted horizons, I persuaded my parents to allow me to channel the one hundred pounds held in trust from my share of the Cabbage Tree Mob's reward money into a 'Sale of Commission', buying me an officer's rank within the British Indian Forces. The decision stirs a whirlwind of emotions within the Brody household, a blend of reluctance, apprehension, and eventual acceptance.

As my father grapples with my decision to venture into uncharted horizons, he sees a reflection of his youthful ambitions. The spark of adventure that once led him to prospect for gold in Snake Gully, Little Bendigo District, intending to earn his fare to the Swan River Settlement of Western Australia, resonates within him. His understanding of my yearning for adventure and a father's concern propels him to action. He cannot refuse my request, recognising the same stirrings of wanderlust that once fueled his journey.

Drawing on his connections and the respect he has garnered in Ballarat, Levi reaches out to Peter Lalor. Lalor, a legendary figure of the Eureka Stockade Rebellion, has since retired from politics but still wields significant influence. His connections reach as far as the corridors of power in England, a testament to his enduring legacy.

The process is set into motion with my father utilising my reward money, his persuasive skills, and Lalor's influential contacts. The result is a Second Lieutenant's commission in the 11th Devonshire 2nd Battalion, serving in the northern province of Punjab, a significant military station in British India.

The commission is a hard-earned victory that symbolises my father's support and Lalor's enduring influence. It begins a new chapter for Sam Brody and my entire family. As I prepare for this new life, I am acutely aware of the sacrifices made and the trust placed in me.

The news of my commission spread through Ballarat, stirring admiration and surprise among those who knew me as a member of the Cabbage Tree Mob. My transformation from a local adventurer to a commissioned officer in the British Army is the talk of the town.

Eleanor, my confidante and beloved, whose love has blossomed in parallel with my academic pursuits, finds excitement in my decision. Her presence has been a constant source of support and inspiration. Introduced to my family as my betrothed, she has endeared herself to them with her intellect and charm.

Eleanor and I speak of plans in the privacy of our unchaperoned meetings under the starlit skies of Ballarat. "I'll make a life for us in India, Eleanor," I promise, my voice a blend of determination and longing. "And once I'm settled, you'll join me, and we'll begin our life together."

Eleanor's eyes, mirrors of our shared dreams, sparkle with anticipation. "I'll be waiting for that day, Sam," she whispers, her words laced with the thrill of the unknown. "Our love knows no bounds, no borders."

As I prepare for departure, my parents, Levi and Isabella, watch with bittersweet pride. My mother's eyes glisten with unshed tears, and my father's hand rests firmly on my shoulder, a silent symbol of his support.

The day of my departure dawns, a tapestry of farewells and promises. My parents embrace me tightly; their faces are a complex canvas of pride and concern. "Make your mark, Sam," my father says, his voice firm yet emotional. "But never forget where you come from."

Eleanor and I share a tender, lingering goodbye. Her touch, gentle yet filled with unspoken words, anchors me to a promise of a future together. "Wait for my call, Eleanor," I murmur, my heart heavy yet hopeful.

As I board the ship bound for India, the silhouette of Melbourne fades into the distance, but my spirit soars towards new adventures. The whispers of the past blend with the call of the future, a symphony of what has been and will be.

India awaits a land of mystery and opportunity. In its embrace, I will carve my path, guided by the lessons of my youth and the unyielding drive for exploration. It is a journey not just of distance but of self-discovery, where the legacy of Levi Brody and the shadow of Jack Riley converge in the forging of my destiny.

In the months that follow, India reveals its wonders and challenges. As an officer in training, I navigate the complexities of military life, each day a lesson in leadership and perseverance. The vibrant culture, the sun's heat, and the kaleidoscope of experiences shape me, moulding the contours of my character.

Letters from Eleanor, filled with love and longing, become my solace. We share our dreams and plans through ink and paper, our bond growing stronger despite the miles that separate us. Our resilient and unwavering love becomes the beacon that guides me through trials and triumphs.

As I rise through my training, earning respect and recognition, the day of Eleanor's arrival draws near. The anticipation builds, a crescendo of emotions that culminates when I see her again, stepping off the ship onto Indian soil. Our reunion will be a fusion of two souls destined to traverse life's journey together.

• • • •

AS ELEANOR EMBARKS on her journey to India, her heart flutters
with a mix of trepidation and excitement. The ship, a majestic vessel
bound for the subcontinent, is a world unto itself. Its decks, bustling
with travellers of diverse backgrounds, offer Eleanor a glimpse into the
myriad lives that intersect on this journey.

The voyage is a symphony of ocean waves and wind, the ship
cutting through the blue expanse with grace and might. Eleanor spends
her days on deck, the salt air kissing her cheeks, her eyes fixed on the
endless horizon. Nights are a tapestry of starlit skies, the gentle rocking
of the vessel lulling her into dreams of the adventures that await.

As the Indian coast appears in the distance, anticipation courses
through her. The port is alive with chaos and colour, a sensory feast
that overwhelms and enthrals. Eleanor steps onto Indian soil, her senses
assaulted by the cacophony of sounds, the vibrant hues of the market
stalls, and the rich aromas of spices and street food.

The journey to Punjab is an odyssey through a land of contrasts.
The train, a marvel of British steam engineering, snakes its way through
lush landscapes and past ancient cities. Eleanor peers through the
window, her eyes capturing snapshots of life in India – children playing
by the tracks, women in brightly coloured saris drawing water from
wells, and men leading oxen along dusty paths.

Arriving in Rawalpindi, Eleanor is greeted by a tapestry of green
fields and the distant silhouette of the Himalayas. The air is scented
with the earthy fragrance of the fields, and the sounds of the bustling
bazaars echo in the distance. I, Samuel, her beloved, await her arrival.
Our reunion is a moment of profound joy, culminating in a journey
that spans continents and oceans. In my embrace, Eleanor feels a sense
of belonging, a deep connection to this land that will now become her
home.

Eleanor's eyes open wide as we travel through the Punjab together. She marvels at the ancient forts and palaces, remnants of long-gone empires. She walks through the bustling markets, delighted by the array of goods, from intricate textiles to handcrafted jewellery.

Eleanor's journey is a landscape passage and an exploration of her spirit. She finds strength she never knew she had and a deep well of empathy for the people she meets. Her conversations with the locals, filled with warmth and curiosity, bridge the gap between her world and theirs.

In the heart of Rawalpindi, Eleanor finds a new chapter of her life unfolding—one of discovery, love, and a deepening understanding of a land that captivates her heart. Amidst India's challenges and beauty, she and I will forge a life together, a testament to the enduring power of love in the face of the unknown.

With Eleanor by my side, India becomes not just a land of duty but of home. We marry in a ceremony that blends our cultures, a testament to our journey and the love that will triumph over distance and time. The sun casts a golden hue over the gardens of the British Residency, where Eleanor and I stand, ready to bind our lives together in a ceremony that is as unique as our journey. The air is perfumed with the scent of jasmine and roses, and the soft murmur of our guests blends with the distant sounds of the bustling streets of Punjab.

Eleanor walks towards me, radiant in a gown that fuses the West's elegance with India's vibrant colours. Her masterpiece of silk and embroidery glimmers in the sunlight, reflecting the intricate patterns of henna adorning her hands and feet. Her smile, a beacon of joy and love, reaches deep into my soul.

As she joins me, our hands meet, and I am acutely aware of the significance of this moment. We stand before an assembly of regimental friends and colleagues, local dignitaries, and a few close Indian friends we've made. Our union is a bridge between worlds, celebrating diversity and understanding.

The ceremony begins with traditional Western vows, our voices steady as we promise to love and cherish each other. The British chaplain, a kind-hearted man who has embraced India's spirit, officiates solemnly and warmly.

As we turn to the Indian part of the ceremony, a local pundit steps forward, his presence commanding yet serene. He recites ancient Sanskrit mantras, their rhythmic cadence merging with the rustling leaves of the nearby banyan trees. The sacred fire, Agni, crackles in the centre of the mandap, a symbol of purity and witness to our vows.

We circle the fire, and each step is a pledge to support and honour each other. The pundit explains the significance of each phera or round, and our commitment deepens with every step. The shehnai's sound resonates through the air, weaving its melodies through the garden.

As the ceremony concludes, the pundit blesses us with a shower of flower petals, their fragrance mingling with the incense that wafts through the air. Our guests erupt in applause, their faces alight with happiness and goodwill.

The reception is a fusion of cultures, with tables laden with an array of Indian and Western delicacies. Laughter and music fill the air, and the evening sky is painted with the vibrant colours of fireworks, a celebration of our union.

As Eleanor and I dance under the starlit sky, our hearts beat in unison, not just to the rhythm of the music but to the rhythm of a new life we embark upon together. India, with its myriad hues and profound mysteries, is now our home, and our love story is just beginning a journey of discovery, understanding, and an ever-deepening bond that transcends all boundaries.

Our story, a tapestry of adventure, love, and destiny, continues to unfold under the Indian skies. It is the narrative of a young man who chose the path less travelled, driven by the spirit of adventure and the power of love. His journey began in the heart of Ballarat and found its fulfilment in the embrace of the East.

Chapter Thirty-Nine

I now find myself in the heart of North India as a lieutenant in the British Forces; my days are spent navigating the complex tapestry of military life in the jewel of the British Empire. With the air thick with the scent of spices and the murmurs of a thousand languages, it is a far cry from the familiar eucalyptus breeze of my homeland.

My duties are demanding and often fraught with the tension of upholding the Raj's might while navigating the undercurrents of local sentiment in Punjab. Rawalpindi's bustling and vibrant streets remind me of this land's diversity and richness. I walk through markets filled with colourful textiles and spices, absorbing the sights and sounds of a vivid and intricate culture.

But it's not just the soldier's life that occupies my thoughts. My heart is intertwined with Eleanor, my wife, who bravely joined me in India. Our reunion in this foreign land is like a story from the pages of a romantic novel. With her adventurous spirit, Eleanor adapts to this new life with a grace and curiosity that amazes me.

Together, we explore this land's complexities. Our home blends English decorum and Indian vibrancy, a testament to our union of two worlds. With her keen mind and compassionate heart, Eleanor quickly earns the respect and affection of our fellow Britons and the local populace. Her efforts in organising events for the officers' wives and Her involvement in local charities bridges cultural gaps, endearing her to many.

Our days are a blend of military obligations and social engagements. We host dinners where British propriety meets Indian hospitality, and our table is a microcosm of the Empire itself. The conversations around our table mix English and Urdu, a dance of diplomacy and friendship.

But our life here is not without its challenges. The political climate in India is ever-changing, and now, as a Captain, I often find myself caught between the orders of my superiors and the realities of life on the ground. The whispers of dissent and the rumblings of independence are impossible to ignore. I grapple with the moral complexities of serving an Empire amidst a people yearning for self-determination.

Amid this, Eleanor and I find solace in each other. Our love, forged in the fires of adventure and solidified in the trials of a new life, remains our anchor. We find joy in the small moments – a shared glance during a bustling bazaar visit, quiet evenings on our verandah overlooking the Punjab plains, and the laughter that fills our home.

My responsibilities have increased as I rise through the ranks, as does my understanding of this land and its people. Eleanor and I continue to navigate the intricate balance of our duties and convictions, striving to impact those around us positively.

Our journey in India, rich with this ancient land's colours, sounds, and heart, becomes a defining chapter in our lives. Here, in the heart of the British Raj, we write our story of love, duty, and the unyielding quest for understanding in a world of contrasts.

As I set foot on the soil of Punjab in 1891, the air was thick with the legacy of empires and the echoes of battles long past. This land, a tapestry of history and turmoil, has been shaped by the hands of conquerors and the will of its people. The Punjab, I now behold, is the result of seismic shifts in power, from the proud reign of the Sikh Empire to the calculated control of the British East India Company.

The battlefields of the Anglo-Sikh Wars, now silent, still whisper the tales of conflict and ambition. The fall of Lahore in 1849 marked a pivotal moment, ending the Second Anglo-Sikh War and leading to the annexation of Punjab by the British. It was a time of transformation, where the might of the Sikh Empire, with its formidable Khalsa army, succumbed to the strategic prowess of the British forces.

The annexation of Punjab opened a new chapter in British India's history. With its strategic location and abundant resources, this region has become a jewel in the crown of the British Empire. Its integration paves the way for greater control over the princely states, creating a chessboard of power and diplomacy.

After annexation, Punjab became a land of paradoxes. Under British rule, it witnessed remarkable advancements in infrastructure and administration. Railways and telegraphs connected cities, while canals and new agricultural practices transformed the landscape. Yet, beneath this veneer of progress, its people still simmer with a spirit of resistance and a yearning for self-determination.

The Revolt of 1857, though primarily concentrated in North and Central India, sent ripples across Punjab. It was a watershed moment, leading to the end of the East India Company's rule and the establishment of direct British governance, marking the beginning of the British Raj. Punjab remained relatively calm during this tumultuous period, its loyalty secured by careful British political manoeuvring and the recruitment of Punjabi soldiers into the British Indian Army.

Walking through the bustling bazaars and the tranquil countryside, I sense the undercurrents of change. The 'Doctrine of Lapse' enables the British to annex princely states and sow seeds of discontent. Stories of lost sovereignties and dethroned princes linger in the air, fuelling a silent resentment against foreign rule.

In this land of ancient traditions and newfound changes, the people of Punjab are resilient and adaptable. The fusion of cultures, blending Sikh, Hindu, and British influences, creates a rich tapestry of life. The grandeur of the Sikh gurdwaras stands as a testament to the Region's spiritual and cultural heritage, while the British cantonments and colonial architecture mark the era of imperial rule.

As 1891 unfolds, Punjab is a region in transition, caught between the remnants of its glorious past and the realities of colonial rule. As a young British officer, I believe this land represents both a challenge and an opportunity. I must navigate the complexities of administration and diplomacy, understanding the delicate balance of power and the aspirations of its people.

My journey in Punjab is not just a military assignment; it's an exploration of a land rich in history, culture, and diversity. As I immerse myself in this vibrant province, I find myself learning not just about the strategies of governance but about the human spirit's resilience and the enduring quest for identity and autonomy. In all its complexity and beauty, Punjab becomes a canvas upon which the stories of empires, wars, and revolutions are painted and where my report finds new chapters to unfold.

• • • •

AS THE SUN CASTS ITS first golden rays over Rawalpindi, the bustling heart of Punjab, I stand on our balcony, surveying a land caught between ancient traditions and the encroaching tide of the British Empire. The distant sounds of the city waking up blend with the aroma of brewing chai, yet my thoughts are consumed by the recent orders dispatching me to the North-West Frontier.

Eleanor, the beacon of my life, stands beside me. She's aware of the looming peril, her expression a blend of concern and fortitude. "The North-West Frontier," she murmurs, her voice hinting at apprehension.

"Yes," I reply, my gaze fixed on the horizon, where the lawless tribal areas lay hidden. "The British aim to quell the rebellions there, to maintain their prestige and control. The tribesmen are fierce, Eleanor, viewing their raids as acts of heroism."

Eleanor's grip tightens on the balcony railing. "And you, Sam, what do you view it as?"

I sigh, a complex mixture of duty and doubt swirling within me. "I view it as a task that must be undertaken, albeit with a heavy heart. These tribesmen fight for what they believe is their rightful freedom."

Our conversation is interrupted by Sergeant Havers's arrival, who brings news that reinforces my fears: "Sir, the Punjab Free Legion has grown bolder, and their influence is spreading to the tribes in the mountains.

The revelation starkly reminds me of the formidable task ahead. As a British officer, I am bound by duty, yet the rebel clans' fierce independence resonates within me, echoing my journey to break free from my family legacy.

Our day unfolds under the shadow of the impending mission. The streets of Rawalpindi, alive with vibrant colours and bustling activity, now appear as fleeting moments of peace in a world braced for conflict.

As Eleanor and I dine together, the tension is palpable this evening. "Every man, woman, and child in these rebel clans see their warriors as champions," I explain, my voice tinged with respect. "They leave for their raids with blessings and return as heroes."

Eleanor listens intently, her eyes reflecting the flames of the oil lamp. "It's a different world, Sam. One where their actions are not seen as crimes, but as valour."

Our conversation drifts into the night, each of us lost in our thoughts about the impending expedition. Eleanor's presence is a constant source of comfort, yet the knowledge of the dangers I must face on the frontier casts a long shadow over our serene home.

The night is restless, filled with unspoken fears and silent prayers. The North-West Frontier's looming presence, with its fiercely independent tribes and the British Empire's relentless pursuit of control, poignantly reminds us of the delicate balance governing our lives here.

As dawn breaks, bringing the promise of a new day, I know the path ahead is fraught with peril and uncertainty. In the heart of Punjab, our story continues to unfold, a tale of duty and love amidst an empire in turmoil. The North-West Frontier beckons, and the fate of countless lives, including mine, hangs in the balance. The journey to the mountains looms ahead, a journey into a land of rebellion and bravery, where the line between hero and outlaw blurs in the eyes of those who fight for their beliefs.

Chapter Thirty-Nine

The dawn in Peshawar, the principal town of the North-West Frontier where I am now dispatched, breaks with a palette of warm hues, painting the ancient city in colours of hope and foreboding. Standing at the edge of the British fortifications, as Captain Samuel Brody, I am struck by this historic town's contrasting beauty and latent tension.

Peshawar, encircled by a formidable British fortress, is a testament to the Empire's might and a buffer against the rebellious tribal areas. As the city stirs to life, its bazaars brimming with vibrant activity and the calls of street vendors, there's an undercurrent of unease that belies the apparent normalcy.

Eleanor, the pillar of strength and grace, joins me on the balcony of our quarters within the British garrison. Her eyes, reflecting the complex tapestry of this frontier city, meet mine. "Peshawar is beautiful yet so fraught, Sam," she observes, her voice carrying a note of worry.

I nod, my gaze drifting to the rugged hills in the distance, a stark reminder of our purpose here. "The North-West Frontier is a land of untamed spirit. The tribes see their defiance as bravery against the British presence, a resistance steeped in their fierce code of honour."

Eleanor's hand finds mine, a gesture of comfort and solidarity. "And you, leading your men into these unknowns..."

Our next day progresses under the looming shadow of a challenging mission. With its bustling markets and ancient fortresses, Peshawar now feels like the calm before a storm. Eleanor and I wander through the streets, absorbing the sights and sounds, each moment tinged with the unspoken knowledge of the dangers ahead.

As we dine in the subduing light of our quarters, I again share my conflicting thoughts with Eleanor. Eleanor listens, her expression one of understanding. "It's a world apart from ours, where their defiance is seen not as rebellion but as upholding their traditions and freedom."

Our conversation meanders, a delicate dance of words revealing our deepest fears and hopes. Eleanor's presence soothes my troubled mind, yet the threat of the impending campaign casts a long shadow over our peaceful abode.

The twilight is restless, filled with unspoken fears and silent prayers for the days ahead. The frontier, with its fierce tribes and the relentless march of the British Empire, constantly reminds us of the delicate balance of our existence here.

• • • •

AS THE GOLDEN SUN DIPS further below the rugged skyline of Punjab, casting long shadows over the bustling streets of Peshawar, I now stand within my modest officer's quarters. The air is thick with the scent of spices and the distant sound of temple bells mingling with the muezzin's call. With its vivid contrasts and enduring spirit, this land has become more than just a station of duty to me; it's a canvas of endless possibilities and hidden stories.

But tonight, my thoughts are clouded, not by the wonders of India, but by a gnawing unease that has taken root in my heart. It's been three years since I left the familiar streets of Ballarat, trading the comfort of my family's home for the uncertain path of a British Army Officer in colonial India. My parents, Levi and Isabella Brody, had hoped for a future of legal prowess for me at Melbourne University, yet here I am, clad in a uniform that bears the weight of an empire.

As I gaze across the horizon, my mind drifts to Eleanor, the woman my only solace in this foreign land. Her words, filled with love and longing, are a balm to my weary soul.

A soft knock at the door breaks my reverie. Sergeant Havers, a loyal comrade and friend, stands at the threshold, his face etched with concern. "Sir, there's been word from the south. A rebel group called 'Punjab Free Legion' has been causing unrest. There are rumours they've been targeting British interests."

I feel a chill run down my spine. The Punjab Free Legion, a name whispered in hushed tones among the ranks, a shadowy force rising from the discontent sown by years of British rule. Their leader, Arjun Singh, a Specter from Punjab's turbulent past, has been rallying disaffected warriors and commoners alike under the banner of rebellion.

"And there's more, sir," Havers continues, hesitating. "There are reports of a killing... an Indian force's clerk journeying to his home. The Legion's handiwork, they say."

"Prepare a unit, Havers. We move at dawn," I command, my voice steady despite the turmoil within.

The night is restless, filled with strategy and silent prayers. As dawn breaks, painting the sky in hues of orange and purple, we set out, a contingent of cavalry under my command, galloping towards the heart of uncertainty. The journey is arduous, and the Indian landscape is a maze of challenges and wonders.

We travel through villages where the air hums with unsaid words, and the locals' eyes follow us with curiosity and fear. The Legion's presence is like a shadow over these lands; its motives are mysterious, and its actions are unpredictable.

As we venture deeper into the heartland of Punjab, I find myself torn between my duty as an officer and the personal quest that drives me forward. The image of Eleanor, solid and resolute, is a constant in my mind, guiding me through the labyrinth of doubts and fears.

Our search leads us to the outskirts of a small village, nestled between rolling fields and ancient forests. The air is tense, the silence of the early morning broken only by the distant call of a peacock. It is here, amidst the whispers of rebellion and the echoes of a land steeped in history, that our journey takes a fateful turn.

As we approach, the village is veiled in the morning mist and appears almost serene, but the undercurrent of tension is palpable. The villagers eye us with a cautious blend of suspicion and curiosity, their daily routines a facade over the unrest simmering beneath. We dismount our presence, a statement of authority and a plea for information, blending into the landscape of apprehension and whispered secrets.

Sergeant Havers and I, flanked by our men, advance towards the village elder, a figure of respect and authority among the locals. His aged yet sharp eyes meet mine, a silent exchange of wills in the quiet of dawn.

"We seek the Punjab Free Legion," I state, my voice cutting through the silence like a sword. "Any information could aid in quelling the unrest that threatens the peace of this land."

The elder lingers on me, weighing my words and intent. After a moment that stretches like an eternity, he nods slowly, a gesture of reluctant acceptance. "The Legion... they are shadows," he begins, his voice a low rumble, "moving unseen, striking without warning. But their leader... he seeks justice for perceived wrongs, a response to the people's grievances."

The information is cryptic, yet it paints a picture of the Legion's motivations, reflecting the complexities and contradictions that define this land. Armed with this knowledge, we press on, tracing the Legion's shadowy trail through the countryside.

The sun climbs higher as we ride, and the heat is a relentless adversary in our quest. The landscape changes from verdant fields to rugged terrain, a testament to Punjab's diverse beauty. Our journey is a blend of vigilance and contemplation, each mile bringing us closer to an inevitable confrontation.

Our scouts report a camp ahead, nestled in a valley surrounded by towering hills—a strategic location, challenging to assault yet impossible to ignore. It is here, amidst the natural fortifications of the land, that we prepare to face the Legion.

The plan is simple yet daring. A small detachment, led by me, will infiltrate the camp under the cover of darkness, seeking to capture the leader and disband this small group without significant bloodshed. The risks are immense, but the potential for a peaceful resolution drives us forward.

Night descends like a cloak, shrouding our movements as we approach the camp. The stars, a canopy of silent witnesses, guide our path through the darkness. My heart beats a steady rhythm of anticipation and fear, the weight of command heavy on my shoulders.

The camp is alive with the low murmur of voices and the crackle of fires—a hive of activity masked by the night. We move like phantoms, our presence unnoticed until the moment of revelation. As we reveal ourselves, the clash is sudden, a whirlwind of motion and sound, taking the camp by surprise.

The small group of camp warriors is caught off guard and surrounded. They rally towards their leader, who appears to resist our intrusion fiercely. But our determination, evident by our raised rifles and fuelled by the desire for peace, proves to be an unyielding force.

In the heart of the chaos stands their leader, a figure of defiance and strength. Our duel is a dance towards death, two warriors bound by duty and conviction. But I hold the power of understanding and recognising common ground.

"We seek not to conquer but to understand," I proclaim, my voice cutting through the silence. "Let us end the likelihood of bloodshed and find a path to peace."

The words, spoken sincerely, resonate with the leader, a moment of clarity in the fog of war. A fragile yet hopeful stalemate takes shape, a first step towards reconciliation and understanding.

As dawn breaks, casting its light over the camp, the small group of Punjab Free Supporters stands down, and it is apparent that the death of the Peshawar clerk was the result of a family vendetta between clans from the farthest mountain regions. This group before us who lean towards the Legions' cause is heard, their grievances acknowledged, and their commitment to move on is given. The journey back to our fortifications is a procession not of conquerors but peacemakers, a testament to the courage and compassion that define the human spirit.

As I return, Eleanor's embrace is my sanctuary; her love is my guiding light. Our story, set against the backdrop of Punjab's majestic beauty and turbulent history, continues to unfold, a saga of adventure, love, and the eternal quest for peace.

The Punjab Free Legion is a clandestine group formed in the shadows of the British Raj's expansion. Its roots lie in the aftermath of the Anglo-Sikh Wars and the Revolt of 1857, drawing members from disillusioned Sikh warriors, local peasants, and former princely state loyalists who lost their autonomy due to the 'Doctrine of Lapse'.

The group is driven by a desire to restore Punjab's sovereignty and resist British control. They yearn for the return of their lost glory and autonomy and feel a deep resentment toward the foreign rule that has altered their homeland's political and cultural landscape.

Their Supreme Leader, the charismatic and enigmatic figure of Arjun Singh, is possibly a descendant of a deposed princely family or a veteran of the Sikh wars. This leader blends military expertise with a deep understanding of Punjab's history and culture.

The Legion employs guerrilla tactics, staging ambushes and raids against British outposts and supply lines. It is skilled at blending into the local population and using the region's vast and diverse terrain to its advantage. Its bases are hidden in Punjab's rural heartlands, possibly in dense forests or rugged hill regions, allowing it to launch surprise attacks and then vanish.

Chapter Forty

As the sun rises over Peshawar, signalling the start of a new day, I am acutely aware of the challenges ahead. Our story in the heart of the North-West-Frontier continues to unfold, a narrative of duty and love amid an empire's ambitions.

My recent journey to the mountains was fraught with danger and uncertainty. In the unfolding saga of Peshawar and the North-West Frontier, the fates of many, including myself, hang precariously in the balance.

As the sun scorches the arid landscape of Peshawar, casting elongated shadows of the city's ancient architecture. The bazaars teem with life, a medley of colours and dissonant sounds. In this vibrancy, a lurking danger brews, unseen yet palpable. I feel it in my bones as I walk through the bustling streets, unaware that today would change everything.

Eleanor, my wife, her spirit as brave as ever, decides to explore the local market alone in the afternoon, her fascination with the culture undimmed by the simmering tensions. Her departure from our quarters feels ordinary, yet fate, it seems, has a cruel twist in store.

Hours later, a sense of unease grips me. I am informed Eleanor hasn't returned. The setting sun casts a foreboding hue over the city, And a chilling fear takes root in my heart. My search leads me to the market, now a labyrinth of shadows and deserted stalls.

The revelation comes like a thunderbolt – Eleanor has been kidnapped. The Punjab Free Legion, seeking to strike a blow against the British establishment and aware of my presence from my recent travels into their territory, has taken her. The news hits me like a physical blow; my world reels.

The Legion's audacity in kidnapping Eleanor, the wife of a British officer, signifies a shift in the conflict's nature. It's no longer just a battle of arms but a profoundly personal fight against an enemy that now holds the most precious part of my life in its clutches.

The gravity of the situation is not lost on my superiors. Colonel Stevenson, my commanding officer, a man of stern countenance, voices his concerns. "Brody, this is a delicate situation. The Legion wants to draw us out, but we must act cautiously."

My mind races, torn between my duty and my heart. "Sir, I must rescue her," I assert, my voice firm with resolve. With the Colonel's reluctant approval, I prepare to embark on this dangerous rescue mission. The Legion's stronghold lies deep in the rugged terrain of the North-West Frontier, a maze of mountains and valleys where danger lurks at every turn.

I quickly assemble a small team of trusted men, their loyalty and bravery unquestionable. We set off on horseback under the cover of darkness, the moon our silent companion in this covert operation.

Our journey is a harrowing test of endurance and resolve. The mountainous paths are treacherous, and the Legion's scouts are ever watchful. We evade their gaze, moving like shadows, our progress slow but steady.

Local informants' faces etched with the hardships of frontier life provide us with vital intelligence. In a dimly lit hut, an old Pashtun man, his eyes reflecting years of wisdom, whispers, "The British Sahiba is held in an old fort, hidden in the valley of death. Be wary, Captain. The Legion's fighters there are fierce and many."

With each step, my resolve hardens. The Legion may be formidable, but my love for Eleanor gives me a strength I never knew I possessed. My mind conjures images of her—her smile, courage, and unwavering love—fueling my determination.

As the stronghold of the Legion looms before us, shrouded in the inky cloak of night, the magnitude of our undertaking unfurls in my mind like a battle standard. The notion of a direct assault is folly, a surefire path to oblivion; our success hinges on the shadows, our movements as silent as the whispers of fate. Under the celestial canopy, punctuated by the glimmer of distant suns, we draw nearer, our every heartbeat a thunderous drum in the silent anticipation of what lies ahead.

As I inch closer to the heart of the fortress, the night air tightens around me, heavy with anticipation of the impending confrontation. The defence, a labyrinth of shadows and stone, looms ahead—a silent giant awakened by the intruders at its gates. My cautious footsteps echo against the ancient walls, a constant reminder of the precarious line between stealth and discovery.

The moon, a sliver of silver in the ink-black sky, casts an ethereal glow over the fortress, revealing snatches of the rugged beauty that belies its dangerous occupants. The occasional flicker of torches along the parapets throws grotesque shadows that dance along the ground, distorting the figures of the guards into monstrous forms that seem to watch our every move.

Every sense is heightened, attuned to the slightest whisper of movement or the softest tread of enemy feet. My ears pick up the low murmur of voices, the clink of metal, and the distant barking of a dog—a cacophony of sounds that vividly depict the fortress's lifeblood pulsing in the dead of night. The air is tinged with the smell of smouldering wood from unseen fires, blending with the earthy scent of the surrounding wilderness.

As we navigate the winding pathways that cut through the fortress grounds, the oppressive weight of the stone structures towers Over us, a constant reminder of the centuries of history and conflict embedded in their walls. I can't help but feel a grudging respect for these structures' fortitude, standing as silent sentinels to the passage of time.

The tension builds with each step closer to Eleanor's presence. My palms are slick with sweat, and I grip my weapon with determination and an underlying current of fear. The reality of our mission, fraught with danger at every turn, presses down on me with an almost physical force.

Suddenly, a shout shatters the quiet, a stark signal that our presence has been discovered. The fortress erupts into chaos, the sound of a bell piercing the night air, rallying the defenders to their posts. My heart races, adrenaline surging through my veins as we prepare for the inevitable clash.

Amid this turmoil, I focus on the singular image of Eleanor, her strength and courage, a beacon guiding me through the darkness. The thought of her waiting, perhaps praying for a miracle in her confinement, fuels my resolve. I push forward, driven by a love that transcends fear, ready to face whatever challenges lie between us and freedom.

The path to Eleanor's chamber becomes a blur, each moment a desperate battle against time and odds. Once a silent maze of shadows, the fortress now echoes with the Clamour of war—the clash of steel on steel, the shouts of men, and the relentless determination of those fighting for their lives.

Three of my best men and I break from our leading group as we navigate the fortress's interior; the path to Eleanor's chamber unfolds like a complex puzzle, each piece fraught with peril. The stone corridors, cold and unyielding beneath our feet, twist and turn, leading us deeper into the heart of this ancient stronghold. Our progress is measured, a silent dance of shadows as we slip past unsuspecting guards and avoid the pools of torchlight that sporadically punctuate the darkness.

The staircase to Eleanor's chamber looms before us, a steep ascent carved from the fortress's stone. Its narrow confines promise no quarter for retreat, a vertical battlefield where the advantage lies with those above. We ascend in silence, the only sound the soft scuff of our boots against the worn steps, each of us aware of the lethal challenge that awaits at the summit.

At the top, the final guardian of Eleanor's prison stands watch—a solitary figure silhouetted against the flickering light of a single torch. His presence is a testament to the importance of the prize beyond the wooden door he guards. With a practised motion, I raise my weapon, whispering a silent prayer to the night as I aim. The shot rings out, a thunderous proclamation in the stillness, and the guard collapses, a life extinguished in the pursuit of our singular purpose.

With the path now clear, we breach the door to Eleanor's chamber. The room beyond is a stark cell, devoid of comfort, lit only by the moonlight filtering through a narrow window. And amidst the desolation stands Eleanor—her spirit undimmed, a defiant flame in the darkness.

The reunion is a moment of profound emotion, relief, love, and unspoken fears. Words are unnecessary; our embrace speaks volumes, a promise of hope and a vow of unyielding defiance. "Eleanor, we must leave now," I urge, the urgency of our situation lending weight to my words.

As we dart through the labyrinthine corridors of the fortress, the air is thick with tension and the acrid scent of gunpowder. Eleanor, her resilience unwavering, keeps pace beside me. Our escape is a desperate race against time; every corner turns into a potential ambush.

Suddenly, a sharp crack of gunfire echoes through the stone passageway, a harbinger of dread. I turn just in time to see James, one of my most loyal men, crumple to the ground, a bright blossom of blood spreading across his uniform.

"James!" I call out, my voice a mix of command and concern. Eleanor's eyes widen in shock, her hand flying to her mouth in horror.

Thomas, another party member, and I rush to James's side without hesitation. His face is pale, his breath ragged, starkly contrasting to the stoic soldier I've known. The bullet has struck his shoulder, a wound severe but not fatal if tended quickly.

"We can't leave him," I declare firmly, meeting Thomas's eyes. He nods, understanding the unspoken bond that ties soldiers in the heat of battle.

Together, we hoist James up, his arm draped over each of our shoulders, his feet dragging limply. His body weight and the urgency of our escape are a physical and emotional burden, but one we bear willingly for a comrade in arms.

Eleanor, her fear pushed aside, assists by taking James's rifle, her determination lending us strength. We move as one unit, a cohesive force bound by duty and desperation. Jimmy, another stoic member, acts as our rear guard, firing at the enemy that pursues us through the corridors.

The fortress seems to come alive against us, its narrow halls now teeming with enemies. Gunshots ring out, stone chips flying as bullets strike the ancient walls. We return fire, moving in a tight formation, protecting our injured comrade with fierce resolve.

Our progress is slow and agonising, each step a battle against time and the encroaching enemy. The fortress within, once a silent sentinel, now roars with the sound of combat, a cacophony that echoes our pounding hearts.

The final corridor to the quadrangle is a gauntlet, a length defended by the fortress's remaining guards. We fight with a ferocity born of desperation, Eleanor beside me, her courage matching my own. Each fallen enemy brings us closer to escape, to the promise of a future beyond these stone walls.

Beside the fortress walls, we join the remainder of our fighting unit; the dawn has turned into a battlefield. The rebels, fierce in their resistance, converge on us with terrifying and awe-inspiring ferocity. The air is filled with the sounds of combat—the ring of steel on steel, the cries of their wounded, and the relentless barrage of sporadic gunfire.

In the thick of battle, I fight as a soldier and a man driven by love and desperation. Each blow I deliver with my sword is fuelled by the need to protect Eleanor to ensure our freedom. She moves alongside me, her courage undiminished by fear. Together, we are a force unto ourselves, our spirits unyielding in the face of overwhelming odds.

As we break through the last of our adversaries and advance in the open, the first light of dawn begins to creep across the horizon, casting a pale glow over the scarred landscape. Now behind us, the fortress stands as a testament to the night's ordeal—a reminder of the cost of freedom and the strength of the human spirit.

As we navigate the rugged terrain towards our tethered horses, James's laboured breathing is a constant reminder of the price of our escape. But amidst the chaos and danger, there is a glimmer of hope. In this moment, we are more than just soldiers; we are brothers, united by a bond that adversity has only strengthened.

Our journey is far from over; the path ahead is uncertain. But for now, we press on, guided by the unyielding spirit of survival and the unwavering resolve to protect one of our own. The sun has greeted us like a long-lost friend. The sounds of pursuit fade behind us, lost in the vastness of the wilderness that now offers shelter.

Our flight on horseback is a blur of adrenaline, a headlong rush towards safety and the promise of a new dawn. We then emerge from the valley, battered but alive. Eleanor's presence seated behind me on my mount is a testament to our love's strength, a love that has endured the darkest of trials.

Our journey from the enemy's fortress is a testament to our resilience, a shared ordeal that binds us even closer. As we distance ourselves from Eleanor's captors, realising that we have survived and are together and free is overwhelming. The physical and emotional scars we bear will heal with time, but the memory of this night, of the love and bravery that saw us through, will remain with us forever.

Chapter Forty-One

As we escape into the rugged wilderness of the North-West Frontier, our hearts racing and our bodies weary, the reality of our situation becomes starkly apparent. The world we knew has irrevocably changed, and the path ahead is difficult. The Legion, infuriated by our defiance and Eleanor's rescue, will undoubtedly seek retribution. We are now in a relentless game of survival that requires cunning, bravery, and an unbreakable bond of trust.

In the cover of a densely wooded area, we lay James down gently, his injury needing urgent attention. Eleanor, her bravery unshaken, tends to his wound with a calmness that belies the chaos around us. "We need to find shelter and regroup," I say, scanning the horizon for any signs of pursuit.

Thomas, his eyes sharp and alert, points to a distant ridge. "There's an abandoned village there. We can take cover and plan our next move." With a nod, we carefully lift James and begin our cautious journey towards the village, each step a testament to our resolve.

As night falls, the abandoned village offers a momentary respite. We gather in a dilapidated hut, the air thick with tension and unspoken fears. The flickering light of a small fire casts shadows on our faces, each etched with the strain of our ordeal.

"Our priority is to get word to the regiment," I declare, my mind racing with strategies. "They need to know about the Legion's plans and our current predicament."

Eleanor, illuminated by the fire's glow, adds, "We must also ensure James's safety. He won't survive another jolting homeward journey in this state."

The discussion turns to our options—a dangerous trek to the nearest British outpost or a covert message sent through trusted local allies. The risks are immense, but we cannot afford inaction.

As we deliberate, a sense of camaraderie and purpose solidifies among us. We are no longer just a British officer, his wife, and his men; we are a unit bound by a shared ordeal, a common enemy, and a mutual desire to see justice served.

We execute our plan the following morning under the guise of dawn's early light. Thomas and I set out to contact the regiment stealthily through the treacherous terrain. Eleanor stays behind with the wounded James and other men, her presence comforting in a sea of uncertainty.

Our journey is a harrowing test of endurance and wit. We evade Legion patrols, navigate treacherous landscapes, and rely on the help of local villagers whose hearts align with our cause. Each encounter, each narrow escape, strengthens our resolve.

As we reach the British garrison, exhausted but undeterred, we are met with disbelief and swift action. The regiment mobilises, their resolve as fierce as ours. Plans are drawn to counter the Legion's influence and to rescue those still under their thrall.

Meanwhile, Eleanor and Jimmy are not idle in the deserted village. Despite the danger, they gather intelligence, crucial in determining the Legion's broader strategy and present whereabouts.

The story now evolves into a complex tapestry of guerrilla warfare, political intrigue, and personal vendettas. With its majestic beauty and lurking dangers, Punjab becomes a backdrop to our relentless pursuit of justice.

Amidst the unfolding chaos, Eleanor and my bond deepened, and our love is a constant flame in the darkness of war. Our story, intertwined with the Punjab's fate and the Legion's machinations, becomes a testament to the enduring power of the human spirit against overwhelming odds.

The rescue journey leading back to Peshawar is a mix of relief and reflection for all. The Legion's attempt to use Eleanor as a pawn in their game has failed, but the cost of our ordeal is imprinted on our souls. We return as survivors and symbols of resilience in the face of overwhelming odds.

As the continuing conflicts climax, with daring raids, strategic alliances, and the culmination of our efforts to dismantle the Legion's hold, we stand at the precipice of a new era. The outcome of our struggle will not only define our futures but will leave an indelible mark on the history of the British Raj in India.

Our journey, a blend of love, courage, and determination, transcends the confines of war. It's a narrative of triumph over adversity, a saga that will resonate through the ages, a tale of an unbreakable bond forged in the crucible of conflict. This is our legacy, a story that will be told and retold, a tale of heroism, sacrifice, and the unyielding pursuit of British justice.

The sun rises over Peshawar, casting its golden light on a city that remains a battleground of conflicting ideologies. But for Eleanor and me, it marks a new beginning, a reaffirmation of our love and our unbreakable bond.

• • • •

AS DAWN BREAKS OVER the sprawling landscapes of Punjab, I find myself standing at the precipice of a new chapter. The British Indian authorities, recognising my role in helping to quell the Punjab Free Legion's uprising, have offered me the position of political emissary. This role fills me with a sense of purpose yet humbles me with its demands.

The task before me is formidable: to weave through the intricate tapestry of alliances and rivalries that shape this vibrant land, engage with its rulers, the local rajahs, and fortify the British presence with a Blend of respect and firmness as Captain Samuel Brody of 'The Viceroy of India', a representative of the British Crown.

The air is charged with the scent of jasmine and the distant sounds of the bustling markets as I ready myself for my first mission. I aim to meet with Rajah Singh, who is renowned for his influence and wavering stance towards the British. The journey to his palace reflects India—vibrant, chaotic, and teeming with life. I ride through the countryside, where the green of the fields clashes with the stark blue of the sky, a reminder of the beauty and complexity of this land.

As I step through the ornate gateway, the Rajah's palace unfurls before me, an edifice of splendour that whispers tales of India's storied past. Its towering spires pierce the sky, while intricate carvings in the sandstone walls depict legends of gods and warriors. I'm led through a labyrinth of corridors, each turn revealing more of the palace's grandeur until we reach the grand hall. The heavy air here is infused with sandalwood and jasmine, an intoxicating blend that seems to slow time.

Rajah Singh sits at the far end of the hall, nestled on a throne that seems to have been carved from the very essence of majesty. He is a figure of undeniable authority, his posture radiating the power that speaks of centuries of rule. He wears an ornate turban adorned with jewels to signify his royal position and richly embroidered robes made from silk with a hand-painted tiger motif. A wide sash studded with gemstones is worn around his waist to symbolise authority and Power, and additional jewellery, such as necklaces, bracelets, and rings, are heirlooms from another century. His eyes, dark and fathomless, fix upon me as I approach, and I feel the weight of his scrutiny like a physical force.

"Greetings, Captain Brody," he intones, his voice rich and resonant. "I have been expecting you."

I bow, respecting the customs of his court. "Rajah Singh, I am honoured to be received by you. I come on behalf of the British Crown, hoping to foster peace and prosperity between our lands."

His gaze remains unyielding, searching as if he seeks to peer into the very depths of my soul. "The British Crown," he muses, hinting at irony. "And what makes you think that you can navigate the delicate intricacies of our alliances and enmities, Captain Brody?"

The question is a challenge, a test of my resolve and understanding. I draw a deep breath, my mind racing to frame a response worthy of his query. "It is not what I bring from the British Crown, but what I hope to build with you, Rajah Singh. An understanding born of respect and a partnership that values the traditions and aspirations of your people."

A flicker of interest sparks in Rajah Singh's eyes, the first crack in his formidable demeanour. "Indeed? And how do you propose to build this understanding, Captain Brody?"

I step forward, encouraged by his interest. "By listening, Rajah Singh. By engaging with your people, learning from them, and ensuring their voices are heard in the decisions that affect their lives. By being present, not as a ruler, but as a partner."

The Rajah's gaze softens, and for a moment, the air between us is charged with the possibility of something new, something transformative. "You speak of partnership, Captain Brody. This concept has been absent from our dealings with the British. If you truly stand by your words, you may find in me an ally."

The promise in his words is a beacon in the night, a sign that the path ahead, though fraught with challenges, is not insurmountable. As our meeting unfolds, we delve into discussions of trade, security, and cultural exchange, each topic a step toward the future we both envision.

When I finally leave the grand hall, the night has wrapped the palace in its serene embrace. The stars above shine a little brighter, reflecting the spark of hope that Rajah Singh's words have kindled within me. The journey ahead is uncertain, but for the first time, I feel that the bridges we seek to build may span the chasms that have long divided us.

In the heart of Punjab, a new chapter begins beneath the watchful gaze of history—one not of conquest but of collaboration. As I navigate the complexities of this land and its people, I am guided by the belief that true strength lies in unity, in the shared dreams that light our way forward.

The initial exchanges are cautious, a delicate dance of diplomacy. I speak of cooperation and mutual respect, invoking the shared interests that bind us. For his part, the Rajah expressed his concerns and aspirations, a leader protective of his people and their traditions.

Our conversation meandered through the complexities of British and Indian relations, each of us probing and assessing. It becomes clear that my role is not merely that of an emissary but of a bridge—a conduit for understanding and reconciliation. I find myself drawn into the cultural and political intricacies of Punjab, each discovery a thread in the larger fabric of its identity.

As days turn into weeks, my engagements take me from the opulent courts of rajahs to the humble dwellings of the common folk. Each encounter enriches my understanding of India, its challenges, and its unparalleled spirit. My wife, Eleanor, stands by my side, and her efforts to improve women's and children's welfare weave another layer of connection between us and the land we now call home.

Yet, as I navigate this complex landscape, a new threat emerges. Disgruntled and ambitious, a radical faction within the East India Company seeks to undermine our delicate balance. Their Machinations, hidden in the shadows of power, threaten to ignite a fire that could consume all we have worked to build.

With the stakes higher than ever, I am thrust into a game of political chess, where each move could determine the fate of Punjab and the British presence in Punjab. My resolve is tested, and my diplomatic skills sharpened against intrigue and rebellion.

But it is not just a battle for political supremacy—it is a quest for peace, for a harmony that transcends borders and disputes. As I stand firm against the gathering storm, I am reminded of the love and loyalty that bind Eleanor and me, the dreams we share for this land and its people.

Our journey is far from over; the path is fraught with challenges and uncertainties. But together, we face the future, ready to forge a legacy of understanding and respect, a beacon of hope in a land of ancient wonders and enduring mysteries.

Chapter Forty-Two

In the heart of Punjab, under the relentless Indian sun, Eleanor Brody embarks on a mission fuelled by the harrowing experience of her recent past and the indomitable spirit of the local populace. Her resolve to forge a path of compassion and change in this vibrant yet tumultuous land sets her on an unparalleled journey.

Eleanor, along with a coterie of local leaders and visionaries, initiates a campaign to transform the lives of women and children. Her crusades are the foundations of schools; each brick laid a testament to her unwavering commitment to education and empowerment. She also gives her attention and resources to scarce and overwhelmed healthcare facilities, which are slowly beginning to flourish under her care.

The challenges she faces are manifold. Cultural barriers and traditional norms often seem daunting. Yet Eleanor navigates these with a grace and understanding that belie her foreign origins. Some may scoff at her efforts, but her genuine desire to uplift the communities she serves gradually wins hearts and minds.

Eleanor's journey is not just one of philanthropy but of profound self-discovery. In the faces of the women she empowers and the children she teaches, she finds reflections of her strength and resilience. The conventions of her time, which once seemed Impossible, now appear as mere stepping stones on her path to making a tangible difference.

Born from adversity, her mission blossoms into a beacon of hope in the Punjab region. Schools are pillars of knowledge and freedom, and healthcare facilities are sanctuaries of healing and hope. Eleanor's legacy, intertwined with the destinies of those she has touched, becomes a narrative of transformation and empowerment.

From my perspective, watching Eleanor embark on this journey of change and self-discovery fills me with a profound sense of pride and admiration. Her courage to challenge the status quo and her compassion for the people of Punjab redefine my understanding of strength and purpose. Together, we navigate the complexities of our roles in this foreign land, united by a shared vision of a better future for all.

Eleanor's mission in Punjab is a chapter of courage, change, and self-realisation. It's a story that transcends the boundaries of culture and geography, highlighting the universal values of empathy, education, and empowerment.

• • • •

NOW, BACK IN RAWALPINDI, the air in Punjab is heavy with unrest, a tension that clings to the dust swirling in the streets. Amid this simmering turmoil, as Captain Samuel Brody of The Viceroy of India, I find myself standing at a crossroads not just of paths but of destinies. With its pulsating heart and veiled secrets, the Punjab has become more than a mere posting; it has become the crucible of my resolve, the test of my allegiance.

As the sun dips below the horizon, painting the sky in shades of crimson and gold, a message finds its way into my hands. The wax seal, embossed with the symbol of the East India Company, belies the storm it carries within. Unfolding the parchment with a sense of foreboding, I discover a plot that threatens to shake the very pillars of British rule in India—a radical faction within the East India Company, disillusioned with London's tightening grip, aims to usurp control over the subcontinent's military and economic arteries.

The revelation sends a shiver down my spine. The faction, a shadowy cabal of officers and merchants, is not merely dissenting; it plans a coup that could plunge Punjab and beyond into chaos. Its grievance with the Crown's directives is its rallying cry, but its ambition veils a dangerous lust for the power it had before the British Crown took over.

My mind races as I consider my next steps. My loyalty to the Crown and the bond I've forged with this land and its people stand on opposing shores. Yet, the path forward is clear—this insurrection must be quelled, not just for the sake of the Empire but for the fragile peace that Punjab has only just begun to cherish.

As I gather a trusted cadre of men assigned by the Punjab Garrison upon my request, the moon rises, silently witnessing the turmoil within me. Among them is Sergeant Havers, whose steadfast presence comforts me in uncertain times. Together, we set out under the cloak of night, navigating the labyrinthine alleys of Rawalpindi, where whispers of rebellion simmer just beneath the surface.

Our mission is fraught with peril. We tread a fine line, seeking to unearth the conspiracy's leaders without alerting them to our pursuit. Each step brings us closer to confrontation, and the air thrums with the tension of unseen battles yet to be fought.

Eyes watch our every move in the shadows. The faction's spies are as ubiquitous as the dust that coats the city, and their intentions are as obscured as the darkened streets we traverse. But our resolve is ironclad, and our purpose is clear. The fate of Punjab, of India, rests in the balance, and I am but a single piece on this chessboard, poised to make a move that could alter the course of history.

As dawn breaks, casting a gentle light over Rawalpindi, we find ourselves at the heart of the conspiracy inside a Dhaba. This rustic roadside establishment serves hearty meals with its simple décor and a sense of authenticity. It serves steaming hot parathas, aromatic curries, and chi in metal cups. With whispered secrets, we converse with our spies planted within the East India Company. When confrontation comes, it will be swift and decisive. Words are weapons, and loyalty is the shield that guards us. The faction's plot will unravel beneath the weight of truth and the strength of our conviction.

Our investigations uncover the birth of a rebellion under vibrant chaos and profound silence. Under the charismatic leadership of Lal

Singh, the 'Kshatriya Sangathan' rises, challenging the British Raj's iron grip, instigated under a coup sponsored by the inside rebels of the East India Company – by their shadowy cabal of officers and merchants. The Kshatriya Sangathan are not just rebels with a cause favouring the breakaway; they're visionaries seeking to stitch together a fragmented nation to reclaim the dignity stripped away by the British Raj.

Lal Singh, a man of noble heritage and profound wisdom in its rich history, is disillusioned by the British's oppressive reign. Watching the suffering of his people, especially during a monsoon season that brings famine rather than relief, ignites in him a fire that no British rain can extinguish. He sees the plight of the farmers, the very soul of India neglected and exploited, strengthening his resolve to fight for justice and freedom.

The 'Kshatriya Sangathan' draws strength from the north's dense forests and rugged mountains. Lal, along with his devoted followers, disrupts British supply lines, cuts through our communications, and fans the flames of nationalism with every act of defiance.

Lal Singh's name has become a legend, whispered in awe and reverence. His fiery speeches inspire a resurgence of patriotism. He dreams of a unified India, free from foreign chains, where every voice is heard, and the wealth of their lands enriches every life.

But we of the British Raj, with our superior military, dispatched troops to suppress their uprising. Yet we underestimated Lal's intimate knowledge of his lands and his people's unwavering support. The Punjab countryside became a battlefield of strategy and resistance.

But Lal Singh's vision transcends mere conquests. He imagines a new India rooted in justice, equality, and a deep respect for their cultural mosaic. Gathering leaders from various communities, he aims to forge a charter for an India reborn, free and sovereign.

As the rebellion gathers momentum, I watch Lal Singh evolve from a warrior to a visionary leader, embodying the dreams of a nation yearning to breathe free. The journey ahead is laden with challenges, but Lal Singh and the Kshatriya Sangathan stand unwavering, their gaze fixed on the dawn of a new India.

My story is a testament to the courage and conviction of those daring to defy the tides of history, a narrative of a people's indomitable spirit to reclaim their destiny. From within my diplomatic duties and allegiance to the British Raj and the British Crown, I should abhor the success and aims of Lal Singh and the Kshatriya Sangathan, but within my heart, as an Australian 'Currency Lad', a 'Pure Merino' (native born) of Irish descent, I feel shame and the pain of the Indian people who have been under colonial rule and exploited by both the East India Company and the British Raj, and financing Briton's Industrial Revolution from 1757 to this present-day of 1892 – one hundred and twenty-five years, with more to come.

As the 19th century wanes in the sweltering heart of India, I find myself caught in a vortex of conflicting loyalties and hidden desires. The emergence of the Kshatriya Sangathan, led by the enigmatic Lal Singh, has sent ripples through the established order, which ensnares this land and its people in chains of exploitation.

As a diplomat, my allegiance lies with the Crown, yet my soul resonates with the cries for freedom echoing across the Punjab plains. The tale of Lal Singh, a nobleman turned rebel, stirs a familiar fire within me. Witnessing his journey from disillusionment to defiance in the face of Britain's oppressive regime mirrors the struggles of my ancestors against the colonial yoke back home and what my father Levi experienced in Ballarat at the Battle of Eureka.

The dense forests and rugged mountains of northern India serve as a backdrop to this drama, where Lal and his band of patriots wage a shadow war against an empire. Their raids on British convoys and the spread of nationalist fervour through the villages speak to a deep-seated yearning for autonomy—a desire that finds an echo in my heart.

Lal Singh becomes more than a mere insurgent; he becomes a symbol of hope, his name a beacon for those yearning to break free from foreign subjugation. His impassioned speeches, advocating for a united India where the wealth of the land benefits all, resonate with a truth I cannot ignore.

Yet, as the British dispatch their forces to quash his uprising, the countryside becomes a chessboard of conflict. My military mind appreciates Lal's guerilla tactics as a strategic genius, yet my position demands I oppose him. The clash of ideals is palpable. Each encounter with the Kshatriya Sangathan is a test of wills, where the line between friend and foe blurs in the dust of battle.

On a fateful night, as Lal leads an audacious assault against a British stronghold—a fortress symbolising the Raj's iron grip—I admire his courage. The fortress falls, a significant blow to British prestige, yet the victory is hollow. True peace requires more than the toppling of strongholds; it necessitates a foundation of justice and equality.

In the aftermath of Lal Singh's transformation from warrior to statesman, his vision for a new India challenges me to reconsider my role in this historical tapestry. As he convenes a council of leaders and drafts a charter for independence like the Ballarat Digger's charter before the Battle of Eureka, I stand at a crossroads, torn between duty and profound respect for a cause that, in another life, I might have championed.

My journey through this turbulent period is a testament to the complexity of empire and the indomitable spirit of those who dare to dream of freedom. Within the echoes of the Kshatriya Sangathan's rebellion, I grapple with the bitter truth that peace is an elusive quarry, sought in the shadows of justice and the light of understanding. As I navigate the intricate dance of diplomacy and intrigue, I am reminded that history is not merely a series of events but a mosaic of human experiences, each striving for a place in the dawn of a new era.

Chapter Forty-Three

A s the Indian sun descends once more, painting the sky in a palette of fire, I stand on the balcony of our colonial residence, the weight of a momentous decision anchoring my thoughts. The air is heavy with the scent of jasmine and the distant hum of land caught between epochs. Eleanor, ever my compass in the storm of doubt, joins me, her hand finding mine.

"In the heart of this land, amidst its pain and beauty, I have found the line between duty and justice blurring," I confess, my voice a mere whisper against the evening breeze. "Our allegiance to the Raj, once a beacon of service, now casts a shadow over the peace we seek to foster."

Eleanor's gaze, deep and understanding, meets mine. "Sam, wherever our path leads, our journey is together. India has taught us much, but perhaps it's time to seek new horizons."

Resolving my commission, a decision that once seemed unthinkable, now feels like the only course true to my heart. The conflict between the Empire's aspirations and the aspirations of a people yearning for self-determination has etched a chasm too vast to bridge from within the confines of my role.

Under the silent vigil of a starlit sky, Eleanor and I sit at an aged teak desk, the quiet of the night enveloping us like a shroud. The only sound is the scratch of my pen against the paper, each stroke a testament to the gravity of our decision. The lamp flickers gently, casting a warm glow over the parchment that holds the future in its lines. I begin, the words flowing with a mix of trepidation and resolve:

"To the Esteemed Office of the British Raj and Viceroy of India,

With a heavy heart and after considerable reflection, I tender my service resignation to both. Profound experiences have marked my tenure, indelibly shaping my understanding of duty, honour, and the complex tapestry of human justice."

I pause, searching for words to bridge the chasm between my duty and conscience. Eleanor's supportive hand on my shoulder gives me the strength to continue.

"In my years of service, I have witnessed the indomitable spirit of the Indian people, their resilience in the face of adversity, and their yearning for self-determination. These encounters have stirred in me a deep respect for India's cultural and political aspirations, which I find increasingly at odds with the role I have been asked to play.

I leave my post not in search of accolades or escape but in pursuit of a peace that respects the sovereignty of all peoples. I hope that in stepping down, I may contribute, in some small measure, to the dialogue of understanding and mutual respect that is the foundation of true peace.

As I return to my homeland, I carry the lessons learned and the friendships forged in this land of incredible diversity and history. I remain committed to fostering relationships built on the principles of equity and justice, transcending the confines of geography and governance."

May the future hold a path towards reconciliation and mutual respect among nations, where the bonds of humanity are celebrated above all else."

Signed: Captain Samuel Brody.

The letter concludes with a promise to those who will read it and unto ourselves. Sealing the envelope, Eleanor and I share a look of solemn determination. More than a resignation, this letter declares our journey forward, guided by the principles we hold dear. As the dawn begins to break, casting a soft light over the horizon, we step into a future unbound by the constraints of past obligations, our hearts buoyed by the hope of making a difference in the world.

The journey back to Australia is not merely a return but a pilgrimage to the essence of our shared values. As the ship cuts through the cerulean expanse, each wave a testament to the adventures we've weathered, I reflect on the legacy we leave behind.

In the Punjab, where whispers of rebellion and dreams of independence mingle with centuries' dust, we leave a piece of our souls.

Our efforts to mend the rifts may not sway empires, but we hope to have kindled a flame of understanding in the hearts of those we've touched.

Australia beckons with the promise of a new chapter, not as a retreat but as an arena for a different service. Our experiences in India have reshaped our vision, imbuing us with a deeper appreciation for the diversity of the human tapestry and the universal quest for dignity and respect.

As we disembark on Australian soil, we long for the familiar scent of eucalyptus and the chorus of the bush to welcome us home—a home where the lessons of India will inspire our endeavours, whether in the courts of law or the halls of advocacy.

In this land of vast horizons and resilient spirits, Eleanor and I commit ourselves to be agents of change with our memories of India's vibrant soul. Ultimately, the quest for peace and justice knows no boundaries, and our journey is a chapter in the more remarkable story of humanity's pursuit of harmony.

Don't miss out!

Visit the website below and you can sign up to receive emails whenever Richard Moorman publishes a new book. There's no charge and no obligation.

https://books2read.com/r/B-A-PZQV-PTRWC

BOOKS 2 READ

Connecting independent readers to independent writers.

Did you love *Golden Bloodline 2*? Then you should read *Golden Bloodline*[1] by Richard Moorman!

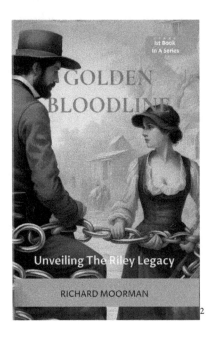

[2]

In the sprawling landscape of the 1800s, a tale of profound consequence unfolds within the pages of 'Golden Bloodline'. The narrative delves deep into the human psyche, where one man's singular act reverberates through time, setting in motion a cascade of events that will change lives forever.

As the story unfurls, it weaves together the voices of its characters - men, women, and the indomitable spirit of a son. Each perspective adds a layer of authenticity, drawing the reader into a world where suspense and intrigue reign supreme.

'Golden Bloodline' doesn't shy away from the stark realities of its era. It lays bare the horrors of slave labour, the fires of rebellion, and

---

1. https://books2read.com/u/mdqg7w

2. https://books2read.com/u/mdqg7w

the shadows of discrimination. It acknowledges the pivotal role these factors played in shaping destinies. It's a mesmerizing journey where every tragedy can be traced back to the singular actions of one man, rippling through the years.

This novel is a must-read for those who relish historical fiction and are captivated by the intricate tales of crime families. Prepare to be transported in time as AI ingenuity transforms this compelling story, earning accolades and acclaim.

'Golden Bloodline' is a journey through history that you won't want to miss.

Novel Length 333 Pages.

Read more at https://books2read.com/Rick-Moorman-Author.

Also by Richard Moorman

Golden Bloodline
Golden Bloodline
Golden Bloodline 2

Standalone
Abandoned Warriors Riding High
The Gravel Pits

Watch for more at https://books2read.com/Rick-Moorman-Author.

Milton Keynes UK
Ingram Content Group UK Ltd.
UKHW020952010424
440421UK00016B/1033